A beautiful quilt. A desperate journey. Jennifer Hudson Taylor's *Path of Freedom* takes readers on an adventure rife with romance and enough suspense to keep you up nights, proving that freedom comes in many forms and is always sweetest when from the heart!
—Laura Frantz, author of *The Frontiersman's Daughter*, *Courting Morrow Little*, and *The Colonel's Lady*.

I looked forward to reading a book about historical quilts. I liked the important part the quilt played in the story. The characters leapt off the pages and straight into my heart. I was sorry to see their story end.
—Lena Nelson Dooley, author of *Maggie's Journey* and *Mary's Blessing*, and winner of the Will Rogers Medallion award

Other books in the Quilts of Love Series

A Wild Goose Chase Christmas
    Jennifer AlLee
    (November 2012)

For Love of Eli
    Loree Lough
    (February 2013)

Threads of Hope
    Christa Allan
    (March 2013)

A Healing Heart
    Angela Breidenbach
    (April 2013)

A Heartbeat Away
    S. Dionne Moore
    (May 2013)

Pieces of the Heart
    Bonnie S. Calhoun
    (June 2013)

Pattern for Romance
    Carla Olson Gade
    (August 2013)

Raw Edges
    Sandra D. Bricker
    (September 2013)

The Christmas Quilt
    Vannetta Chapman
    (October 2013)

Aloha Rose
    Lisa Carter
    (November 2013)

Tempest's Course
    Lynette Sowell
    (December 2013)

Scraps of Evidence
    Barbara Cameron
    (January 2014)

A Sky without Stars
    Linda S. Clare
    (February 2014)

Maybelle in Stitches
    Joyce Magnin
    (March 2014)

Other Books by Jennifer Hudson Taylor

Highland Blessings
Highland Sanctuary

PATH OF FREEDOM

Quilts of Love Series

Jennifer Hudson Taylor

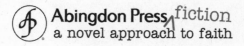

Abingdon Press fiction
a novel approach to faith

Nashville, Tennessee

Path of Freedom

Copyright © 2013 by Jennifer Hudson Taylor

ISBN-13: 978-1-4267-5263-6

Published by Abingdon Press, P.O. Box 801, Nashville, TN 37202

www.abingdonpress.com

Library of Congress Cataloging-in-Publication Data

Taylor, Jennifer Hudson.
  Path of freedom / Jennifer Hudson Taylor.
    pages cm. — (Quilts of love series)
Includes bibliographical references and index.
  ISBN 978-1-4267-5263-6 (book - pbk. / trade pbk. : alk. paper) 1. Quakers—Fiction.
2. Underground Railroad—Fiction. 3. Fugitive slaves—United States—Fiction. 4. African
Americans—19th century—Fiction. I. Title.
  PS3620.A9465P38 2013
  813'.6—dc23

2012040008

Printed in the United States of America

1 2 3 4 5 6 7 8 9 10 / 18 17 16 15 14 13

To my mother, Janice Sarah Robbins Hudson,
Thank you for being my spiritual mentor and
leading me on my journey with Christ.
I'm so glad you shared your childhood memories with me,
especially those of my great-grandmother, Flora Sarah
Saferight, and our Quaker ancestors.

There is neither Jew nor Greek,
there is neither slave nor free,
there is neither male nor female;
for you are all one in Christ Jesus.
(Galatians 3:28)

ACKNOWLEDGMENTS

I would like to thank my husband for brainstorming with me about this story as we drove down the highway, and for taking me to places to visit and do research about our Quaker history and the Underground Railroad.

Celina, thank you for putting up with me as I lived with one foot in the present and the other in 1858. You are a wonderful daughter, and I'm so very proud to be your mom.

I appreciate the rich history of Centre Friends Meeting of Greensboro, NC, and Mendenhall Plantation of Jamestown, NC, which were both used as settings in my novel. The wagon on which I based the wagon in my novel was given by a Quaker family who attended Centre Friends Meeting. I appreciate Mendenhall Plantation for allowing me to visit and take photos of this wagon.

I'd like to thank my beta readers for such a quick turnaround and for your insight into the story and characters. I treasure your honesty.

I'm grateful to Ramona Richards, my editor, for having the vision of the new Quilts of Love line at Abingdon and for allowing me to be part of this great opportunity. And to Terry Burns, my agent, your unfailing prayers and encouragement are a great inspiration to me.

Dear Readers,

Since the plot in *Path of Freedom* involves the Underground Railroad and a secret quilt map, I'd like to address a couple of controversial topics argued by historians. The first is the idea that quilts were used to display secret codes in the Underground Railroad to guide slaves on their journey to freedom. Since most slaves couldn't read, some believe this was one way they communicated. On the other hand, some insist that this idea is a myth and that there is no historical evidence that quilts were used in this manner. Others say that very little evidence regarding the Underground Railroad survives since it was so secretive and most evidence would have been destroyed to protect those involved. Therefore, there is no evidence to support the Secret Quilt Code and no evidence to disprove it either.

The story of the Secret Quilt Code began with the 1999 publication of a book entitled *Hidden in Plain View*. Prior to this book, there was no mention of a Secret Quilt Code. In interviews with freed slaves in the 1930s and earlier, no mention was made of a Secret Quilt Code. Still, I loved the idea as an element of a plot for a novel. (See http://ugrrquilt. hartcottagequilts.com/rr6a.htm for more information.)

The second controversy concerns the involvement of Quakers in the Underground Railroad since they were against slavery as something that was antithetical to faith. The truth is that some Quakers were, but not all. Some Quakers didn't believe in breaking the law or lying, even to protect slaves. They believed in advocating to change the law, not breaking it. One way Quakers could legally free slaves was to buy them and become slave owners themselves. They taught their slaves a trade and set them free.

I grew up in an area where Quakers had a prominent history of buying slaves and setting them free. In fact, my mother's ancestors were Quaker and were most active at Centre Friends Meeting in Greensboro, NC. A false-bottom wagon used to transport slaves to Ohio and Indiana was in the possession of a family at Centre Friends, and they donated it to Mendenhall Plantation. I used the history of this wagon in my story. (See http://www.mendenhallplantation.org for more information.)

While Levi Coffin was one of the most famous Quakers who worked with the Underground Railroad and was regarded as the "Father of the Underground Railroad," others were just as active but less known. Levi also lived in the Greensboro, NC, area before moving to Indiana. On July 19, 1816, Charles Osborne organized the North Carolina Manumission Society, an organization of Quakers and other abolitionists, whose main objective was to help free slaves and teach them how to support themselves. George Mendenhall was the largest slave owner in Guilford County. He owned as many as one hundred slaves, trained them as craftsmen, and set up a special school for slaves to teach them to read and write in order to prepare them for emancipation. His cousin, Richard Mendenhall, was the owner of the surviving Mendenhall Plantation, which is now a museum where the Underground Railroad wagon is housed. He allowed his slaves to operate and manage his store before he set them free.

For my non-Quaker readers, there are times when I use the term church in the book for clarity, but most of the time I use the term meeting to refer to the church or services. As with the Amish and Mennonites, Quakers varied from region to region. Some had organized services or meetings, while others sat in congregated silence and waited for the Holy Spirit to move individuals to speak and to share what was on their hearts. Some had leaders who were known as pastors, ministers, or preachers, but none of them were officially appointed. They took on the role because they felt led or called by God. Also, unlike people of other faiths, Quakers were open to women ministers since the beginning. In 1647 Elizabeth Hooten became the first female preacher.

In *Path of Freedom*, the quilt was made by Quakers who were familiar with the Underground Railroad route and wanted to provide a way for others to follow it. While most runaway slaves from Greensboro, NC, escaped to Indiana or Ohio, in my story they take a nontraditional route to Charlestown, PA. My story is fiction. The heroine is named for my great-grandmother, Flora Saferight, but the real Flora Saferight wasn't born until after the Civil War in 1890. She was Quaker and attended Centre Friends Meeting, where she was buried.

I hope you enjoy *Path of Freedom*.

Blessings,
Jennifer

1

A shiver of excitement rushed through Flora Saferight at the thought of their upcoming trip to Virginia. It had been at least two years since she'd seen her aunt and uncle, and even then they had traveled as a family by wagon. Now she and her younger sister would be making the trip by train.

"I think this is sensible for our journey." Standing in Gilmer General Store, Irene held up a red shawl with a lining. Her blue eyes shone bright in the hope of Flora's approval. Blond curls framed Irene's heart-shaped face beneath her white bonnet. With a delicate nose and smooth skin heightened by a blush of enthusiasm, Irene was considered the beauty between them.

"Mother would prefer a sensible cloak," Flora said. "Charlottesville can get awfully cold in the fall."

Her sister bit her bottom lip and lowered her gaze in disappointment. A dramatic sigh slipped from her lips. Flora glanced around the general store and spied a rack of cloaks by the front counter.

"Why not try one of those?" She pointed beyond a table displaying hats and bonnets, hoping to lift Irene's spirits. "Since we don't have time to make a new cloak and thee has grown out of thy clothes from last winter, I'm sure Mother would approve."

"True." A bright smile lit Irene's face as she sailed over to investigate. "Now that I'm taller than thee, I won't be inheriting thy clothes."

The shop door opened, ringing the tiny bell at the top.

"Good morning," Mrs. Edwards, the store clerk, called from where she stood on a small step stool, stacking bolts of fabric on the wall shelves.

"Morning." Bruce Millikan stepped inside wearing a white buttoned shirt, tucked into a pair of black trousers. His reddish-blond hair lay against his neck beneath his tall black hat. Flora's stomach shuddered at the thought of another confrontation with him. She took a deep breath, eager to escape before he noticed her.

Bruce glanced back to ensure that the door had closed properly. Flora gulped and turned, taking advantage of his momentary distraction to hurry behind a shelf of oil lanterns.

"Flora Saferight!" His deep voice flowed over her like bittersweet honey before she reached her destination. She waited for the sting of a familiar insult. Other girls may have enjoyed his teasing and attention growing up, but she hadn't. She closed her eyes, cringing as his booted footsteps charged across the wooden floor.

"Flora?"

She clenched her teeth and forced a smile as she squared her shoulders and prepared to greet him. Staring into his broad chest, Flora had to lean back to gaze into those amazing green eyes. Had he grown taller since she'd seen him eight months ago?

The freckles she remembered had faded beneath a ruddy complexion and a slight tan. A smile eased his lips, revealing straight teeth—too perfect, in her opinion. If only he would smile a little wider, then she'd have the satisfaction of seeing the gaping hole on the left side. Too bad a fall from a tree had been responsible, for she would have dearly loved to claim the honor—especially after he'd teased her about her two front teeth.

What was wrong with her? Guilt sliced through Flora. Her thoughts were much too bitter for a proper Quaker. They had been children. Still, all his barbed words had cut her to the core and continued to sting like a nasty bee buzzing around inside her soul. "Good morning, Bruce Millikan. I wasn't aware thee was back in town."

"I arrived home a fortnight ago." He blinked and his smile waned. "For a moment, I thought thee might be trying to avoid me."

Flora lifted her chin and met his gaze. "Do I look like I'm avoiding thee?" She folded her arms across her chest and glared at him with what she hoped was her best disapproving look. "Goodness, Bruce Millikan, thee acts as if I knew thee would walk right through that door. Since when has thee known me to back down from anything?"

His lips curled as two thin lines framed each side of his smile. He shook his head in slow motion. "No, Beaver Face, no one could ever accuse thee of ignoring a challenge." He gave a reminiscing chuckle. "Thee is the most headstrong girl I've ever known—and foolhardy at times." He folded his arms and stared down at her as if she were still a wayward child.

"Foolhardy? Beaver Face? Really, Bruce, one would hope thee would eventually grow up and leave the childhood name-calling behind." Flora bristled, his words scalding her heart like a new flesh wound. "We may only be a year apart in age, but thee hasn't changed one bit."

"Come on, Flora, I didn't mean it like that. It's more of an endearment now." He stepped closer, leaning forward. "The rest of thy teeth have grown in and are now perfect." He glanced behind him as if to see if anyone else was listening. "I'm sorry. I wish I'd never called thee that. I've sure spent every day since paying for it."

She stepped back, confused by his nearness and stunned by his apology. Flora swallowed, clearing her mind. The childhood taunts she could forgive, but the idea that he would insinuate she was foolish when she'd worked so hard to become a proper young lady of eighteen chafed her.

"Apparently, thee isn't sorry. For thee just called me fool-hardy. I'll have thee know, there's a good doctor in Virginia who thinks very highly of me. As a midwife, I will, he believes, complement his practice rather well." Clint Roberts had only mentioned it once in a letter, but she chose to interpret his words to mean that. No need in letting Bruce know she exaggerated.

"What doctor?" The light left his green eyes and his lips dropped in a frown. "Is thee courting a doctor?" He shifted, placing his fists at his side.

Irene walked over with a dark purple cloak draped over her arm. The bell rang and a new customer walked in, greeting Mrs. Edwards.

"It's true," Irene said. "Flora met him two summers ago when we were visiting our aunt and uncle. They've been corresponding ever since."

Thrilled that her sister would come to her aid, Flora beamed at Bruce. "See? Perhaps thee is the only one who harbors such an opinion of me." She stepped around him and over to her sister's side. "I'm content to live with the knowledge that I'll always be an ugly Beaver Face girl to thee, and thee will always be a mean-spirited bully to me—a childhood nightmare I'm more than happy to forget."

She linked arms with her sister and turned, leading Irene to the front counter. "For that, dear sister, thee may have a purple cloak. Thee deserves something a little less . . . plain today," Flora whispered in her ear.

"Flora, thee has an imagination to feed a pack of were-wolves," Bruce called from behind. "Thee is twisting my words. It isn't like that."

"Indeed," she mumbled loud enough for only Irene to hear. "Over the years it has been much worse."

It took three trips, but Bruce finally hauled all the supplies he'd purchased to the wagon parked out front. He dropped the last twenty-pound bag of flour in the bed and rubbed the dust from his hands.

An image of Flora Saferight came to mind. She wasn't as plain as she thought. In fact, she had grown into a beautiful woman, but he couldn't give her the satisfaction of knowing he thought so. Flora possessed blue-gray eyes that could captivate a man until he lost his senses. Her coffee-colored hair matched her spirited personality—vibrant and alive.

Why had he called her foolhardy? He touched the palm of his hand to his forehead in disbelief. Now she had another grievance to hold against him in addition to his long list of past sins. While some of her decisions were impulsive, and she needed more time to mature, he didn't think of her as a child, either. Flora was an enigma, with the cunning ability to challenge and frustrate him. Yet, in spite of being an annoyance, she intrigued him.

Wagons and carriages rolled by, crunching pebbles and dirt in the road. Two women stopped to converse on the corner in front of the barber shop. He strained to see if they were Flora and Irene, but when they turned, he realized it was a mother and daughter.

Disappointment fueled a fire his chest. He wanted to find out more about the doctor in Virginia. Was she serious about this man? Bruce strolled around the wagon and prepared to pull himself up into the seat.

"Good day, Bruce Millikan," a familiar voice called from behind.

Bruce turned to see Pastor John Allred striding toward him from across the street. He had to dodge a rider before he reached Bruce. They shook hands in a firm grip, greeting each other with smiles.

"Glad to see thee back. When did thee arrive in town?" John asked.

"Almost a fortnight ago. I'm sorry I missed meeting last week, but I plan to be there this Sunday. It was a long trip to Indiana. I've been trying to catch up on some chores around the farm."

"No need to explain." John shook his head and waved his hand to dismiss the issue. "Thee is doing important work for the Lord. That's the main thing. Was the mission successful?"

"Yes, but I'm looking forward to seeing everyone again and catching up on all the news. I just ran into Flora and Irene Saferight."

"I heard they're about to leave on the train to Virginia." John rubbed the back of his neck. "Speaking of which, there's something I'd like to discuss with thee. Would thee be willing to come over for supper tonight?"

Bruce rubbed his chin. What would Flora's trip to Virginia have to do with him? Curious, he nodded. "I'll tell Mother not to expect me for supper when I return. Flora mentioned a doctor she met up there two summers ago. Does thee know when they'll be leaving?" Bruce hoped his voice sounded casual. "I thought she was planning on being a midwife around here."

"I don't reckon her plans have changed." John shook his head, his brown eyes lit up, and a smooth grin spread across his face. "In fact, she helped Hazel Miller birth her latest child. I think Flora will prove to be one of our community's best assets."

Not if she moves away to Virginia. The sudden thought made Bruce's stomach churn. She was too young. What was she thinking? He'd only been gone eight months. How could things change so fast?

"Well, Pastor John, I'd better get these things home and put away so I can make it over to your place in time for supper."

"Good idea, Bruce." John slapped him on the shoulder. "I'll see thee in a little while."

Bruce gave him a nod and climbed into the wagon. He took the reins, unset the brake, and guided the horse down the street.

⁂

Flora didn't slow until the post office was in sight. Her sister breathed heavily from their brisk pace, hauling her new cloak over her arm.

"I still don't see why thee wouldn't let me stop long enough to put my cloak in the wagon. Besides, I thought we had more shopping to do." Irene glared at Flora while they waited for a buggy to pass before crossing the street.

"I promise. We'll go back and finish our shopping after I'm sure Bruce Millikan is gone." Flora charged into the street and stomped across the dirt road.

"Thee cannot avoid him forever. Forgive him for the past and let it go. He's right. It was a long time ago."

"It's true that Beaver Face was a long time ago, but his calling me foolhardy this morning isn't." Flora blew out a puff of air. If it were possible for a human being to explode, she'd be in a million pieces right now.

She swung open the post office door and an elderly woman stumbled out.

"Oh! Pardon me." Flora reached for the woman's elbow to steady her.

"Goodness!" The gray-haired woman righted herself and smoothed her skirts. She lifted her chin and glanced up at Flora and then Irene with brown eyes of stone. "You young people need not be in such haste. I daresay, this post office won't grow legs and walk, you know."

"We're sorry." Flora pressed her lips together to keep from laughing.

Inside, Flora blinked, adjusting her eyes to the darkness. She strode toward the open window, where Joseph Miller, the clerk, greeted her with a genuine smile.

"Howdy, Miss Saferight and Miss Saferight." He nodded to Irene standing by Flora. "Hazel and the baby are doing very well. You did a fine job delivering my baby girl." He rubbed the top of his bald head, which sported a thin layer of brown hair stretched from ear to ear.

"I'm glad to hear it. I hope to stop by for a visit before we leave on our trip to Virginia," Flora said.

"Hazel would like that. I think the confinement is starting to bother her."

"It won't be long before she'll be able to go out into society again." Flora pulled out a folded letter addressed to her aunt. "I need to send this to Charlottesville, Virginia."

"That will be one penny."

Flora dug into her skirt pocket and handed him the required change. Once they finished their business at the post office, they stepped outside the small wooden building into the bright sun. She shielded her eyes. She loved North Carolina in the fall. Soon more color would fill their world and cooler weather would bring in the harvest.

"I promised Mother we'd stop by the train station and find out the prices of the tickets," Flora said as they made their way toward South Elm Street.

"This is exciting!" In a sudden burst of energy, Irene caught Flora's pace as a smile tilted the corners of her mouth. "Just think, we'll be going through the capital city of Raleigh and then into Virginia in comfortable passenger seats. No slow, bumpy wagon with a hard wooden seat for days on end."

The sound of a distant train whistle bellowed through the air. Smoke shot into the sky over the gray roof of the wooden train depot as they neared. A shiny black engine appeared beyond the building, hauling several linked train cars. They took off in an eastward direction. More steam unleashed its power, hissing and groaning against the wheels attempting to churn over the rails. The massive iron machine started out slow, but gained speed and momentum with each thrust.

They reached the side of the depot and rounded the corner of the building to the front entrance. Flora collided with a moving object and gasped, straightening her bonnet.

"Oh, dear, please excuse me," a woman said.

Flora glanced up. Concerned green eyes met her gaze. Wisps of auburn hair framed the young woman's face beneath a white bonnet. Recognition gripped Flora's muddled brain as she took a moment to sort through her childhood memories for a name.

"Kimberly Coltrane?" Flora tilted her head and gulped, hoping she'd remembered correctly.

"Yes." She blinked, and after a moment her eyes widened. "Flora and Irene Saferight?" Her mouth dropped open, and she covered it with a delicate hand. "How long has it been?"

"It seems like thee moved from Centre to New Garden four or five years ago," Irene said. "Thee has turned into a beauty."

Her rosy glow deepened and she looked down. While she wore a simple gray skirt and white blouse, Flora agreed that Kimberly could never be considered plain.

"What brings thee to Greensboro?" She glanced from Irene to Flora, arching an eyebrow.

"Shopping," Irene said, holding out her new cloak.

"It's lovely," Kimberly ran a gentle hand over the purple garment. "I wish I was in town to shop. I came with my father. He's inside buying a ticket for a business trip to Raleigh. Earlier I had to wait on him in the hardware store." Her eyes brightened, almost like sparkling emeralds. "Guess who we ran into?"

Irene and Flora exchanged knowing glances.

"Would it happen to be Bruce Millikan?" Flora asked, trying not to show disdain in her expression or tone.

"Exactly!" She grinned, blinking in surprise. "He's changed so much. He's as tall as my father now. They discussed farming methods in the hardware store."

"Indeed, we saw him in the general store." Flora shifted in discomfort as Kimberly's expression transformed to a dreamy daze.

"Who would have ever guessed that Bruce Millikan would turn out to be so handsome?" Kimberly touched her hand to her chest. "He's such a gentleman and so attentive. I hope he meant it when he said I've grown into a sophisticated woman and he'd stop by and call on us when he's in town again."

"He called thee sophisticated?" The question tumbled from Flora's tongue before she could hold it back. Disappointment stabbed her anew, twisting her heart.

"Yes." Kimberly folded her arms as if hugging herself and her smile widened. "Father seems to be impressed by him as well. He's talked of nothing else since."

Rare jealousy sparked a flame in Flora's wounded heart. She had always wondered if Bruce Millikan was incapable of tenderness and pleasant gallantry. Now she had proof. He was more than capable—just not with her. The realization brought anger and then a fresh wave of bitterness.

———

Bruce rode past fields of tobacco and rows of tall corn until, by early afternoon, the two-story gray house came into view.

His mother came out onto the porch, shielding her brown eyes from the sun. Her plump form was a welcome sight as she pulled her tan shawl tight around her and patted the silver bun on the crown of her head.

"Looks like thee brought the whole store back from town," her soft voice teased. She hurried down the porch steps toward the wagon and peered over the side.

"Just half of it." Bruce winked, giving her a grin as he jumped down. When she smiled back, a ring of wrinkles encased her loving eyes, reminding him of how much she had aged in the last two years.

With two older sons and a daughter grown and married, his parents were now sixty. Only Bruce and Silas, his younger brother, remained on the farm.

"I ran into Pastor John while I was in town. He asked me over for supper. Said he needed to discuss something with me." Bruce laid a hand on his mother's shoulder. "So don't make a plate for me this evening." He kissed her cheek.

"I hope he doesn't have another mission for thee so soon. Son, I believe in the work thee does for the Underground

Railroad, but after so many months of traveling, thee needs a break. Can he not find someone else this time?" His mother wrung her hands as she followed him to the back of the wagon, where he unhitched the latch and pulled down the gate.

"I'm not sure, but I'll be fine, Mother. Thee knows if I don't go, Father will. He's content to let me take his place, but he won't stand by and let the Millikans miss out on what he thinks is an opportunity to save a life."

"It's so dangerous!"

"Which is why Father should stay here. He can't handle the outdoor elements and the vigorous running and climbing over the mountains like he once did."

"Holly!" His father rode his horse in a canter toward them.

Bruce and his mother walked to meet him where he had slowed to a stop. With the sun casting him in a silhouette from behind, his gray whiskers and sideburns looked white rather than gray beneath his black hat.

"Some of the cows escaped." He took a deep breath. "Part of the fence must have been weak."

"I'll help thee round them up," Bruce offered.

"Thee can help after unloading." His father nodded toward the wagon. "Where's Silas?"

"He was in the barn working on that harvest machine that Bruce made a while back," Mother said. "Can't get it to work right."

"I'll need his help. He can work on that later." Father started to pull away, but she reached up and laid a hand on his arm.

"Eli, Bruce has another meeting with the pastor this evening."

His father paused, and his hazel eyes met Bruce's. "Do I need to be there?"

"He didn't mention it," Bruce said.

"Well, all right, then. Let us know if it's another mission." His father rode away.

"I wish thee didn't have to go." His mother sighed, watching her husband ride toward the barn.

"It may not even be about a new mission. Pastor John may only want a report on the last mission to Indiana."

She grabbed his arm and smiled with relief. "Thee is right. I hadn't even thought of that. Perhaps that's all it is."

2

Bruce pulled up behind another wagon in front of Pastor John's small one-story house. Who else could he have invited? After a busy afternoon of putting away supplies and helping his brother round up cattle that had escaped through the broken fence, he was glad he'd had the foresight to bathe and dress in some decent, clean clothes. While he believed in the Quaker ways of dressing plain, he also believed in cleanliness and being presentable, especially in mixed company.

He set the brake and glanced up at the waning sun casting its pinkish glow across the evening sky. Crickets sang from nearby bushes. Fireflies glowed with blinking yellow lights.

Jumping to his feet, John's black Lab barked from the front porch. Bruce grinned at Shadow's tail wagging in excitement. Once Bruce had hopped down and walked around the wagon, the animal ran over and leaped up on him, greeting Bruce with a long, wet tongue. Bruce managed to turn his face just in time.

"Shadow, down!" Pastor John gave a stern warning, as he stepped out onto the gray porch and crossed his arms. The dog dropped to all four feet and whimpered, lowering his head and walking back to his master, his tail no longer wagging.

"Sit down." John pointed at the ground beside his feet. "That's no way to greet our guest."

The dog plopped down into the exact spot with a pouting sigh.

"Sorry about that." John grinned and slapped a hand on Bruce's shoulder when he reached the steps. "Hope I caught him before he caused any damage."

"He's fine. I like dogs, and he knows it. I think he remembers me from my last visit."

"Come on in." John opened the door and waved him inside.

"I didn't know thee cooked." The smell of chicken and dumplings teased his nose, mingled with the aroma of an apple pie. His tongue watered, and he gripped his rumbling stomach. He followed John through the living room and into the hallway.

"I don't. At least not well, but as a bachelor, I've learned to get by." He stepped into the kitchen and motioned around the room. "But the Saferight ladies took pity on me and brought over some good food tonight."

Flora turned from the counter and her blue-gray eyes met his as she carried two steaming bowls and set them down in front of two empty seats. Irene placed silverware around the table.

"I've heard about thy mother's good chicken and dumplings." Bruce rubbed his hands in anticipation. "I'm looking forward to trying it."

Flora straightened, her eyes piercing him with a glare as her hand flew to her slim hips. "I suppose thee will have to keep waiting." Her voice dripped with sarcasm. "Tonight we only have MY chicken and dumplings, and we all know how disappointing a meal by a foolhardy girl can be."

"Flora?" Irene's eyes widened in surprise. "Thee doesn't sound like thyself."

Lifting her chin in a testimony of defiance, Flora twisted her lips and turned to grab the other two steaming bowls waiting on the counter.

Bruce stood in place, realizing with trepidation how he must have sounded this morning. He hadn't meant to hurt her, and now he'd just insulted her again by not even giving her credit for having prepared the meal.

"Well, it smells delicious. I'm sure thy cooking is superb, since thee has learned from the best." He forced a smile, hoping to lighten her mood. "I'm starved."

A silver spoon crashed to the floor, splitting his ears. "I'm sorry." Flora bent to retrieve it.

Irene cleared her throat and gestured to the chairs. "I made an apple pie for dessert. Go ahead, gentlemen, please have a seat."

John pulled out a chair at the square table. Bruce took the seat opposite him, glancing in Flora's direction, but she ignored him as she poured water into cups. Irene set the cups on the table. She sat on his left and Flora on his right.

"Let's give thanks to the Lord." John bowed his head. The two women followed his lead, as did Bruce. "Lord, we thank thee for the abundant meal we receive this night and for the friends gathered here. Give us wisdom. Help us to see thy plan and to follow thy guidance. In Jesus' name, amen."

Everyone lifted their heads, and John looked around the table, his gaze shifting from Flora to Bruce. "Thanks for coming tonight. Go ahead and enjoy the meal, while I share the main reason we've all gathered."

Bruce dipped his spoon and lifted a portion of chicken and a small dumpling. He shoved the bite into his mouth and savored the taste of tender meat and the soft chewy bread immersed in a buttery broth.

"Mmm . . . this is quite good." The compliment rolled off his tongue.

No response followed. Unspoken tension filled the air, and he wondered if there would ever come a time when he would be able to reconcile his mistakes with Flora.

"Oh!" Flora jerked, jarring the table, and glared at Irene. Her pale cheeks struck a rosy glow that amused Bruce. "Um, I thank thee."

It was a begrudging admission and one that Bruce assumed must have come from Irene's kick under the table. He grinned. How many times had he longed to do something similar when Flora wasn't behaving as he wanted her to?

"So, John," he lifted his glass of water and forced his gaze upon their pastor, "tell us why we're here."

"I have an important mission." John leaned forward, placing his elbows on the table and linking his fingers. "In a fortnight a slave couple will arrive, and I need someone to take them to Pennsylvania by way of Virginia. Since Flora and Irene already have an upcoming trip to Charlottesville, I thought it would be less suspicious if thee escorted them and the slave couple."

"And Flora," John turned to his left. "The slave girl is pregnant. We'll need thy midwife skills if anything goes wrong and she goes into early labor."

Bruce stared at his pastor. Shock vibrated through his system. His jaw slackened and dropped open. How could he get out of this without offending anyone?

———∞———

Flora sat still as disbelief pooled in her brain like a muddy swamp with no way out. Her pulse coursed through her body, pounding her limbs into numbness. The idea of being part of the Underground Railroad and doing something so meaningful for God thrilled her, but carrying the mission out with Bruce Millikan was impossible. They would kill each other, or worse, argue themselves into discovery, and then where would they be? Lives were at stake. No, this mission was too risky.

"But Pastor, Flora and I were planning to travel by train," Irene said. "We were just there today inquiring about ticket prices. It's well known that the train is our plan. Would that not cause some suspicion if we were to suddenly change our minds?" Irene's surprised expression mirrored Flora's own feelings. She felt sorry for her sister, knowing how much she'd been looking forward to the train.

"Has thee already purchased the tickets?" John asked, his gaze flitting from Irene to Flora.

"No, but we were both so excited to be traveling by train that we've been telling everyone." Irene touched Flora's wrist, soliciting her support. "Haven't we, Flora?"

"Y . . . yes," Flora said, struggling to find her voice. She risked a glance in Bruce's direction, but he stared down at his bowl as if entranced. In spite of his rugged coloring from being out in the sun, he looked a bit pale. She had heard that Bruce was an avid abolitionist and his trips were in support of the cause. At least that was one thing in his character for which she could find no fault. If he was already active in such missions, she didn't want to stand in his way. His lack of silence could only mean one thing—he wasn't in favor of the idea any more than she.

"Irene, I'm sorry thee wouldn't be able to go by train. I know it's a huge disappointment, but think of the three souls thee could save in the process." John touched her elbow. "There will be other opportunities to travel by train. This couple and their baby may not get another chance. They've already run away from their master. If caught, they could be beaten to death. We have to help them. Please consider it."

Irene looked down, but not before Flora saw her trembling chin. How could one argue with the pastor's compassionate plea?

"I already know where Bruce stands on the subject of slavery, and what the Saferight family believes as a whole, but I've yet to hear an opinion from thee, Flora." She could feel Pastor John's gaze upon her.

Lifting her attention from the table, she realized Bruce's green eyes watched her in silence. Her face grew warm under his scrutiny. Whatever was he thinking? Why wasn't he talking? She took a deep breath and licked her lips.

"Like my family, I strongly believe that no human being should own another. However, I've no experience in such matters, and I feel this mission is too important for me to be the midwife. Thee has made a wise decision in selecting Bruce. He's more than capable and well-respected in the community for completing his commitments."

John finished chewing and swallowed as he weighed her words.

Bruce continued to study her, an eyebrow cocked and his eyes widened with an expression of curiosity. She ignored him and took a bite of her chicken and dumplings. In spite of how much she disliked him, if he expected her to lie—even about his abilities—he was quite wrong and didn't know her as well as he thought.

"Know what I think, Flora?" John lowered his spoon. "I think thee is not recognizing thy God-given gifts." He pointed in her direction with a grin. "Thee has a heart to serve others, and that is why thee was called to midwifery."

"True. I cannot deny it." She nodded. "But perhaps I'm not ready. This is a lot of responsibility. How would we travel? The risk and danger keep weighing on my mind. Irene is only sixteen. Has thee spoken with Mother and Father?"

"Not yet." He shook his head and took a deep gulp of water, while Bruce and Irene ate in silence. He set down his glass. "I wanted to first broach the subject with thee and Irene before I asked their permission. No need to do that if thee and thy sister are opposed."

"We believe in the cause. I'm just not sure if we are the right people to be involved," Flora said.

"The circumstances are perfect. Thee and Irene are already scheduled to travel to Virginia. All thee must do is change the way thee would travel. We have a special wagon with a compartment beneath the wagon bed. The slaves would hide in there while Bruce appears to be escorting thee and Irene to visit your family in Charlottesville. We've used this special wagon in lots of other missions, which were all successful. Believe me, Flora, there is some risk, but this is the least suspicious way."

"Will we be camping the whole way?" Irene twisted her lips, obviously displeased at the thought. Flora smiled, knowing her sister was already mentally comparing the comfort of a train to the outdoor elements.

"We have Quaker families along the way who will receive thee with open arms. They will give thee a place to sleep, a warm bath, and food. But there will be some camping. I won't deny that." John looked from Irene to Flora. "Will thee at least consider it? I need to know in a couple of days so I'll have time to make other arrangements, if not."

Flora sighed, her chest feeling heavy. She glanced at Bruce, who gulped his water like a man who had gone too long without a well. "Bruce is very quiet. I'd like to know his thoughts." She raised an eyebrow, plopped her chin on her palm, and waited.

He grunted, wiping his mouth with the back of his hand, and sat back in his chair.

"For once, I agree with thee, Flora." He scratched his reddish-blond sideburns. "This is an excellent cause, but Pastor John, the risk of danger is too great with two innocent women without any experience."

"See? It's just as I said." Flora tried to ignore the sting to her pride. His response had been just what she thought it would be. He didn't want her along any more than she wanted to go. "I know it's rare that Bruce Millikan and I agree on anything, but in this case we're united."

Pastor John scooted his chair back, the legs scraping against the wooden floor. A mischievous grin played at his lips. His brown eyes lit with interest as he stared at Flora and then Bruce. He rubbed his stomach in satisfaction.

"Well, I happen to disagree." He pointed at Bruce. "The same danger existed when thee first started out on these missions. Where does thee think experience begins? It always starts with innocence. I think this mission is perfect for both Flora and Irene—and it isn't so different from Mr. and Mrs. Saferight's first mission years ago."

Flora gasped. "Mother and Father are part of the Underground Railroad?" She exchanged a look with her sister.

After Flora and Irene said their good-byes and disappeared down the lane, Bruce slipped his thumbs through his suspenders and leaned against the porch column. "John, may I speak with thee a moment?"

"I was hoping thee would." John turned to assess him in the lantern light hanging above them.

Moths flew around the lamp as crickets chirped nearby. The lower evening temperature gave a slight glimpse into how much cooler the days would soon become.

"Have a seat." John stepped down, sat on the top step, and patted the area beside him. Shadow nudged his hand and flopped down, settling on the step below him. He scratched the dog's ears.

Bruce lowered himself beside John and leaned his elbows on his knees, linking his hands. Where should he start? "Flora Saferight hates me." He blurted the statement before he realized what he intended to say.

"I doubt it's that bad." John chuckled. "But the tension is hard to miss. What's the story?"

"There isn't a story, other than she hasn't forgiven me for some childhood taunts." Bruce rubbed the back of his neck, unsure when the uncomfortable ache had begun. "I don't really think she ever will."

"It may not be that she hasn't forgiven thee as much as she doesn't feel she can trust thee," John said.

"Which is why we shouldn't go on this mission together," Bruce pointed out. "Trust is critical on a dangerous mission like this. And besides, I'm not convinced she's mature enough. Her behavior is too erratic—at least where I'm concerned."

John rubbed his chin as silence lengthened between them. After a few moments, he gave Bruce a sideways glance. "I want the honest truth. Does thee believe Flora could do this if someone else besides thee was to escort them?"

The thought of another man escorting them, spending each day in Flora's company in such close proximity, soured his gut. He rubbed his irritated stomach and turned his head to cough, his throat suddenly dry. Instead of answering, he asked, "Even though I'm the one who's experienced, thee would replace me instead of the Saferights?"

"The mission is tough on anyone in excellent health, but especially burdensome on a pregnant woman. I'm told she may not last until the end of the trip before she goes into labor.

Flora has to be there. I don't know any other midwife young and healthy enough to make the grueling trip."

"I see." Bruce stood and leaned over the rail.

"Don't get me wrong, Bruce," John said. "Thee is my first choice as a guide, but Flora is my first choice as a midwife. I prayed about this, and I believe I've chosen the right people."

"She'll fight me every step of the way. If I decide something, she'll go against me just to spite me." Bruce dropped his head back and gazed up at the stars. "As much as I hate to admit it, Flora would probably do fine with anyone else guiding them." He glanced down at John's dark head. "Who does thee have in mind?"

"Thee—and that's the problem. Each time I prayed over the matter, thy face is the only one that kept coming to mind." John shook his head and linked his fingers around his bent knee. "That's why I'm so baffled by thy reaction—and hers."

"Believe me, everything concerning Flora Saferight *is* baffling." Bruce allowed sarcasm to creep into his tone. "I've done everything I know to do. I've apologized—although I'm not sure of all the misdeeds I've committed to apologize for. The woman can hold a grudge and has a memory that will forever haunt a man."

"Has thee tried talking to her?" John asked. "Just to get everything out in the open and to air the peace."

Bruce chuckled, thinking how quickly and smoothly she could twist his words to justify her behavior. He took a couple of steps closer to John and squatted down on his haunches.

"Flora won't stay in my company long enough for a decent conversation, and if she did, I'd manage to offend her before we'd get that far." Bruce rubbed his face, his eyes suddenly heavy and tired. "Yet I can't think of another soul I'd trust to do the job."

"What about Bob Blankenship? He's trustworthy." John scratched the side of his head.

"Yes, but temperamental." Bruce shook his head. "The first time Flora flared up at him, he might lose patience."

"There's George McGee—he's a good fellow," John suggested.

"Last year I saw him staggering out of a tavern with a wench hanging on his arm. He doesn't do it often, but I'm afraid the girls wouldn't be safe with him." Bruce folded his arms and paced across the porch. His boot heels clicked against the wood.

"Matthew Hunt," John said. "He's trustworthy, and we'd never find him in a tavern. I feel confident he believes in our cause."

"Yes, but he's too passive, and any kind of danger could befall them." Bruce continued to pace as he stroked his chin. No one suitable came to mind.

"Everyone else is getting on in years, Bruce." John rose with a sigh. "I think thee should pray about this and search thy soul. Why does thee really object to this trip with Flora? Is it truly because thee believes she's too immature, or is there something deeper? No other man seems to meet thy approval." He laid a hand on Bruce's upper arm. "Son, I'd like thee to try and talk to her. We have lives at stake here. Whatever differences there are, I'm sure thee can work them out to do the will of God."

3

Flora followed her sister into the house and untied her bonnet. She slid it off her head, handing it to Irene, who hung both their bonnets on a wall peg in the foyer.

"Flora? Irene?" Mother's voice called from the living room. "I've been worried. It's getting late."

The smell of tobacco floated through the air and she knew her father was smoking a pipe. As tobacco farmers, the men in the Saferight family, as well as their neighbors, often indulged in smoking a pipe or rolling a cigar. Flora wrinkled her nose, hating the way the tobacco smoke lingered on her clothes.

"Why didn't thee tell us about thy work in the Underground Railroad?" Irene demanded as she stomped into the living room to confront their parents. Flora followed on her heels, wondering the same thing.

"Why would Pastor John tell thee something like that?" Her father looked up from his newspaper, his spectacles perched low on his nose. The paper rattled as he folded it over and set it on a small table.

"Because he's asked us to go on a mission." Flora sat in the rocker across from her mother by the empty hearth. "We were both shocked. How did thee hide it from us all these years?

Why not trust us?" She glanced from her father's blue-eyed gaze to her mother's gray eyes. Hurt beat in her heart.

Her parents were still quite young, in their midforties. While there was a bit of silver at her mother's temples, most of her hair was still dark brown. Her father's blond locks showed no hint of gray, only a small patch in his long beard and on the tips of his mustache. Was it true they were getting too old for such a mission?

"We didn't want our girls having to bear the burden of lying if questioned." Father leaned forward, straightening his posture. "Thee and Irene were so young when we went on our last mission. It was easy to plan, as thee stayed with thy grandparents and were well cared for."

Flora rocked, trying to process everything. She remembered staying with her grandparents, but she'd never suspected a thing.

"Well, I don't want to do it!" Irene flung herself on the couch. "I was so looking forward to the train ride. And besides, the whole thing sounds dangerous."

"The risk is worth it to save lives and bring others to freedom." Flora waved her sister's concerns away. "What has me worried is Pastor John wants Bruce Millikan to guide us."

"Isn't he the one who used to call thee Beaver Face?" Mother tilted her head and wrinkled her nose.

"The very one." Flora nodded, rubbing her arms as if to ward off a chill. "Why on earth would I want to spend the next two months in his company? Depending on him for protection? I'd rather face a bobcat."

"Flora, boys do change when they become men. Thee should give him a chance." Father gave her a pointed stare meant to reprimand her. "Forgive him."

Fury rippled through her as her face and neck heated. Why did everyone have to defend him? Even her own father took his side over hers. She rocked harder. "I've forgiven him, but that doesn't mean I have to like being around him." She brushed at a strand of hair that had fallen in her eyes. "Just this morning he called me foolhardy."

"I was there, and he didn't mean anything by it, Flora." Irene sat up. "In fact, he was a perfect gentleman all through dinner at Pastor John's house."

"He was there?" Mother asked, looking from Irene to Flora.

"Yes, and he's quite handsome, too." Irene smiled as she gazed off into the distance.

"Flora, tell me the details," Father said. "Exactly what is this mission? Who's involved and where will thee be going?"

She spent the next few minutes retelling their dinner conversation at Pastor John's house. Her parents nodded, asked more questions when they needed something clarified, and often exchanged glances. When she finished, they sat in silence while her father stroked his beard and considered all that she'd told them.

"Just because they need a midwife doesn't mean I have to go," Irene said, her tone a lingering pout.

"If thy sister decides to do this," Mother said, "she can't go alone with a man. It wouldn't be proper. No one will know the slaves are with them and it will appear as if she's traveling alone with Bruce Millikan. Thy presence is required for propriety's sake."

"So this whole thing will be Flora's decision? I don't have a say-so?" Irene's lower lip quivered.

"Irene and Flora, I want thee to stop thinking about thyselves and consider the Lord's will in this and the lives at stake," Father said. He turned his attention to Flora. "If I was going instead of Bruce Millikan, would thee do this?"

Flora gulped and stopped rocking. She imagined an anxious couple, a woman desperate to save her unborn child, and conviction shamed her selfish pride. Dropping her head, she whispered a silent prayer in her heart: *Lord, please forgive me for being so inconsiderate.*

"I would." She took a deep breath and met her father's gaze.

"Then thee must do what is right." Father gave her a nod of approval and sat back in his chair, settling the matter.

The rooster crowed. Bruce bolted straight up in bed, the air whooshing out of him. Disoriented, he rubbed his eyes, still swollen from sleep.

"That bird sounds like he's standing on my window sill." His hoarse voice cracked through the nip in the air. It was cold enough to start a fire this morning. He rubbed his hands together and blew his warm breath on them.

He glanced at the window, where the curtains left a slight opening. Darkness still lined the edges of the skyline above the trees. Blinking, he tried to push the sleep from his eyes. Bruce flipped the cover to the side and grimaced as the cold prickled his legs and arms. A chill raced up his spine, and he shivered as he swung his feet over the side and stepped onto the cold wooden floor.

Footsteps passed by his door. His brother would beat him downstairs this morning—a rare occurrence. He squinted in the dark to make out the shadows of his dresser and trunk at the foot of the bed. He bent, feeling for the latch, and raised the lid. The hinges creaked.

Bruce pulled out a pair of clean pants and a button shirt. He dressed and went to the wash basin to clean his hands and face. The cold water jarred him awake as he groaned from the impact.

If he hadn't spent so much time pondering how he was going to approach Flora Saferight, he might have gotten more sleep. The girl, no, woman—the woman had a way of paralyzing his nerves. He had once thought of her as a girl, but after spending time in her company last night, he would never be able to think of her as a girl again. She cooked as well as his mother and had tried to argue her way out of going by highlighting his good qualities when she could have chosen to use his flaws against him. If only he'd been as considerate to her over the years. He grabbed a towel to dry his face and neck.

Then there were the physical changes in Flora. Her coffee-colored hair now contained sandy highlights, and wisps of it kept falling from her bun and framing her square face. As a child her face had seemed too wide, but as a woman her features had softened. The freckles he remembered had smoothed into her skin and her wide nose seemed smaller.

Her blue-gray eyes were bright and full of intelligence when she assessed him, claiming his attention almost to the point of distraction. Each time she had glanced at him, he had lost his thoughts on the conversation. He had kept quiet so it wouldn't be so obvious.

The worst part had been when she had stood and walked from the table. No plain clothes could hide the curves of her figure as her skirts swayed when she glided into the living room. Once again Bruce had lost his tongue. Flora Saferight was no longer the annoying brat he remembered, but a woman with a power she didn't yet understand—an attraction that tugged at him like the current in a raging river.

Bruce left his room and made his way downstairs, his footfalls resounding on each wooden step, announcing his arrival. The aroma of fresh-baked biscuits and sausage milk gravy drifted through the air as he made his way to the kitchen. Low voices rumbled in conversation.

The warmth of the kitchen welcomed him, as did the smiling faces of his family as they paused in conversation to look up and greet him. Silas shoved in a huge bite, while his father pushed his empty plate aside and sipped his coffee.

"Just in time for a fresh plate of warm biscuits and gravy." His mother poured two large spoonfuls over steaming biscuits.

"There's coffee left in the pot and some cool milk in a pitcher." Father nodded his head toward the gray container on the table.

"I'll take the coffee." Bruce walked over to the counter, grabbed a clean cup, and poured the hot brew. "Everything smells delicious."

"Then eat all of it." His mother beamed as she handed him his plate. She leaned over and kissed his cheek. He grinned and took his place at the square oak table. Bowing his head, Bruce prayed over his food. He cut into his biscuit and speared his first bite.

"I told thy mother what Pastor John asked of thee last night." His father raised a gray eyebrow. "Has thee made a decision on what to do?"

To keep from answering right away, Bruce shoveled in his food and enjoyed the savory taste of his mother's good cooking. The soft milk gravy and buttery flakes of bread softened the sting of the spicy sausage, giving it a nice flavor. He swallowed, well aware of his father's hazel eyes watching him, waiting in patience.

"Eli, let the boy eat," Mother said. "He just sat down."

"Sure is good," Silas paused long enough to say. "Think I'll have another plate." He winked at Mother, standing up to help himself.

A year younger than Bruce, Silas had dark brown eyes and sandy brown hair. With an oval face and an olive complexion that was darker than Bruce's, he was the real charmer in the family. He favored their older sister, Deborah, while Bruce, with his reddish-blond locks and green eyes, took after their two older brothers.

Bruce picked up his black coffee and sipped the warm beverage, enjoying the heat pooling in the pit of his stomach. After a few moments, he cleared his throat. He couldn't avoid answering his father forever.

"I hope I don't live to regret it, but I've decided to try and talk some sense into Flora Saferight. Pastor John seems convinced he needs her midwifery skills and there isn't another midwife young enough for the rough travel. Maybe I'll approach her next Sunday at Meeting."

"That's very sensible." Father nodded. "I'm proud of the decision thee made, son. I know things have been difficult with Flora in the past, but thee must admit that part of the blame falls with thee."

He didn't need reminding.

"Yes, all the times thee called her Beaver Face kind of branded her among all the kids." Silas sat down with another plate piled high. Bruce wondered how his brother managed to stay so thin. "Thee even had the other girls calling her that."

Setting his coffee down, Bruce rubbed his eyebrows, a sudden headache coming on. "If only that was all I was guilty of. Yesterday morning I called her foolhardy." Bruce rubbed his temples. "How could I help it? Before I went on my last mission, I caught her walking in the snow without a proper cloak. If I hadn't given her a ride to shorten her trip, she would have frozen to death."

"Bruce, she told thee it was an emergency. Irene had borrowed her cloak and she couldn't find it." Mother shook her head. "If she hadn't returned with the doctor when she did, her mother may not have made it through that spell of pneumonia."

"Still, she should have done something to protect herself." Bruce stabbed his fork into his gravy biscuit. "To me, that is foolish behavior and it makes me question if she's the right one for this mission."

"That's between Flora, the pastor, and God," Father said. "For thy part, thee needs to apologize to Flora for past wrongs and set her mind at peace that thee won't provoke her on this mission."

What if she provokes me?

"Why not go over there today?" Silas asked. "I could come along."

"What for?" Bruce turned to assess his brother, irritation gnawing at the back of his neck. All he needed was further distraction. Silas had a way of turning everything into a game, not to mention his flirting habits with the ladies. Flora had never seemed affected by his brother's charm, but how would she react now that she'd changed so much? No, he needed complete concentration when next he approached her. And today, he wasn't in that frame of mind.

"The only time I ever get to see them is at Meeting, and most of the time that's across the room, since the men and women sit on separate sides. I miss our school days. Now we can hardly talk to a young lady without someone assuming we're courting. We belong to The Society of Friends—why must it be more than that with a woman friend?" Silas glared at Bruce across the table, a rare expression on his usually joyful face. "That is . . . we would still be good friends if thee wasn't always taunting and arguing with Flora."

Bruce could feel his skin turning a shade darker. "That was a long time ago." He took another drink of his coffee and stood, pointing at Silas. "Not today. It's a bad idea. I'm going out to the barn to get a head start on the chores."

Flora woke to beams of light shining through the two windows in her chamber. She groaned, flipping onto her stomach and slamming her pillow over her head.

Throughout the night she'd struggled to sleep, and when she'd finally dozed, a childhood nightmare haunted her—all too similar to her real memories. Her weeping must have awakened Irene, for she came in and tried to comfort her.

Once again Flora was eight, and Bruce Millikan was nine, leading a pack of kids who chased her through a dark forest, calling her Beaver Face. The remnants of the chant pounded against her aching head, deepening the wounds of her scarred heart.

Before the dream ended, Bruce transformed into a man. He folded his arms over his chest and laughed, his shoulders shaking with mirth. "Flora Saferight, thee will always be a Beaver Face." His taunting voice sliced her to the core. In her dream, she'd touched her mouth and had felt two large teeth hanging over her bottom lip. Tears had blinded her vision, until everything faded.

Was it a sign that she shouldn't go on this mission? She placed her hands over her ears as if to make the memories and dreams disappear, but they remained, threatening her confidence in making a wise, unbiased decision. Fear coiled in the pit of her stomach. Why did she keep worrying about Bruce's opinion of her? This was ridiculous. She was a grown woman, and she didn't need Bruce's approval. Pastor John had complete faith in her midwifery skills. Shouldn't the pastor's opinion matter more?

In all honesty, she knew Bruce would do his best to protect her and Irene. He had a reputation to keep if he wanted to continue on these missions. The real challenge would be getting along with him and not allowing his insults to hurt her. She could try to pretend that she was immune to him, but she knew the truth. He affected her in more ways now than he did when they were younger.

An image of Bruce's dangerous smile burned in her brain, charming a path directly to her heart. Her pulse responded by quickening to a rapid pace. Of course, things would be so much easier if he hadn't grown into such a handsome man. A complete distraction, Bruce could rile her with his sharp tongue until she wanted to thrash him, or tip her mind into a daze with a simple glance.

A soft knock echoed through her chamber.

"Come in," Flora called.

The lock clicked, and Irene poked her head inside. "Mother wanted me to check on thee. It's an hour past dawn and the rest of us have had our breakfast. She made thy favorite—apple butter jam with biscuits."

"I'm getting up." Flora yawned and stretched her arms over her head. "I don't want to get behind on my chores for the day."

"I'll tell her." Irene closed the door, and the sound of her footsteps carried down the hallway.

With a deep sigh, Flora forced herself from the luxury of her bed and padded over to the window in her bare feet. She fingered the pale yellow curtains. The bright morning sun greeted her, casting a golden glow on her cream-colored walls. A gentle breeze swayed the oak tree branches that barely reached the height of her second-story window. A few leaves had already faded to half green and yellow. Soon they would all be full of brilliant colors, highlighting the fall season.

She shivered and rubbed her arms as she hurried to her armoire and pulled out a simple brown gown. Trembling from the nip in the air, her cold fingers struggled with the buttons once she'd donned the garment. As she washed up using the basin, she cringed from the icy water. That task complete, she grabbed the brush on her dresser. It slipped from her fumbling fingers and tumbled to the hard floor.

Another knock sounded at her door, this one more sturdy. "Flora, is thee all right?" her mother called.

"Yes, come in." The door opened as she bent to retrieve her brush. "My fingers are so cold, I couldn't hold it."

"Allow me." Mother carried a navy blue quilt in her arms and deposited it on Flora's unmade bed. She took the brush from Flora's hands and slid it through her hair, taking her time when she reached the tangles toward the ends.

"Thank thee." Flora closed her eyes, enjoying the feel of each stroke, as if she was once again a child being soothed by her mother.

"Irene told me about thy difficult night," Mother said.

"I'm fine." Flora clenched her jaw, determined to make the words true. If she didn't concentrate on it, perhaps the insecure feelings would dissolve. Eager to find something else to discuss, she glanced at the folded quilt on her bed. "Thee didn't need to bring me another quilt. I have plenty in my trunk."

"This is a special quilt. It doesn't belong with the others." Mother twisted her hair and coiled it around Flora's head, slipping in pins to hold it in place. "There, that should do." She patted the side of Flora's head.

"Special? How?" Flora walked to her bed and lifted the quilt, studying it more carefully. "I don't believe I've ever seen this one. When did thee make it?"

"When thee was a little girl. Let's open it all the way up. I have something I want to show thee." Mother helped her unfold the quilt and they spread it out over the bulk of her existing bedcovers.

"It's beautiful!" Flora stared at it, noting how this quilt didn't contain her mother's usual abstract patterns. "Thee stitched a road with several houses and a star by each one." She fingered the stitched star over the first house. "What does it mean? I bet it represents how all the towns and villages are somehow connected through the path of life." A wistful mood came over her, as she traced the detailed stitching with her fingers.

"Not exactly." Mother shook her dark brown head and glanced over at Flora, who had the same heart-shaped face as Irene. At forty-two, her mother still showed signs of beauty, with smooth skin, intelligent gray eyes, and a small mole at her right eyebrow that gave her a distinguished look. "I stitched this quilt after thy father and I went on our last mission. It's a secret map to thy cousins in Charlottesville, Virginia."

"Are they part of the Underground Railroad as well?" Flora searched the quilt for their house.

"Indeed. They've been helping slaves escape these many years even after we stopped going." Mother sat on the edge of the bed. "Each star represents a station, a safe home where thee may stay, eat, and hide. The trees along the road are where thee will need to camp. I've included towns on the side of the path in case thee needs to find food, temporary shelter or a doctor, but there are no stations in these places. Thee will need to be very careful and hide the runaways in the woods if thee must go to one of these towns."

"Mother, this is brilliant," Flora said. "I've never seen any-thing like it."

"Listen, Flora, we've kept this secret because it must stay secret. Not all Quakers believe as we do. Some feel harboring slaves and helping them to freedom is breaking the law and causes us to lie in order to protect them. Do not trust anyone, no matter if they are Quaker, unless they are at one of these stations."

"I understand." Sudden fear stabbed her chest at the serious expression on her mother's face.

"Here is our house." Mother pointed to a white house at the bottom of the quilt. "And this is Jamestown, thy first stop. It's called the Mendenhall Station. The next one is New Garden." Her mother paused, looking at her. "After New Garden thee will enter into the wilderness and cross into Danville, Virginia, here." She pointed to the next house. "Thee will camp for a while until thee reaches Lynchburg, then Charlottesville."

The map came to an end, and Flora worried her bottom lip. "But Pastor John said this mission will go all the way to Harrisonburg and end in Charles Town, Pennsylvania. Do we not have a map for the rest of the trip?"

"Thy cousins will give thee instructions when thee reaches Charlottesville." Her mother cupped her cheek. "Don't worry. We'll give thee all we can to make this a successful mission."

Relief flooded Flora as she stared again at the quilt. "Thee has named all thy other quilts. What is this one called?"

"Midnight Star, since thee must travel at night and follow the stars." Mother folded the quilt and patted the bed beside her. "There is more I must tell thee."

Flora swallowed, the responsibility of what they wanted her to do weighing upon her. She looked up at her mother with so much love and respect, waiting.

"When thee is talking about an Underground Railroad mission in front of others, thee must refer to the safe houses as stations. The special wagon thee will be using is called a train. Bruce will be referred to as the conductor since he will be the main driver. The runaways are referred to as baggage or cargo."

"But that seems demeaning." Flora frowned, trying to understand why they would go to this much trouble to free people and treat them as equals if they were to be treated in such a way.

"It's only to protect them, I assure thee." Mother laid a hand on her arm. "We had to come up with terms that others wouldn't recognize. If caught, the runaways could die and thee, Bruce, and Irene could go to prison. Thee must keep the code words. I've already talked to Irene this morning while thee slept."

"I understand." Flora nodded.

"Patience is key. If anything unexpected happens, wait. Thee will travel mostly at night and hide and sleep during the day. Remember, if anyone tries to track thee, water will make the dogs lose their scent. That's why I've included rivers on the quilt." Mother leaned over and kissed her forehead. "I love thee, and I'm so proud of thee and Irene."

Her mother spoke as if the matter was settled. How could she back out now? The last thing she wanted to do was disappoint everyone when so many were counting on her. She would be responsible for denying a young pregnant couple a chance at freedom if she refused to go. The thought filled her soul with too much guilt. Most of all, she didn't want to disappoint God. Long ago she had made the commitment to sacrifice her personal wants and serve God's will and the needs and desires of his people. This mission would be that very thing. It was the right thing to do.

"We'll do our best, Mother." There, the words were said. She had made a verbal commitment.

4

Bruce shook off his mounting frustration as he closed the side door to the kitchen and bounded down the wooden steps. No one understood his current predicament with Flora, least of all his charismatic brother, who had a way of winning women's affections. Bruce had an undeniable past of teasing Flora. He enjoyed watching her get riled up and unleashing her angry wit. Their sparring debates were interesting, challenging. No other girls ever compared.

His most dangerous flaw was the fact that he didn't like to lose. He shook his head at himself, remembering back to how prideful he was, especially when he feared being bested by a girl and possibly losing Flora's respect and admiration. Now he realized, perhaps too late, that his vicious behavior had ended up pushing her further away.

Morning fog still clung to the landscape. The rising sun cast beams of light through scattered tree branches, glistening upon the sprinkled dew. He breathed deep, smelling the drifting smoke from the woodstove pumping through the chimney above the house. Several robins whistled and sang, fluttering from limb to limb. "Lord, sometimes I wonder if thou created the mornings just for me."

He shoved his hands in his pants pockets and headed toward the arched stables to the left. Cattle called from the distant pasture. Bruce grinned, feeling peace ease back into his soul. He rubbed the bridge of his nose as he approached the wide threshold. His feet pressed into the packed dirt of the stable yard.

If he was truthful with himself, he didn't like the idea of Flora being with some doctor in Virginia, and the thought of another man leading them on the mission had turned his stomach into knots. A jolt of realization seized him, and he paused, peering into the shadows of the rows of stalls on each side. If he craved Flora's affection for himself, he was doomed to disappointment. She hated him. Cold fear slithered up his spine, his momentary peace gone with one simple thought.

One of the horses neighed and flicked his tail. Bruce set about refilling the feed at each stall and pouring fresh water. Once the chore of feeding the horses was complete, he lit a lantern and approached the final stall on the left, where his new machine was stored. He hung the lantern on a nearby peg and looked over the field reaper machine he'd been working on since his last mission.

"Son, I think I know why thee doesn't want Silas to go with thee." Eli's voice echoed through the barn.

Bruce glanced around the stall wall. His father strolled toward him. He walked with a determined gait, an expression of fatherly concern in his wise hazel eyes. Eli Millikan stroked his gray beard in thoughtful contemplation, a look Bruce had come to recognize as a sign he was about to be questioned.

"I might have overreacted. He can come along if he wants." Bruce hoped his quick agreement would end the subject.

"Why does thee struggle with getting along with Flora?" Father angled his head and met Bruce's gaze. "The Saferights are a good and respectable family. Flora and Irene have been raised well and are fine young ladies. It may be that God's will for thee and Flora is to put thy past aside and start a fresh new relationship with complete forgiveness and acceptance."

"I'd like that. Really, I would." Bruce walked around the reaper and bent to access the bottom rollers. "She says a doctor in Virginia wants her to come work with him as a midwife and be his helper."

"A doctor?"

"Yes, she has her sights on some doctor who lives near her cousins in Charlottesville. I don't think she's planning on staying in Greensboro to be an asset around here."

"And that upsets thee?"

"No." Why did his father always have to be so direct? Bruce sighed. "It will seem strange here without her. And what if she doesn't like it there?" Bruce gripped the iron jaws that gathered hay and wiggled them—sturdy with no breaks. Then he checked the chain on the pulley. One of the links was rusted. Maybe that was the reason it kept getting stuck.

"She can always come back," Father said, leaning over him.

"I think I found the problem," Bruce said, changing the subject. "Looks like I'll have to replace this link in the chain with one that isn't so rusted to keep the kinks out of it when the machine pulls it through."

"I have a suggestion," Father said.

"Does it involve more humiliation on my part?" Bruce backed out from under the machine and rubbed the muddy rust from his palms.

"No, but is thee too prideful to suffer a little humiliation?" His father stepped back, allowing him room to check other parts on the machine.

"Believe me, Flora has made sure I've had some moments with my share of it. She has a tongue sharp enough for a double-edged sword." Bruce shook his head with a grin. "She's the only person who can make me lose my head and temper. Yesterday I called her foolhardy, and I don't know why I did it. I only meant to tease her, but I guess it didn't come out that way."

"I see." Father chuckled. "I take it she's not too pleased with thee."

"That's an understatement." Bruce looked away as heat climbed his neck and face. "She doesn't want to go on the mission because of me." A dull ache burdened his chest. The knowledge made him feel like he'd already failed the Lord and everyone else.

"She'll come around." Father patted Bruce's shoulder. "Thee just might have to visit and apologize."

Apologize?

The thought sent a wave of nausea to Bruce's gut. A rushing headache pierced the back of his head. His apologies hadn't gone so well in the past. Instead of graciously accepting his regret, she'd ended up insulting him out of anger and stomping away.

"I wish it were that simple. Flora is a grudge holder, and I don't know if she'll ever forgive me."

"Perhaps thee should view this trip as an opportunity to prove thee can be trustworthy again," Father said. "Just think about it. Guess I'll go on back and leave thee to finish working on thy machine."

"Hope to have it back up and running by this afternoon." Bruce rapped his knuckles on the side of his hand-built machine. Once he fixed the link in the chain, he would hook it up to a horse and test it out.

"Good," his father said while walking away. "Then thee will have time to visit Flora Saferight tomorrow and make things right."

Bruce took a deep breath, not ready to commit to such a daunting task. "I think I'll wait till Sunday. She might be in a better mood at Meeting after prayer and meditation on God's word."

He hoped.

Sunday morning Flora sat on the hard wooden benches on the fifth row beside her mother and Irene at Centre Friends Meeting. Her father had settled on the opposite side of the aisle with the men.

She loved Sunday meetings, where she got a chance to see and talk to friends she couldn't visit with during the week. It was a time to reflect on God's word, pray, and fellowship with friends.

Pastor John Allred walked down the center aisle toward the front, where a long table sat against the pine wall. In the middle of the simple oak table stood a hand-carved wooden cross with two lit candles on each side. At the far right side of the table sat Elizabeth Osbourne with a feather quill in hand and a bottle of ink next to her book of recordings. Throughout the Meeting, she would record all the discussions. The sanctuary grew silent out of respect as all eyes turned toward the front.

"I would like to read a scripture from Leviticus 19:18," Pastor John said. "Thou shalt not avenge, nor bear any grudge against the children of thy people, but thou shalt love thy neighbor as thyself."

He paused, allowing them to meditate on the scripture he'd read. Flora contemplated the word *grudge*. Forgiveness was something she had learned to give as a young girl, but she didn't see the point in putting herself back into the clutches of a friend who couldn't be trusted. An image of Bruce Millikan came to mind. She didn't dare look over her shoulder. Earlier she had seen him arrive with his family and had tried to avoid eye contact.

Even if she had forgiven him for his past deeds, she hadn't forgotten them. Resentment filled her heart at the thought of him. Did that mean she still harbored a grudge against Bruce Millikan?

Lord, please forgive me.

It was a sin from the heart. Tears of guilt stung Flora's eyes. The last thing she wanted was to be disobedient to God. Her dislike of Bruce had almost cost her the chance to do the Lord's work on this mission. She didn't want anything holding her back from doing God's will and helping others.

Flora bowed her head and concentrated on her plight. She could let go of past wrongs, but feared letting her guard down and being caught unaware by new hurts. How could she trust a man who had just called her foolhardy only a few days ago? It wasn't a childhood jibe. She truly believed that Bruce Millikan thought her foolish.

Pastor John's voice broke the silence. He prayed aloud for their community. Flora let his voice fade into the background as she whispered a silent prayer of her own.

One by one other friends prayed aloud or shared an enlightening experience as they felt led. Afterwards the congregation received a new family who had transferred from another Virginia Quaker church. A woman was disowned for marrying outside the Quaker faith. Friend Elizabeth dipped her quill. It scratched against the paper as she raced to record all the details.

Pastor John announced a wedding that would take place in three months and informed the congregation that Widow Hodgson had suffered a stroke and could use some assistance around her house. Once his announcements were finished, he bowed in closing prayer and dismissed everyone with a brief nod and smile.

Conversations buzzed around them, and people stood. Some lingered in further discussions while others filed into the aisle and out of the building.

"That was quite refreshing," Mother said with a contented sigh. "Now I believe the afternoon meal will do us all some good."

"I agree." Irene touched her middle. "My stomach rumbled so loud I thought for sure everyone would hear it."

"If thee had taken time to break thy fast, then thee might not feel so famished." Mother glanced over her shoulder, her gaze drifting past Flora to Irene.

"I only wanted to look presentable," Irene said, lowering her voice, drawing out each syllable as if she were tempted to whine.

"Thy vanity is starting to concern me," Mother said. "I believe this trip will do thee some good. Nothing like a little humbleness and a charitable deed for someone else to bring one back to reality."

They stepped into the aisle, smiling and greeting others, inching their way to the back door leading outside. A few moments later, bright sunshine greeted them along with a slight breeze that Flora welcomed. With the church building located on a hill, they were able to view the other families in various conversational groups or making their way to their country wagons and black carriages.

"Where could thy father have gone?" Mother shielded her eyes. "I see him. He's over by the graveyard. Visiting our three babies, no doubt."

"Go on and join him." Flora touched her mother's arm. "I need to speak with someone."

"I believe I shall." Mother patted her hand and moved off in that direction.

"What about me?" Irene asked.

"Thee is welcome to come witness me humble myself or thee can go visit with one of thy school friends."

"I believe thy humbleness will be much more entertaining." Irene's lips twitched.

"I figured thee would see it that way." Flora nodded in the opposite direction. "Come on."

With her heart outpacing her, Flora set off down the hill to where the Millikans were preparing their carriage on the side of the dirt road. Eli Millikan adjusted the harness and reins around the family's two horses. Holly Millikan was the first to notice their approach. A smile lit her face, and she hurried toward them, her hands outstretched in greeting.

Nearing sixty, Friend Holly's silver hair framed her face beneath her black bonnet. Her brown eyes held a deep regard and warmth that gave Flora encouragement. Thin lines etched her eyes and mouth without detracting from her looks, but rather enhancing her years of wisdom. Hers was a comforting expression that made one want to confide in her.

Warm hands gripped Flora's and then reached out to welcome Irene as well. "Good to see thee this morning. I'm so glad I got a chance to greet thee both." She squeezed Flora's hand in emphasis.

"Indeed," Flora nodded. "I hope thee is doing well?"

"I am." She leaned close and lowered her voice. "Although I had hoped to have my Bruce home a little longer before he set out on one of those dangerous missions again. I've put him in the Lord's hands, but a mother still worries." She lowered her eyes and shook her head as if ashamed that she couldn't help worrying.

"I understand." Flora's heart filled with compassion, and she rubbed Holly's arm. "If I had a son, I'd feel the same way."

"Oh, Friend Flora, now I shall worry about thee as well. And thee, too, Irene." She glanced from her to Irene. "But I do have one small favor to ask."

"Anything," Flora said, nodding.

"Will thee make sure my Bruce eats well? I fear he lost too much weight on his last mission and there weren't two nice young ladies such as thyselves to feed him."

"On that score, I believe I can put thy mind at ease." Flora gave her hand a reassuring pat. "I'll make sure he eats plenty."

Bruce and Silas walked up and greeted them with wide grins. Bruce walked with assurance and Silas with a nonchalant swagger.

"We were thinking of calling on thee," Silas said. "Perhaps this afternoon will do? The weather is perfect for a buggy ride after the midday meal."

"I promised Mother I'd help her cook the midday meal and then we must can some of the vegetables for winter." Flora glanced at her sister, who was gazing up at Silas with wide, admiring eyes. "I thank thee, but perhaps Irene would?"

"I'd love to," Irene said, her face flushing a pink as bright as their spring garden roses.

"Friend Bruce, may I speak with thee about the mission?" Flora asked, pinning her gaze upon him before she lost her newfound courage.

His eyebrows rose and his lips dropped into a frown.

"In private?" Her chest beat like a drum against her ribcage. "Please?"

"Excuse me." He nodded to the others and stepped away with her.

They walked down the road side by side. As the silence lengthened, their arms grazed. Warmth flooded her. She imagined her face turning the same color as Irene's had a moment earlier.

"Flora, I know thee didn't want to go on a stroll. What's on thy mind?"

His tone wasn't unkind, but it was inquisitive. She took a deep breath. "I'm sorry. I just wasn't sure where to begin." She stopped and glanced up into his green eyes. His reddish-blond hair was combed gently over to the side of his forehead beneath his black hat. His oblong face now fitted his man's frame very nicely. Irene was right. Bruce Millikan had turned out to be very handsome indeed.

"Flora?" He leaned forward, his gaze searching hers in concern.

"I'm sorry . . . for not forgiving thee as I should." She scratched her eyebrow and brushed a strand of hair aside. Her fingers trembled, and she hoped he hadn't noticed. "When I heard the scripture this morning, I realized I don't want to be a grudge holder or have unforgiving thoughts linger in my heart. I want to be obedient to the Lord. Please know that I forgive thee and will not begrudge thee for thy past."

"I'm sorry, too." He rubbed the back of his neck and looked down at the ground. "I was hoping we could come to some kind of truce for the success of this mission. In spite of what thee must think of me, I've a sincere desire to serve the Lord and see slavery abolished, and I'll do anything in my power to help the cause of freedom."

"That's why I've come to admire thee so much." She offered a smile, hoping she wouldn't come to regret those words.

"Does this mean thee is willing to follow my lead in the wilderness? I don't want thee feeling like I'm bossy, but I need to know I can depend on thee."

"Bruce Millikan, I'll always speak my mind. If I don't agree with thee, I'll tell thee. I do not blindly follow any man." She took another deep breath. "But I promise to consider thy view-point if I'm tempted to defy thee."

A week later, Bruce rode up to Pastor John's house. The slave couple, Marta and Jim, had arrived with a Quaker from South Carolina on his way to market. Unable to stay, the man dropped them off and headed back south.

Bruce tethered his horse to a tree in the front yard. The Saferight's wagon was also parked out front. He walked around the side of the house toward the brown barn, where he heard voices. Flora laughed at something. The hearty sound lifted his mood. He hadn't known what to expect the next time he saw her. After her genuine confession at Meeting on Sunday, he couldn't help wondering if she would change her mind once she had more time to reflect on her decision.

His respect for her had risen a notch. He still wasn't convinced that she was the most experienced midwife for this mission, but it seemed he had been overruled on that matter. Now he would just have to make the best of it, and he had no doubt he could do so with the Lord's assistance.

Shadow barked, running out to greet him. Bruce smiled and bent to rub the dog between the ears. The excited animal circled him, shaking his tail in approval.

"Good to see thee." Pastor John stepped out from the shade of the barn entrance and extended his hand. Flora followed with her sister, Irene, and both her parents. They all nodded with greeting smiles. Bruce took John's hand in a firm grip and then shook Will Saferight's hand.

"Allow me to introduce thee to Marta and Jim. They arrived last night," John said, stepping aside and gesturing to a young black couple.

Marta didn't look much older than fourteen or fifteen. She gazed up at him with hazel eyes, a mixture of hope and trepidation lingering in her expression. He imagined she didn't trust people very easily. Her round belly protruded from a thin, malnourished frame in a ragged gray dress. Bruce swallowed in discomfort, wondering how she'd made it this far. Her frizzy black hair had escaped a single braid as if she had been through a difficult trip.

Blinking back a bit of moisture and swallowing his compassion, he offered a smile. "Glad to meet thee, Marta. I'm looking forward to helping thee."

Next, he glanced at the man standing beside her. His skin was much darker than Marta's, and he stood a few inches taller than Bruce. His dark eyes held a hard glint as he assessed Bruce, looking him up and down.

"Glad to meet thee as well, Jim." Bruce offered his hand.

Jim stared as if he wasn't sure he wanted to touch it. He scratched the side of his head, covered with bushy hair. Something flickered in his eyes, and he tilted his long face, giving Bruce a better view of his wide nose and full lips.

In an awkward silence, Bruce started to pull his hand back when Jim finally extended his in a sure handshake. That's when Bruce noticed that a "W" had been branded into the skin rippling over a muscular upper arm. He followed Bruce's gaze and grinned.

"A gift from my mastah, Mr. Wheaton. He brands all his property."

Bruce swallowed the rising lump in his throat and nodded. "I've seen similar things before, but remember, thee belongs to no one but God."

"That's why I'm determined to have my baby in freedom," Marta said, a fierce light shining in her eyes. She reached out and touched Flora's arm. "An' this sweet lady's going to help me."

"Indeed, I'll do my best," Flora said, meeting Bruce's gaze. "If it would be all right with everyone, I'd like to go into the house and examine Marta and ask her a few questions. It appears she's much farther along in her pregnancy than I'd anticipated."

"Of course," Pastor John said, nodding. "The guest chamber is on the west side of the house. It's a bit smaller than the master chamber, so if that won't suit thy purpose, feel free to use mine."

"No, the guest chamber should be fine." Flora glanced up at her mother. "Would thee please accompany me?"

"I'll come as well," Irene offered.

"Very well, I'll no doubt need thy help on this mission." Flora glanced at Bruce. "It's good to see thee again." Without giving him a chance to respond, she looped her arm through Marta's and they traipsed off toward the house.

Unexpected pleasure filled Bruce as he rubbed his chin. The woman confounded him. Was she sincere or would she turn on him the moment they pulled out of the presence of Pastor John and her parents? As soon as the question arose, a brief memory of her gentle refusal of his brother's offer of a buggy ride filled Bruce with satisfaction. Flora Saferight was the only female who had never fallen for Silas's charms. Her affections wouldn't be easily won. The thought sent a jolt of realization reeling through his system. His father had suggested he view this trip as a chance to gain her trust, but if he was honest with himself, he hoped for much more.

"Uh, Bruce?" Pastor John cleared his throat.

Still staring after the ladies, Bruce scratched his sideburn, knowing his face burned with embarrassment. What must her father be thinking of his besotted behavior? He'd have to be less obvious if he wanted to carry out this mission with success and earn their respect.

"I was just wondering if we'll be able to make it before she goes into labor," Bruce said, speaking his other thoughts aloud, hoping to distract the others from suspecting his interest in Flora.

"Yes, that was a concern of mine as well. I'm eager to hear Flora's thoughts on the matter, which is another reason I'm glad she'll be going with thee," John said, walking into the barn. "I wanted to show thee the special wagon we've built specifically for this kind of mission."

He led them to a green wagon with a canvas covering. The spoked wheels were tall and sturdy for uneven ground and long travel. Upon first glance, the wagon appeared like any other. John walked toward the back. He bent and slipped his hand underneath. The sound of a lock sliding back caught Bruce's attention as he leaned forward to get a better look. A door popped open, revealing a false bottom under the wagon frame. Grinning, Bruce squatted on his haunches and peered inside a dark compartment, long and wide enough to carry two people lying down beside each other. The conditions would no doubt be cramped, but Bruce knew it would be worth it if the method led them safely to freedom.

"Very clever. I've heard of such wagons, but I've never seen one," Bruce said.

"This one is used often for the Ohio and Indiana missions. It was built like the one Levi Coffin used about thirty years ago—with a few minor improvements."

"Such as?" Bruce raised an eyebrow as he stood, glancing from Will Saferight to Pastor John and then to Jim.

"I've drilled a few holes from the bottom to give them more fresh air, and it's a couple of inches wider," John said.

"What about Marta? Will it be wide enough for a pregnant woman?" Bruce asked, folding his arms.

"It'll have to be." John sighed, shaking his head and rubbing his neck. "It's the best we've got."

5

Flora folded a quilt and laid it on top of the others in the trunk. She wanted to be sure to pack enough for all of them when the cold weather set in, as well as for Marta and Jim. Irene packed another trunk full of cooking pots and utensils. Their mother checked off a list she held in her hand.

"I still wish we were going by train." Irene closed the lid and slid the lock in place. "This one's packed."

"Thee will get over thy disappointment soon enough." Mother removed her spectacles from her nose and waved them in the air. "I'm beginning to worry about thy priorities, Irene. Should I be concerned?"

"Of course not!" Irene sat on top of her trunk. "I'm only disappointed, is all."

"She's still young, Sarah." Father folded his paper and set it on the end table by his cushioned chair. "There's plenty of time for her to develop a conscience about such things."

"Young and fanciful." Mother walked to the couch and sank upon it, turning to gaze out the living room window.

"We'll have plenty of other opportunities to travel by train," Flora said, laying her folded cloak in the trunk. "I must admit, I'm a little disappointed as well, but after meeting Marta and

Jim, I'd much rather be helping them. I can't bear the thought of them or their newborn living in slavery."

"Someone is coming up the drive." Mother leaned over the back of the couch and squinted. "It looks like Rebecca Williams. Flora, was thee expecting a visit from the midwife?" Mother met her gaze.

"Not that I can recall." Flora shook her head and shrugged. "Perhaps Rebecca heard of our mission and has come to deliver some parting advice. I must confess, it would be most welcome. I'm afraid Marta will go into labor before we cross the border into Pennsylvania."

"Pastor John took thy concerns to heart," Father said. "He may have taken it upon himself to confide in her." He stood and stretched his arms above his head. "I think I'll take myself off to the barn so thee may talk about birthing as needed."

"And I shall make us some tea and forage for some refreshment to serve." Mother rose and hurried to the kitchen.

Father opened the door and stepped out onto the front porch to greet their guest. Flora and Irene both followed.

Once the carriage pulled to a stop, the door opened and out peered Rebecca's gray head, covered with a white bonnet. Father bounced down the steps and went to assist her. She wore a white blouse tucked into a charcoal-colored skirt. Her sturdy black boots stepped upon the pebbled drive that circled the front of their white two-story house.

"Good day, Friend Will. I hope thee is doing well?" She glanced up at Father with a curious smile, her gaze sliding to Flora and Irene standing on the porch. She winked and Flora couldn't suppress a grin at the woman who had taught her so much. "I came to see thy girls. Pastor John paid me a visit and told me about their upcoming mission. I confess, I'm a bit jealous. Wish I were young enough to go. It's such a bold and noble cause."

"Indeed, it's their inexperience that gives me cause for concern." He held out his hand. She accepted it as she stepped down, moving much slower than Flora remembered. "But I trust that this is the Lord's will, so I won't get in the way," Father said.

"Good." She patted his arm and pointed above her carriage. "Would thee be so kind as to bring in my trunk? I've brought some supplies for Flora that may be helpful should the slave girl go into labor."

While her father retrieved the trunk, Flora went to Rebecca and wrapped her in a warm hug. "Thee didn't have to go to such trouble."

"Nonsense." Rebecca waved a hand and lifted her skirts to climb the porch steps. "It was no trouble at all." She paused beside Irene. "And how is thee? Excited about this important mission?"

"I was when I thought we were going by train." Irene dropped her gaze and stepped to the side to let Rebecca pass through the threshold.

"I see." Rebecca chuckled as she swept into the house. "Just think about all the tales thee might have to share with thy future husband and children, even thy grandchildren. I'm sure thee will come upon some special adventures thee might not experience on a train."

"Like what?" Irene followed Rebecca as she found a seat in the first chair she came to and plopped down with a weary sigh.

"Let's see . . . bobcats, tracking hounds, bounty hunters."

Irene's eyes widened, and she turned to Flora, the first suspicion of fear flickering in her blue eyes. A blond eyebrow rose in a question as her mouth dropped open without a sound.

"Friend Rebecca, has thee come to scare my sister?" Flora walked over to Irene and wrapped an arm around her shoulders. "She's only trying to instill a bit of excitement in thee. Cheer up!"

"But such things are a possibility." Rebecca lifted a finger in warning.

"Here's thy trunk." Father hoisted her brown trunk up over his shoulder and set it next to the one Flora had been packing. Relief flooded Flora at the brief interruption. Perhaps now Irene would forget about what Friend Rebecca had said. The trunk thumped against the hardwood floor and something rattled inside. "Hope there aren't any breakables in there."

"No, not at all," Rebecca said. "I thank thee, Friend Will."

"Well, I'm off to the barn." Father made a quick escape.

"I've brought some tea and biscuits." Mother had appeared with a tray. Saucers and cups were stacked with a teapot on one side and a plate of homemade biscuits with jam, honey, and a slab of butter on the other side. Flora could almost taste the warm flakes and the sweet buttery flavor.

"How delightful." Rebecca scooted to the edge of her chair. "I brought a few supplies that will be helpful to Flora on this mission." She nodded toward the trunk.

"We're most appreciative." Mother followed her gaze and smiled. "I've been in fervent prayer for the girls and this whole mission ever since I've heard about it." Mother poured a cup of tea and handed it to Rebecca.

"I imagine thee has." Rebecca sipped her tea as her gaze lingered in Irene's direction. She swallowed. "Has Irene ever been in a birthing room? Flora may very well need her assistance."

"No, she hasn't." Mother dropped her gaze, and for the first time Flora realized how concerned her mother was in letting Irene go. "Irene is only ten and six. It has been so long since I lost my little ones. She doesn't have an interest in midwifery like Flora."

"No matter. There may come a time when she'll be needed out of necessity. We must prepare her as best as we can." Rebecca's brown gaze met Flora's. "Of course, I hear that handsome young man Bruce Millikan will be escorting thee. He's very capable. Few know this, but a year ago he patched up a slave with a gunshot wound on a mission. He isn't afraid of blood and will know how best to stop the bleeding if there are complications. Out in the wilderness, thee must forget about protocol. It doesn't matter that he's a man and not a doctor. Ask for his help if thee must. Survival comes first."

Bruce shoved his fists against his sides and stared at all the trunks Flora and Irene expected to take on the trip. He couldn't stop his jaw from dropping open in acute shock.

"What's wrong?" Flora demanded as she strolled to a stop beside him, her arms folded across her chest in defiance.

"This!" He gestured toward their loaded wagon. "We're not going on a pleasurable trip. We need to take as little as possible."

"I only packed what was necessary," she said through tight lips.

Disappointment plowed through him as he pivoted back on his foot and rubbed his shaved jaw. He should have expected this. Hadn't he been concerned that she was too immature for such a mission? Here was the proof stacked before him. What had her parents been thinking to let her pack this much?

He glanced over at the Saferights and Millikans, talking to Pastor John by the barn. Why weren't they helping him manage Flora?

They were expected to leave within the hour, but now he realized it wouldn't happen. The Saferights' wagon still needed to be unloaded and transferred to the special wagon, but first he'd have to convince Flora and Irene to leave some things behind.

It was almost dusk, and cooler temperatures hugged his body, causing his skin to rise with goose pimples. He wasn't sure if it was due to the cool air or the idea of another confrontation with Flora—so soon after their recent truce.

Silas walked up beside him with his hands in his pockets, a sharp whistle upon his lips as he shook his head in disbelief. "Looks like thee will have thy hands full on this trip."

"What's that supposed to mean?" Flora leaned around Bruce, and the fragrance of cedar teased his nose. Her eyes pierced his brother. Any other time, Bruce would have found the situation humorous, but right now they were losing daylight. The last thing he needed was Silas antagonizing her.

"I could leave behind a dress and a few more pots," Irene offered as she leaned over the side of the wagon. "And maybe a quilt."

"No!" Flora glared at her sister. "We need all the quilts we've brought."

"Like I said, thee will have thy hands full." Silas shook his head and slapped Bruce on his shoulder. "I'm glad it's thee and not me."

"Silas," Bruce's voice sliced through the air, "thee isn't being helpful."

"And neither is thee, Bruce Millikan." Flora pursed her pink lips. "We went to great pains trying to determine what to bring. In spite of what thee must think, we put many things back."

"Flora, I appreciate all thee has done to prepare for this mission, but we only have one horse available." He pointed to the animal hitched to the green wagon beside them. "This is too much weight. We'll kill the poor horse. The special wagon isn't

68

designed for two animals even if we wanted to hitch another one."

Without waiting for a response, Bruce unlatched the back, pulled it down, and hopped up onto the bed. He opened the first trunk as the lid squeaked. "Silas, bring me a lantern."

"Stop!" Flora scrambled to climb into the wagon. Her long skirts tripped her, and she fell to her knees and crawled toward him. "Those are our personal things."

Worried she would hurt herself, he reached down to assist her, but she jerked her elbow away. "Don't touch me."

He hated the hissing tone she used. Dread pooled in his stomach. With a sigh, he turned from her and bent toward the trunk. "These are hardly personal." Bruce lifted a stack of four pots. "Two will be sufficient." He separated them, making two stacks.

Glowing light appeared, swaying toward them. Crickets sang all around them. The skyline dimmed to a pink line over the trees. A crescent moon brightened against the charcoal sky as tiny white stars dotted the heavens.

"Here's the light thee wanted." Silas held up the lantern.

"Thanks." Bruce accepted it, catching a glimpse of Flora's angry glare now that she had righted herself on her feet. She blinked and an unexpected flicker of fear shadowed her glistening eyes. A sudden urge to stroke her cheek in an attempt to comfort her stilled him.

"Why is thee looking at me like that?" She shifted in discomfort and looked down. "A couple of those trunks have some unmentionables in them."

An owl hooted in the distance, mocking him as understanding dawned. "I'm sorry. I should have realized thy concern, but we still have to leave more things behind."

"We don't need these." He turned and lifted eight tin cups. "I packed five for us, as well as plates."

"Forgive me for not imagining thee as the cooking type." Flora's dry tone dripped in sarcasm. "What about utensils?"

"I have them." Bruce dug deeper into the trunk and pulled out other containers they didn't need.

"My brother is quite resourceful, Flora Saferight." Silas leaned over the side of the wagon next to Irene. "He thinks of the little details that most of us men would never consider. I'm sure thee will find him to be a great blessing on this mission."

"I've no doubt of his attributes, but it appears that he has a great deal of doubt about mine." Her voice lowered. "I suppose some things will never change."

Bruce paused, disliking the hurt in her tone. "We should have given each other a list of what we planned to bring. I'm sorry I didn't consider it before now."

"No matter. We need a solution before it gets too late." Flora moved toward him and dropped to her knees. "Finish going through this trunk and pull out anything that duplicates what thee has packed. Since Irene and I will be doing most of the cooking, we'll keep the food we brought and leave behind any food thee has brought." She pointed to a trunk behind her. "These two trunks contain quilts, dresses, shawls, bonnets, cloaks, and personal items. We won't part with anything in them."

"Good idea. I'll go to the other wagon and pull out the extra food supplies we brought," Silas said.

"What about that one?" Bruce pointed to another trunk.

"It's my midwifery supplies. If Marta goes into labor, and I believe she will, I'll need everything in that trunk to pull her through it. I've also brought some diapers for the baby."

Impressed with her ability to shift from a victim of insult to a problem solver, Bruce stared at her reflection in the lantern light as darkness increased around them. Her silhouette showed a chin set in determination; she was a woman who wouldn't be easily deterred by persuasion, but only by reason.

"Is there anything thee might consider parting with? Did thee pack something extra?"

She stared at him in silence.

"Please, Flora. Help me lighten the load our horse must carry."

"I packed extra food in case we are detained for some reason." She looked down at her folded hands. "And lanterns. I don't like the idea of being without light."

"I'll get the lanterns and take them to Mother," Irene said.

"The extra food we can leave behind. I plan to hunt game as we need it."

"Thee brought guns?" Her breath hissed as she swung her head up to gaze at him. "I disapprove of such weapons. Thee cannot."

"Flora, be reasonable. We have to eat, and we can't carry that much food. Besides, we could be ambushed by criminals, and we must have a means of protecting ourselves."

"But Quakers don't believe in fighting . . . or killing." Concern filled her voice. "Would thee truly shoot another man?"

"I wouldn't want to and one could aim for a limb to stop an attacker, but not mortally wound him."

"Bruce, thee has surprised me." She turned away, crossing her arms.

He hated the disappointment in her tone. It made him feel unworthy in her sight. Bruce touched her chin, nudging her to look at him.

"For myself, I wouldn't fight back." He lowered his voice, "But for thee, I cannot say in all honesty that I would not."

They said good-bye to their parents and Pastor John an hour later than planned. Irene burst into tears when she hugged Mother good-bye. Flora embraced her next, holding her tight as she closed her eyes and breathed in her lavender scent. "I'll take good care of her," Flora whispered.

"I know." She squeezed Flora's shoulders and pulled back. Even in the dim lantern light, Flora could see tears shimmering in her eyes. Her father engulfed them both, one arm draped around each daughter.

Flora witnessed a tender moment between Bruce and his mother. Tears streaked her weathered cheeks, and Bruce kissed each side, promising her he'd be home soon. He shook the hands of his father and his brother before grabbing them in a warm embrace.

Jim assisted Marta into the dark compartment. She lay on her side with the quilt Flora had given her. "I'm ready!" she called. "Jim, come on. I don't wanna be in this dark alone."

"I'm coming." He laughed, gave everyone a brief wave, and climbed in beside her. Bruce closed the door and latched the lock as John had shown him. "Don't forget 'bout us now."

"We won't," Bruce said. He touched Flora's arm. "Let's go." She nodded, grabbing Irene's arm.

Hours later, the wagon bumped along an uneven dirt road, jostliong them. Only a sliver of light from the crescent moon guided them on their path toward the Mendenhall plantation in Jamestown. The stars in the sky twinkled like scattered diamonds. As they passed beneath trees, the limbs and branches hid the magnificent view.

Irene yawned, and Flora lifted an arm around her shoulders. Taking it as an invitation, Irene dropped her head on Flora's shoulder. "I'm so tired." Her words ended on another yawn.

"Go ahead and sleep. It'll be a couple more hours before we reach the station." Flora patted her sister's arm, hoping to encourage her. Unlike Bruce, she and Irene would need some time to adjust to these hours.

Flora glanced up at Bruce's profile. He stared ahead, with his black hat casting his expression in complete darkness. Earlier, his declaration about protecting her had taken her by such surprise, and she hadn't known what to say. If his intention had been to silence her, he'd succeeded. What had he meant exactly? Did he mean he would fight for any woman who needed protection or was she an exception? The temptation to hope for more nagged at her, and she kept trying to divert her thoughts.

"Thee might want to get some rest as well." Bruce leaned toward her, his voice more gentle than usual.

What was wrong with him? Was he pretending to be nice to trick her into letting down her defenses? It wasn't like him to be caring and concerned for others—at least not for her— truce or no truce.

"Thanks, but I'm fine." She stiffened, straightening her spine. The slight movement startled her sister and caused her to stir. Flora rubbed Irene's arm, encouraging her to relax and go back to sleep.

"Perhaps it's best." Bruce shrugged. "Thee may sleep better after we arrive and daylight comes. Will Saferight told me about thy mother's quilt. May I see it when we stop at the next station?"

"Yes, it's beautiful." Flora thought of the details of the map her mother had sewn into the quilt. "It's called Midnight Star."

They fell into an amiable silence and arrived at the Mendenhall station an hour before dawn. Flora was sorry the darkness didn't provide enough light for her to view the place. She had heard a lot about Dr. Mendenhall. He was a well-respected gentleman in the community among both Quakers and non-Quakers.

Bruce pulled the wagon around to the back of the house, which looked like a two-story structure with a wraparound porch on the side. Another large structure came into view, and judging by the shape of the outline, Flora assumed it was the barn. A lantern appeared at the back door. The light moved as if someone carried it toward them.

"Bruce Millikan? Is it thee?" A man's voice floated through the darkness.

"Indeed," Bruce said. "Where should I pull the wagon?"

"Once we've seen to everyone, we can take it to the barn and care for thy horse." He cleared his throat. "I'm Richard Mendenhall and this is my wife, Mary. Let's get the cargo into the house where it's safe and comfortable."

"What happened?" Irene said, waking with a start, a slight gasp escaping her lips. She bolted upright to a sitting position.

"Nothing." Flora gently squeezed her arm in an attempt to ease her fear. "We've arrived. That's all."

"I thought the cargo would stay in the barn?" Bruce tilted his head, only his outline visible. "Considering the danger."

"We have a basement under the house where they'll have a warm fire in the hearth and a decent bed," Richard said. "It's the least we could do under the circumstances."

"That sounds even better." Flora scooted to the edge of her seat as Bruce set the brake. "Marta could use the rest. I can't imagine what she must be enduring in those cramped quarters with all the bumps along the road—especially in her condition."

"Yes, I heard she's expecting," Mary said, stepping forward, her voice a gentle whisper. "I have some warm goat's milk waiting in anticipation of thy arrival, and some buttered bread with a slab of ham."

"That sounds divine." Irene perked up at the mention of food.

"Let's get them out of there," Richard said to Bruce, who hopped down and joined him at the back.

Irene rubbed her sleepy eyes as she peered down, then she crawled over the side. Flora followed as the door latch popped open. Jim emerged first and leaned back inside to assist Marta. Her labored breathing concerned Flora. She groaned in pain as she stepped out and tried to stand, clutching her back.

"Marta, is thee all right?" Flora rushed to her. "Where does it hurt the most?"

Marta grabbed her arm and squeezed until Flora feared the blood flow would stop in her veins. "I hurt everywhere, but we got to keep going." She forced the words through her teeth and paused as she winced, leaning further on Flora. "You hear me? Don't let Jim stop 'cause o' me."

"Let's get thee inside." Flora braced herself to bear Marta's weight, but Jim rushed over and swept Marta into his arms.

"I got her." His large frame cradled her as if all his hope in life depended on Marta. Tears swam in his dark eyes, red-rimmed from a lack of sleep and consumed with worry. "I ain't gonna let nothing happen to her." He looked down at Marta, his voice breaking into a whisper, "It can't."

Flora's heart melted with compassion as an ache welled up in the back of her throat. She couldn't give him false hope. All she could do was her best. She tried to swallow so she could respond, but her vocal cords constricted.

"Jim, we'll pray for both Marta and the baby." Bruce laid a hand on Jim's shoulder. "When things are beyond our control, that's when we must turn to God."

"Follow me," Mary said, her voice floating through the air. Gray peeked through the morning sky revealing her silhouette, which hadn't been visible a moment ago.

Once inside, Jim settled Marta on a simple wood-framed bed in the basement. He built a fire while Flora tucked her in and sat on the edge to talk to her about her pains. The others went upstairs to the kitchen to have breakfast.

After Flora sent Jim out of the room, Mary brought some warm goat's milk and a ham biscuit for Marta. She sipped the liquid with hesitation as if forcing it down.

"What's wrong?" Flora asked.

"I should be starvin, but I'm not very hungry right now."

"That's all right," Flora said. "It may be that thy body needs sleep more than nourishment. Try to eat what thee can and then rest."

"I never knew white people can be so kind. Not 'til I met the Quakers." Emotion swirled in Marta's innocent voice. Tears filled her hazel eyes as she looked up. "Not even my own father thought enough o' me to treat me with kindness."

"Thy father was white?" Flora asked, realizing why Marta's eye color was different and her skin much lighter than most blacks she'd seen.

"Yes'm. My mother was his slave, and he raped her." Marta paused to swallow a bite of her ham biscuit. "The mistress must have known, but she pretended not to."

"Well, thee will soon be free." Taking a deep breath, Flora touched her arm. "Keep thinking on that."

"And my baby." Marta's face lit with a bright smile that momentarily masked her fatigue. "My baby'll be born free. That's all that matters."

A fierce determination filled Flora. In spite of the fact that Marta was seven months pregnant, showing signs of the baby coming early, and despite the difficult road ahead of them, Flora vowed she would do everything in her power to help Marta's dream come true.

"Lord, help me make it so," Flora whispered as she followed Mary upstairs.

6

Bruce stared outside the window as beads of rain pelted the glass and slid down the pane. Last night when they had left the Mendenhalls in Jamestown, he wondered if Marta needed more rest, but she had seemed to recover and her pains subsided by the time they arrived at his sister's house in north Greensboro. He slept through most of the morning until a clap of thunder woke him. Now he worried it wouldn't slack off before they had to leave that evening.

Steady footsteps passed by his open door. They stopped. Deborah, his sister, leaned against the door frame with a raised eyebrow. "I thought thee was asleep."

Even though she was eight years his senior and the mother of two small children, his sister looked much younger. She tucked a strand of blond hair behind her ear, where it had fallen from its coil.

"The storm." He gestured toward the window as two quick flashes of lightning lit his chamber. "How are the others? Have they been able to sleep through this?"

"Marta and Jim haven't stirred from their attic chamber. Irene slept all morning." She crossed her arms with a sigh. "Flora slept in her chamber until little Karen toddled in and woke her. Jack was supposed to be watching her since he can't do much on the farm during the storm, but he got distracted by Elias wanting to play a game."

Bruce grinned at the thought of his two-year-old niece waking Flora. He rolled his shoulders back and stretched out his arms. "Well, I suppose I can keep Karen occupied for a few hours, while Flora gets some rest."

"Go ahead and try." Deborah grinned, stepping out into the hallway, where he joined her. "Karen has formed an attachment to her. Flora made her a new doll out of some fabric scraps, and Karen is quite enamored."

"But I gave her a real doll last Christmas." As they entered the living room, Bruce wondered how Flora's doll of scraps could have become Karen's favorite. Before Deborah could reply, Karen ran to him and wrapped her small arms around his legs.

"Look, my dolly!" Karen chimed as she held up a creative-looking doll made of woven fabrics in the shape of a human. The arms and legs flapped in no particular direction.

"What happened to thy other doll?" He bent to peer into Karen's bright eyes.

"Goodness, Bruce. One would think thee is jealous of a doll." Deborah stepped around him. "I'm going to the kitchen to see what we might have for dinner."

"Too hard." Karen scrunched up her nose. "I hug this dolly." She slammed her prized possession against her chest and squeezed it in a fierce embrace.

A feminine chuckle brought his gaze up. Sitting on the floor by the burning hearth, Flora covered her mouth with her hand in an attempt to suppress her grin. Her blue-gray eyes glistened with mirth, and her dark hair hung in waves around her shoulders, highlighted by the fire behind her. She looked as if a halo surrounded her.

Not since they were children had he seen her hair down, but now his reaction was much different. Then, he hadn't paid much attention. Now, he couldn't stop gazing at her with his mouth dropped open like a simpleton. Fluid emotions pooled in his chest, drawing him to her. He wanted to be near her—to touch her and feel if she was real.

Was this the Flora Saferight he'd known all his life? Since when had she become so alluring? She wore a simple gray gown that fanned about her legs like a blanket but that accentuated her tiny waist. He blinked. Flora did nothing to make him think of her like this. What was wrong with him? He rubbed his face with his hand.

"Bruce?" Flora's smile faded into a frown. "Why is thee staring at me like that? What's wrong with me?"

His voice failed him as he groped for a reasonable excuse for his odd behavior.

She glanced down at her gown, felt around her chest and shoulders, and then touched her face. When her long hair fell into her eyes, she gasped. "Oh, it must be my wild hair." She patted her head as her cheeks turned crimson. "Thy niece pulled the pins out of my hair, and I'd completely forgotten about it. I'll go attend to it."

"No, it's fine. Really. There's no need." He swept his niece up into his arms. She giggled and wrapped him in a warm hug. He savored the moment as he stepped toward Flora and lowered himself beside her.

She trembled in awkward silence as she moved to her knees in an attempt to rise. Fearing he'd made her uncomfortable, Bruce clasped her arm with his free hand.

"Don't go because of me. In spite of what everyone says, there's nothing improper about a woman letting down her hair."

"Thy expression would indicate otherwise." Flora jerked away from him, her voice hardening, "I've always known my plain looks to be unappealing, but I try to console myself that I fit in better with the Quaker way of life. Women like Irene and Kimberly Coltrane have to work much harder than I do at appearing plain. But I never actually thought of myself as being repulsive—until now."

"Repulsive?" Bruce wrinkled his brows in shock. "Is that what thee believes I was thinking?"

Flora stood, moving away from him. His chest constricted as he scrambled to set Karen aside, hoping to stop Flora before she left the living room.

"Deborah sent us from the kitchen. She caught us eating a snack before dinner." Jack walked in and sat down in his favorite chair by the fire with his son, Elias, on his heels.

"Uncle Bruce! We can play a game. Father says he's tired of games." Six-year-old Elias gazed up at Bruce with hopeful eyes.

"As soon as I finish a discussion I'm having with Friend Flora." Bruce rubbed the top of the boy's brown head.

"Our discussion is over, Friend Bruce." Flora forced a smile as she emphasized his name. "I'm going to go rest for a while, and then I'll make myself presentable for dinner." She strode toward the hallway.

"But I'm not finished," Bruce said, following her.

"Yes, thee is." Flora increased her pace. "I'm heading to my chamber. I'm certain that Jack and Elias will provide thee with ample entertainment. And don't forget to watch Karen."

Bruce clenched his jaw in determination. She would not win this one.

"Does thee intend to follow Flora to her chamber?" Jack chuckled.

Bruce paused in midstride. Sighing, he slowly turned. "I suppose not, but for a moment, the thought did have merit." He attempted a teasing grin for his brother-in-law's benefit, but inside, his heart ached at the thought that Flora believed he could find her repulsive. Impossible!

After they left Deborah's house, they traveled most of the distance in silence, bumping along the dark road. Only the sound of a coyote howling and an occasional bird flitting among the tree branches rose over the sound of the wagon wheels as they crunched over the dirt road. They had passed one rider on horseback, who tipped his hat in passing.

"It's now dawn." Bruce steered the horse into the woods off the main road. "We need to set up camp, eat some breakfast, and get some rest until this evening." The wagon rattled over tree roots and fallen leaves, as they rode deeper into the forest. "Hold the lantern up higher," Bruce said to Flora as she leaned toward Irene to avoid a low-lying branch. "We'll settle over there by that hedge. It'll provide a bit of cover." They rolled to a stop, and Bruce set the brake.

"By the way, I didn't get a chance to say this at my sister's house, but I could never find thee repulsive. I've no idea how such a thought ever got into thy brain." He jumped to the ground, leaving Flora to ponder his words. He kicked up a pile of leaves as he walked to the back to let out Marta and Jim.

"I'll find something for breakfast," Flora said, landing with a thump on the other side. The man baffled her. A secretive smiled played upon her lips. At least Bruce didn't think as badly of her as she had feared.

"I'll help thee." Irene scrambled down behind her.

"Miz Flora!" Marta called from the back.

Flora grinned as she lifted her skirt to walk toward their voices. No matter how many times she'd explained to Marta that Quakers didn't use distinguishing titles with their names, she still called Flora and Irene by Miss before using their given names. Perhaps a habit that had been ingrained in a person's character would take time to break. In her opinion, many non-Quakers put too much importance on man-made titles.

"I need some privacy." Marta grabbed her arm, her eyes wide.

"I haven't had a chance to survey the place yet." Bruce shook his head. "It may not be safe. Give me a few moments."

"I can't wait!" Marta's anxiety increased as she gripped Flora's arm even tighter. "Please."

"Bruce, she's waited for hours and a pregnant woman needs more breaks." Flora pointed toward the east where the sky began to dawn through the leaves. "We'll go that way."

He shoved his hands to his sides and gave a reluctant sigh. "All right, but don't go far."

Flora led Marta deeper into the woods. As they walked, the sound of water could be heard. Excitement bubbled in Flora's chest at the thought of replenishing their water supply and being able to wash their pots and dishes.

"Marta, I believe we may be near a river." Flora turned her back as her friend squatted to take care of her personal needs.

"I hear it, too," Marta said, joining her a moment later.

"It doesn't sound far. Let's see if we can get to it from here. We need more water." Flora motioned for Marta to follow.

They came to a clearing. Below them a dark river poured over a hill of rocks, winding through the earth like a snake. The bank's surface wasn't as smooth as Flora had hoped, but not impossible to maneuver. She would have to return with Irene. It would be too much for Marta.

A growl rumbled across the moving water. Flora looked up, and her gaze met the dark eyes of a dog standing on the other side and showing a set of fangs. He stood still, watching her as his body tensed, fully alert.

Marta gasped. A piercing bark broke through the sky, followed by more growling. A man stood from where he'd been fishing on the side of the bank. He squinted and leaned forward, pointing at them.

"Hey, there! Why're y'all on my property?" He waved his hand in the air, his Southern drawl full of suspicion. "Ain't no houses for miles 'round here, so y'all can't be a-visitin'.'"

"Miz Flora, we got to go back." Marta's voice whined with fear.

"Shush, we've got to stay calm," Flora whispered. She took a deep breath. "I beg thy pardon, sir. We were just passing through and will soon be on our way."

"A Quaker!" He raised a fist above his head and shook it with fury. "I know what you people do. Helped my Negro escape, and I won't stand for it happening again on my property!"

Flora closed her eyes, wishing she had altered her speech in spite of her convictions. Wouldn't it have been worth it to save their lives? Now she'd put them all at risk. If only she'd had a little more time to consider her options and the consequences.

"Go get 'em, Jethro!" The man dropped his fishing pole and bent toward his dog, waving the animal into the river. Like a dutiful pet, the hound barked at them and ran leaping into the water with a splash. Flora glanced at the width of the river, measuring the short distance. She wished it was wider—it wouldn't buy them much time if they were being pursued across it.

"I'm going to catch y'all!" He bent and retrieved his rifle, aiming it at them.

"Run, Marta!" Flora turned and stepped in front of her friend, hoping to shield her and the unborn baby. She closed her eyes waiting for the pain to slice into her back as the sound exploded through the air, echoing through the woods. The dog growled as he swam.

Once they were out of sight, Flora grabbed Marta's hand and pulled her east. "This way."

"That's the wrong way." Marta jerked back toward the wagon.

"No, listen to me." Flora chased her, grabbing her arm and tugging her east again. "We can't lead him back to the others. This way they'll hear the gunshots and will have a chance to escape." Flora tugged her arm again. "Please! We have to do this for our loved ones. Thee wouldn't want Jim to die, would thee?"

"No." Marta shook her head, now following Flora, tears streaming down her face. They shoved branches aside. Marta almost tripped over a root. Flora paused long enough to steady her, but she cried out, gripping the lower part of her round belly.

"Don't give up, Marta," Flora urged her. "We must survive this for the baby's sake."

Marta whimpered but kept moving. Her labored breathing worried Flora, but she couldn't allow her to rest. Not yet. It was still too dangerous.

The dog started barking again. Flora groaned, knowing he'd crossed the river and would soon be upon their heels. The barking grew closer. Flora cringed, realizing he must have picked up their scent once he'd left the water. What could she do? *Lord, help us!*

As they ran, her mother's words came back to her about how water would cause hunting dogs to lose their scent. She hated the thought of doing so, but they would have to jump into the river if they wanted to lose this dog before his owner caught up with him.

"Marta, can thee swim?"

"Naw." She forced the word between gasping breaths.

"We're going to have to jump in the river to make him lose our scent." Flora led her back to the sound of running water, twisting from a briar that had caught her skirt. "Trust me."

They came to the bank where water poured faster over the rocks along the edge. Flora spotted a smooth ridge where they could ease in without jumping from a high distance.

"What 'bout snakes? I'm scared o' snakes." Marta jerked her arm back and hesitated.

"It may be too cold for snakes. Besides, we don't have a choice. Just keep praying for the Lord to protect us."

The cold water soaked their clothes as they gasped from the frigid shock. Flora took deep breaths, determined to convince her body that it wasn't as bad as it felt. The water was only up to their chests in this part of the river. They traveled along the edge until Flora saw a fallen tree wedged between some rocks in the water. She pointed. "We'll hide under that."

"Looks . . . like a . . . beaver dam . . . to me," Marta said between shivers. "God . . . be with us."

"Here, hang onto this tree trunk." Flora pulled Marta's hand over the bark where a strong branch jutted out and would hide her. "Thee should be safe here until Bruce can come back for thee."

"You can't leave me 'ere like this!" Marta grabbed Flora, her tone frantic.

The dog's barking grew louder.

"It's too small for us both. I'll try and find a place to hide on the other side, or nearby." Flora lifted a finger over her lips. "No matter what, be quiet."

85

Flora held her breath and ducked under the water with the intention of surveying the other side. The current gripped her skirt and sucked her toward the middle, where it was deeper. She floundered, groping for any steady object she could hold onto, but there was none.

Finally, she rose to the surface and gasped for air, flailing her legs and arms. If only she had learned to swim. The bubbling water carried her forward, and she slammed into a rock. Pain ripped through her elbow as the current pulled her back under.

—⁂—

Bruce paused at the sound of a rifle echoing through the woods. It vibrated through him like blood thundering in his veins. His gaze met Jim's and then Irene's. Both their eyes widened in fear.

"I'm going after 'em." Jim turned in a circle and sprinted east.

"No!" Bruce dropped his load of firewood. Jim was quick, but Bruce managed to catch him before he got too far. Jim tried to yank free, but Bruce held his shoulders tight, both men breathing hard.

"Listen to me. It may only be hunters, and we can't risk exposing Marta and Flora if they haven't yet been discovered." Bruce shook Jim to make him pay attention. "We can't panic. We need to stay calm so we can think clearly. They're depending on us. All right?"

Jim nodded, breathing heavily.

"If I let thee go, will thee agree not to run after them?"

"Yeah, but what's we going to do?"

A dog barked. The sound of limbs thrashing about alerted Bruce to how close they were to being discovered themselves.

Bruce tried not to tremble as he imagined Flora and Marta running through the woods, frightened.

"Let's get out of here. I need to get thee and Irene to a safe place so I can come back and look for them." Bruce nudged Jim toward the wagon.

"Not without me." Jim said, his jaw vibrating as he blinked back tense emotion. "If anything happens to her, I don't know what I'll do." He shook his head, wiping tears from his face.

"Keep thy faith." Bruce gripped his shoulder, ignoring the dreaded pool of concern in his own gut.

When they reached the wagon, Irene clutched her stomach as silent tears streamed down her face. "I'm so worried."

"I know," Bruce said, pointing at the small campfire. "Pour some water over that and cover it with dirt. And if anyone asks, thee is my little sister and we're visiting relatives outside of Charlottesville."

"Thee would have me lie?" She wiped her wet face, staring at him in shocked confusion.

"No, for we are brother and sister in Christ." Bruce opened the false-bottom latch and swung the door open. "Hurry, Jim. We don't have much time."

Jim slid inside. Bruce and Irene climbed onto the seat. He flicked the reins and clucked his tongue. The horse lurched forward, always quick to obey. "Good boy," Bruce said.

He traveled at a brisk pace, guiding them back onto the main road. Irene sniffled, wiping more tears from her eyes. He wished she had a similar constitution to her sister. Flora wouldn't be weeping and falling apart but trying to help solve things. An ache seized his chest, an empty void at the realization that Flora wasn't sitting on this wagon bench with them where she belonged.

"Lord, keep them safe and lead me to them." The prayer came out in a whisper.

"What?" Irene leaned toward him, inclining her ear.

"Thee should try to stop crying so thee won't raise suspicion if we pass anyone."

"I'm sorry." She wiped the rest of her tears with her sleeve. "Thee is right. I should try to be strong like Flora." She straightened her back and lifted her chin, then folded her hands in her lap.

Guilt sliced through him. How had she known what he was thinking?

When he felt that they had gone far enough, Bruce pulled off the road and cut a path into the woods. He found another secure spot and set the brake.

"This time I'm unhitching the horse and riding back for them. It's too far to walk and time is of the essence. I'm leaving my hat here. No need to draw attention to my Quaker roots right now."

"What about Jim?" Irene asked, her eyes red-rimmed. She pulled her shawl tight around her as she trembled.

"Don't let him out until I return. He'll be too tempted to come after us and search for Marta." Bruce jumped down and unsnapped the harness. "If anyone happens by, tell them thee is waiting on thy brother to return and that we're only looking for a place to camp."

Inside the covered wagon, he pulled the saddle he'd thrown over his supply trunk and worked fast to ready his horse. His hands shook with worry. He'd never struggled with fastening a saddle around a horse as he did now. He took a deep breath and slipped a foot into the stirrup and swung his leg over and settled in the seat.

Irene walked toward him. Her shoulders continued to tremble and her eyes swam with tears, but he didn't have time to comfort her. "Irene, I know thee is scared, but I need thee to be strong and pray."

"I will." She nodded. "I'll pray by the wagon so Jim can hear me."

"There's a good girl." Bruce gave her an approving smile before whirling his horse around. He nudged his heels into the animal's sides and clicked his tongue, signaling him into a gallop.

Bruce prayed as the cool wind rushed against his face. As he drew near, the sound of a barking dog alerted him to the direction to take. Bruce dismounted and tied his horse to a tree and proceeded on foot, stepping around leaves and branches as softly and slowly as he dared.

"Well, Jethro, looks like we lost 'em."

Bruce peered around a tree to see a man in his mid-thirties carrying a rifle. He bent down and patted his white and brown spotted hound. "I didn't get across the river in time." He sighed, lifting off his brown hat and scratching his shaggy brown head.

The dog grunted, wagging his tail.

"Well, come on. The wife will have breakfast waitin'." The dog circled him and followed him west.

Bruce waited until they were out of sight and hearing before venturing toward the sound of water. The man had said he'd crossed the river. Why would he do that if he hadn't seen them by the river? He hadn't been wet, so maybe he'd taken the time to cross by bridge further down.

On instinct, Bruce trekked east. If the man hadn't found them, perhaps they went the opposite way, which would mean he didn't track them far enough. At twenty paces he ran into a sign nailed to a tree. "Private Property—No Trespassing." That might explain why the man had not gone any further.

Bruce had no choice; he kept going. He scanned the banks, straining his ears for any unfamiliar sounds or sights. Not even a piece of ripped clothing gave him a clue. The longer he looked, the harder his heart thumped with fear. He wondered if it would be safe to call their names at this point. Only the sounds of running water and an occasional bird flying through the air.

He kept going and stopped after another twenty paces. Looking around, he didn't see any signs of human life. He listened to his heart, paying attention to all his instincts. It was safe. "Flora!" He kept his voice low enough so it wouldn't carry too far but would reach her ears if she was nearby.

"Mister Bruce!" Marta called.

Hope lifted in his chest as he ran toward Marta's voice. He saw a fallen tree, squinted, and spotted her dark head bobbing out of the water. No sign of Flora.

"Oh, Lord, please let her be safe." He whispered the prayer as he hurried down the bank, careful not to lose his footing.

Marta burst into tears.

"I'm coming! Hold on." He stumbled into the water, grateful it wasn't over his head and he wouldn't have to swim to reach her. The cold water took his breath away.

When he reached her, she let go of the log and threw her arms around his neck, crying so hard he couldn't understand her words. He had to calm her so he could ask about Flora. She sputtered and sniffed, making her words unintelligible.

"Irene and Jim are safe at the wagon. I've moved it to a better location." Bruce swept her into his arms, thinking she might be mumbling about Jim. Her trembling was so violent, he realized he would have to get her back to the camp and warmed up by the fire as soon as possible or hyperthermia might set in.

Once they reached the bank, Bruce paused to take a deep breath. "Marta . . . where's Flora?"

"I don't . . . know. She said . . . there wasn't enough . . . limbs to cover us both. She went under the log . . . and I ain't seen . . . or heard from her since."

"Let me take a quick look for her. Wait here and be as quiet as possible. I'll be right back." He set her down and covered her with his coat, then hurried back to the river where the log lay.

"Flora!" He scanned the water, looking for a piece of clothing, any sign that Flora might be nearby. No response. Anxiety slithered up his spine, leaving a trail of worry. He shivered. "Flora!" Still no sound. He walked a little further down. "Flora!" No response.

After a few moments, he realized he'd better get Marta to safety and warmth. His steps were heavy as he returned to Marta. "I'll get thee back to Jim and Irene. Then I'll come back for her."

Hoping he'd made the right decision, Bruce set the horse in motion. His heart pounded to their galloping pace. Flora was strong and full of wisdom. She had to be all right. He couldn't imagine anything else. His heart wouldn't allow it.

7

Flora bobbed between rocks and crevices, skinning her knees. She stayed afloat long enough to catch her breath. "Help . . . Jesus!" Back under she went. Her heart pounded against her bruised ribs as the air in her lungs pressed for freedom.

Moments later the water calmed, and she drifted into a boulder. She kicked until her feet found the soft bottom. Out of breath and energy, she sagged against the huge rock. She glanced over at the bank and groaned. Blinking to clear her blurry vision, she tried to judge the distance. It looked too far. What if there were places over her head between here and there? She couldn't take the risk, at least not so soon. She would have to wait until she'd rested and regained some of her strength. Flora shivered, eager to climb upon the rock and rest in the sun.

"Help me . . . Lord." Her ragged voice rasped between breaths.

Flora's skirt tangled around her knees when she tried to lift her legs, and they sank back into the water as if chained. She wouldn't give up. Gritting her teeth, Flora jumped up and grabbed onto a knob on the rock. Her hand slipped and the hard surface bit into her fingernails, cracking and pulling on them until she managed to haul her body up, soggy skirts and all.

Her breaths came in quick gasps as she crawled on sore knees to the center of the rock where it was safe. She collapsed onto her stomach. "Argh!" Pain sliced through her ribs. Flora turned on her side when the pain subsided, making it easier to breathe. Her chest expanded and contracted, but more slowly with each gasp.

"Lord, please protect Marta," she whispered. "Don't let anyone find her but Bruce."

An image of Marta's hazel eyes as Flora was leaving came to mind. Frightened. Worried.

Guilt stripped Flora of all thought as she squeezed her eyes shut and tears trickled through her lashes. "Please forgive me. I didn't mean to cause this."

She wondered how long Bruce would search for them. He would probably find Marta first. Flora knew he'd keep searching for her, but for how long before he thought it endangered the mission? Would he make the decision to go on without her? Once Irene told him she couldn't swim, he would probably assume the worst.

Fear gripped her heart in icy terror, sending another tremor through her body. The sun had helped, but not fast enough. She couldn't keep her lips from quivering. Turning to face the sun, Flora let the heat embrace her face, no longer caring if her pale skin darkened with color. Warmth was all she craved at the moment. Once she achieved that, she'd concentrate on the next step.

Flora closed her eyes and breathed slowly and deliberately, thankful for each breath of fresh air. She listened to the steady flow of water all around, strangely calmed by it after nearly drowning earlier. As her shivering faded, a languid fatigue soothed her body. Her worn muscles felt as if someone had tied a fully packed trunk to each limb.

"Lord, please keep the others safe. Lead Bruce to me before he gives up and assumes the worst." The whispered plea fell from her tongue and ended in a sigh as she realized the irony of it all. To think how many years she had spent avoiding Bruce Millikan. Now she lay here in dire need and the one person she prayed would find her—was none other than Bruce. She laughed aloud at her own folly. A bird flew across the sky chirping, as if mocking her.

Would Bruce chastise her for not hiding her Quaker speech and keeping them all from danger? Would he be angry at her for running to the river rather than back to the wagon? Perhaps he would be livid at her for separating from Marta. At any rate, no matter what she could have done, Bruce would no doubt feel she had made the wrong decision. She'd never been able to please him.

Wrapping her arms around her, Flora consoled herself with the thought that God was the only one she needed to please. In her heart, she knew she had done what she thought was best. The one thing that she could have done differently was conceal her speech. Would such an act of deception be worth saving their lives? Where was her faith? Flora rolled over on her side, allowing a single tear to slip out of the corner of her eye and down her temple, where it trailed the hairline to her ear.

"Father, where does one's faith meet the common sense thee gave us?" She bit her bottom lip in worry. "Is the line truly as blurry as it appears right now? Please forgive me and help me see thy will more clearly."

Flora's rampant thoughts grew distant as she struggled to stay awake and alert. Fatigue claimed her senses until she could no longer keep her eyelids open. She yawned, unable to resist the slumber that seized her.

"Flora!" Where could she be? Bruce climbed over the rugged path banking the river. His booted foot slipped in a patch of mud. He braced himself, throwing both arms out to regain his balance as he kept going. Something moved in the water. It looked like a torn piece of cloth snagged on a piece of driftwood. His heart skidded with a start. Bruce plowed into the water, gasping as the cold wetness seeped into his clothes and against his skin.

Irene had warned him in a tearful state that Flora couldn't swim. He pushed through the water, pressing through the current until it was deep enough to swim. Bruce swung his arms and kicked as hard as he could, chasing after the log. The current was strong, but he wouldn't give up.

He reached out to grab the log, but it rolled from his grasp. Swinging his other arm around, Bruce gripped it tight. He pulled himself up and grabbed the gray cloth, recognizing a piece of Flora's skirt.

"God, please don't let anything happen to her." He closed his eyes and squeezed the cloth. Panic pulsed through his chest, slicing through fear and guilt. Should he have waited to take Marta back? For a moment, he couldn't breathe, and he held onto the log, allowing the current to carry him in the direction it would have most likely carried Flora. "Father, help me find her," he whispered, his voice raspy and strange to his ears.

As he floated on the log, Bruce scanned the area around him, looking for any other movement or more clothing—anything. The current shifted and swirled him, and then he saw her, lying on a rock, face down. Was she conscious?

"Flora!"

She didn't move.

Bruce pushed off of the log and swam toward her, hope giving him renewed strength. He reached the boulder and hoisted himself up beside her. "Flora, speak to me." Bruce brushed her damp hair from her face. Water dripped from his hand onto her closed eyelids. She gasped and jerked, blinking and wiping her face.

"I'm sorry," Bruce said, breathing a sigh of relief. "I was worried when thee didn't answer."

"Bruce?" Her blue-gray eyes widened. "Thee found me!" She tried to sit up, a mixture of relief and excitement replacing her groggy state. At the sudden movement, her face fell into a frown, and she winced. "Marta?"

"She's fine." He leaned forward to help her, but she held up her palm. "I'm fine. Only bruised . . . everywhere." She wrinkled her face as she forced herself up with a groan. "I lost count of the number of rocks I crashed into."

Her gaze fell where her skirt had ripped, exposing a two-inch bloody gash on her knee. She pulled the rest of her skirt over the area.

"My elbow is just as bad." She held it up, as if trying to distract him. Indeed, she had scraped it well, and blood caked her skin. It didn't appear to be broken since she could move it, but he still wasn't sure about her leg or ribs.

"Flora?" He touched her chin, but she turned away, unwilling to trust him.

"I told thee, I'm fine."

"No broken bones?" Ignoring the disappointment, he raised an eyebrow, watching her stubborn countenance as she set her lips in a thin line and shook her head. "I need to make sure before I try to move thee, so I can figure out how to get thee back to camp."

"I ought to know if I have any broken bones." She softened her tone and met his gaze with a wince. "I fear I may ache all over for days to come. I'm sorry, Bruce." The whispered words made his heart constrict.

"What for?" He brushed her hair back to better see her profile, not caring if she slapped him. She kept blinking, but no tears fell from her long lashes. Again, he took her chin and turned her toward him. "Why, Flora?"

Her red-rimmed eyes swam, but she gulped back her emotion as he'd seen her do countless times before—as a child when others were teasing her. She took a deep breath, her spirited determination returning. "Because I almost exposed the mission, but I promise it won't happen again."

In that moment, Bruce wanted to kiss her. With all she'd suffered to save Marta, Bruce's esteem of her grew beyond his secret infatuation. Marta had told him everything—how Flora had jumped into a river, knowing she couldn't swim, so that the dog trailing them would lose their scent. Now she expressed more concern over the mission than her own wounds and discomfort. He had been wrong and Pastor John had been right. Flora Saferight was the perfect woman for this job—now he just had to find a way to keep her safe so she wouldn't risk her life again.

He stared at the endearing freckles across the bridge of her nose, dotting the tops of her cheeks. Her full pink lips looked swollen, as if she'd been biting her bottom lip in distress. He leaned forward.

"Bruce?" She touched her fingers to her lips. "Why is thee staring at me like that? Did I cut my face? Do I look dreadful?" She trembled and scooted away from him, unwilling to meet his gaze. "Don't think me vain, but I was never a pleasant sight to behold. I hope I haven't gone and made things worse."

How could he admit that he had been about to kiss her? She'd probably find enough energy to slap him right off this rock. Hadn't she already made it clear that she didn't want him to touch her? Well, for the time being she would have to bear it. She needed his help getting back, but he didn't have to humiliate himself with an admission of how he felt or what he'd almost done.

"Believe me, Flora Saferight, there is nothing plain about thee other than thy clothes."

"My bonnet." She touched the top of her head. "I lost it in the river."

"No matter. Looks like thee lost part of thy skirt as well." He chuckled, dropping the piece of cloth he'd found onto her lap.

"Where did thee find this?" She wrinkled her lips as she picked it up with two fingers.

"Hanging on a floating log."

"God answered my prayer." She smiled, her eyes sparkling and rendering him as still as a tree trunk. "This ripped from my skirt to give thee something to follow."

"Hasn't thee always believed in prayer?" Bruce bent one knee and wrapped an arm around his leg.

"Of course, but not like this. It was so immediate and here's the evidence." She held up the torn material. "I was frightened that thee would believe that the worst had happened and go on without me . . . for the sake of the mission."

Remorse shuddered through him in waves of past memories. He had once left her hiding during a game of hide-and-seek, convincing the others she had gotten angry and gone home. How could she know that he would have turned this county upside down looking for her?

He leaned toward her, taking her hand in his. For once she didn't jerk away, but merely stared at their hands as if he'd just grown fur. "Look at me, Flora." He waited as her hesitant gaze traveled up his shirt, to his chin, and met his eyes. "If anything like this ever happens again, I give thee my solemn promise not to leave thee behind. I would have to see proof of thy demise before I would carry on without thee. No matter what, I'll always come back for thee."

She stared at him, openmouthed. He waited, but she made no response.

"Flora, does thee understand me?" He squeezed her hand for emphasis. "Please believe me."

Her slender hand trembled in his. To his disappointment, she pulled away from his grasp and folded her hands in her lap. She gave him a skeptical stare. "Careful, or else I might be tempted to think thee has become a true gentleman after all these years." A mischievous grin curled her lips.

"Indeed, I have." Hope smoldered inside Bruce.

Flora licked her bottom lip as if contemplating her next words. She lifted her chin. "I'll never believe it."

Afraid of drowning again, Flora didn't argue with Bruce when he instructed her to place her arms around his neck. He swam to the shore with her on his back. She tried to kick so she wouldn't be such a burden, but her muscles felt like heavy iron. Now she wondered if this had been such a good idea.

She didn't want to choke him and moved her hands to his shoulders. His strong muscles rippled through his wet shirt beneath her cold fingertips. The strength he exuded impressed her, but not as much as his gentle heart. She had expected him to rant at her over how she had almost ruined the mission. He could have criticized her choices, but he did none of those things. Bruce Millikan had seemed more concerned with having found her alive and the state of her health than anything.

His reaction broke the chain of all her childhood memories of them together, leaving her uncertain and vulnerable. Was it possible that Bruce Millikan had grown into a different man than she'd thought? The idea both pleased and frightened her.

His labored breathing came hard as he reached shallow water now that they'd crossed the river. He stood and patted her hand. "Is thee . . . all right?" He paused to catch his breath, turning to look at her, his gaze carefully assessing her.

"Yes." She nodded. "But I'm not the one who just swam across the river hauling a heavy woman on my back." She touched his arm in concern. "Bruce, thanks."

Something flickered in his eyes, and then he turned from her. "We've got to get thee to a warm fire and into some dry clothes. I still don't know what wounds thee may have suffered."

"I told thee. I'm fine." She took a step to follow him, but her sore knee gave out on her. She stumbled, splashing water around her.

Bruce turned. "Fine, huh?" He bent and swept her up into his arms. "It isn't like thee to lie, Flora Saferight."

"I didn't lie!"

He enveloped her against his hard chest. She listened to his fast-beating heart where she had laid her head. For now she would behave. She had caused the poor man enough hardship. "My legs may be sturdy on dry ground."

He didn't answer as he stepped from the water and climbed the muddy bank. He slipped once, but kept a steady hold on her. He readjusted her in his arms after regaining his balance.

"Thee is bleeding again," he said, glancing down at her exposed knee, where red blood bubbled and made a zigzagging trail down her leg. "I believe it will need stitching. Irene will have to sew it up."

She gasped and tried to cover her leg.

"Stop wiggling before I drop thee," he snapped, irritation straining his voice. "The last thing we need is more injuries.

Now, be still." His tone softened as he glanced down at her and their eyes met.

His green gaze penetrated her heart and stirred her senses as warmth filled her flesh. His reddish-blond hair now looked a shade darker wet, and stood on end all over his head. Water dripped down his forehead and into his eyes. He blinked. Flora reached up and wiped her fingertip across his brows to prevent more water from slipping into his vision. Her finger tingled.

"Thee will be the death of me before it's over." He stared at her with a serious expression she couldn't fathom. Was he angry?

"I'm sorry," she whispered. "I only meant to keep the water from thy eyes."

"I know." His voice was low. "But there was a time when thee wouldn't have cared."

"We're grown now. We can be civilized—at least." She gestured down. "Let me see if I can stand on solid ground."

He lowered her with gentle ease. Flora held onto his arm as she attempted her weight on her injured leg. Pain sliced through all the nerves in her knee, causing her to wince.

"Let me . . ." Bruce tightened his grip on her.

"No." She shook her head. "Just allow me to lean on thee. I can make it." Flora glanced around, seeing no horse or wagon. "How are we getting back?"

"I brought the horse," Bruce said. "We can make better time if thee would allow me to carry thee."

"I can do this." She took another unsteady step.

"At this rate it will be nightfall before we reach the others."

Flora glared at him. He twisted his lips in an attempt to keep from smiling, but failed. A half-grin lit his expression.

"I never thought anyone could be more stubborn or determined than I, but I believe thee has proven me wrong." He shook his head in disbelief, his arm brushing against hers. "I don't want to be gone too long. We need to get back to the others."

"Thee always was a bully," Flora teased. "Always making people do things thy way."

"Well, if I was such a bully, I wouldn't have ever set thee down. We'd be on the horse by now almost to camp." He shrugged, risking a quick glance in her direction. "I thought thee would be eager to see how Marta is doing after all the stress she's endured."

Alarm slammed through Flora's brain, and she paused. "I thought thee said she was back at camp? What happened?"

"She is, but I certainly didn't have time to question her. I left right away to find thee." He ran a hand through his short, damp hair, combing it back. It wasn't often Flora saw him without his black hat. His round head gave him a boyish look that she found endearing.

Her wet garments were heavy and scratched against her sensitive skin as she moved. She was so busy adjusting the collar of her blouse that she didn't see a root and stumbled into Bruce.

He turned and caught her in time. "That's it." He slipped an arm around her waist and one under her knees and lifted her up.

"I didn't do that so thee would carry me." Flora slid her arms around his neck to hang on as he jostled her along.

"Of course not." A look of irritation crossed his face as he sighed and set his jaw at an angle and stared ahead. "For we both know that if thee could, thee would avoid me for the rest of thy life."

Flora swallowed in discomfort. Perhaps that was once true, but no longer. Today he had eased her fears and given her a sense of trust in him. Once he'd arrived, her loneliness disappeared. His gentle care had been most unexpected, but appreciated.

Rather than arguing further, Flora laid her head on his shoulder, reveling in the strong feel of his arms wrapped around her—protecting her—if only for this short, temporary walk.

8

Bruce arrived back at camp and lifted Flora off the horse. Thankful she didn't protest, he carried her to the wagon. He knew she had to be in pain, but she didn't complain. Instead, she wrapped her arms around his neck as if she feared being separated.

Irene wept with relief while she assisted Flora into dry clothes. Even with Flora's instructions, Irene proved to be too unsteady with a needle to sew up Flora's knee. In the end, Bruce took care of the task, casting propriety aside out of necessity.

Flora gritted her teeth and closed her eyes, but never cried out in pain—only wincing and groaning. She refused the laudanum he offered, saying Marta may later have need of it. He couldn't fathom how she managed not to jerk on reflex as he pulled the needle and thread through her skin. Bruce tried to keep his tone, as well as his touch, gentle and soothing.

He hoped his nerves didn't show. If ever he needed to be a pillar of strength and comfort for her, it was now. Once he tied off the last stitch, he breathed a sigh of relief, glad the ordeal was over. He risked a quick glance in her direction, worried he'd hurt her too much.

She sat very still, her eyes remaining closed.

"Flora, it's over," he said. "I'm sorry if I hurt thee."

"Bruce, I'm very grateful." Flora met his gaze as she lowered her voice to a whisper, "I know she meant well, but Irene was killing me."

The tension inside him eased, and he grinned, holding out his hand. "Come on. Let's get some food. That might make thee feel better."

An hour later, Flora left half her plate of beans uneaten.

"I suppose three meals of plain beans are enough to make anyone lose their appetite," Bruce said. "I thought thee wouldn't want any fish after spending so much time in the river today, but tomorrow I'll go fishing for all of us." Bruce sipped from his cup of water, pleased with his idea. He was quite tired of beans as well.

A giggle lifted in the air. Bruce lowered his cup, his gaze shifting from Irene to Flora. Marta had already succumbed to exhaustion earlier, so it had to have been one of them. Irene frowned as she carried the dirty dishes to a pot of water full of soapsuds. Flora beamed with a mischievous glint in her eye.

"If I recall, thee might catch us some baby fish, but thy brother is the one to catch the real meat." She folded her hands in her lap and waited.

Was Flora Saferight teasing him?

He searched his memory back to a hot summer afternoon when he and his brother had gone fishing. Bruce was twelve and had just started taking notice of Flora. He had hoped to impress her with his fishing skills, but all he'd managed was two small fish—one for himself and one for Flora. Silas had caught eight strapping trout. Both Flora and Irene had eaten from his brother's pile. Bruce had suffered the humiliation of being bested by his little brother.

"That's right. I forgot. Thee prefers a fine catch from my brother's hand." Sudden irritation assailed him. He tipped his cup and gulped the last of his water, then wiped his mouth with his sleeve.

"Well, today thee accomplished an even bigger feat. Christ tells us to be fishermen of men." Flora gestured to herself. "Friend Bruce, thee fished me out of the river, and I'm very grateful. I hope thee isn't too disappointed I wasn't a rainbow trout."

Jim chuckled, listening to their banter. "So, Friend Bruce done become a fisherman of women instead of men."

"We Quakers often believe that general references to man in the Bible are often meant for all mankind, men and women alike." Flora straightened her back, ready to go into teaching mode. Bruce had seen it often in the last few weeks, especially with Marta.

"How come yous don't believe it says exactly what it says?" Jim angled his head, a look of confusion on his face as he scratched the side of his head.

"We do, but every piece of the Bible must be read in context with other pieces of the Bible." Flora leaned toward him, eager to help Jim understand her faith. Bruce smiled, admiring her. "For instance, if I ask thee for some water, thee wouldn't know how much water or what I'd want it for, right?"

"Yeah, a cup to drink." Jim nodded.

"But thee assumed. What if I wanted a bucket of water for a bath or a cup of water to give to someone else?" Flora asked. "But thee wouldn't know if thee didn't read beyond that statement to discover more of the story."

"Friend Jim, there is a passage in the Bible that might help thee understand what Flora is trying to tell thee. It will also sum up why we Quakers believe men and women are equal, as well as blacks and whites." Bruce went to get his small Bible from his pack and brought it and a lantern back. He flipped to the section in Galatians and found chapter three. "There is neither Jew nor Greek, there is neither bond nor free, there is neither male nor female: for ye are all one in Christ Jesus."

Jim sat in silence, staring at the ground. After a few moments, he looked up at Bruce and then at Flora. "I don't remember my master's preacher ever giving that verse."

"It's also one of the reasons some Quakers allow women pastors," Flora said. "We're very different than other Christian religions, but the same in that we believe Jesus Christ came in the form of a man and died on the cross as the Son of God to save us from our sins."

"That part sounds like what we believe. I likes yous Quakers." Jim smiled, his yellow teeth glowing in the firelight as he stood and stretched. "I'll go check on Marta. She's been sleeping for a while now."

Beside the wagon by the lantern light, Irene splashed water as she washed the dishes. Flora and Bruce were left alone.

"How does thee feel?" Bruce asked.

"I don't think there is one part of my body not aching, but I'll be fine." She covered her mouth as she yawned.

"Thee should get some rest. We'll be leaving within the hour," he said.

Bruce walked to the back of the wagon and reached inside for a quilt. He made a pallet by the fire. "Here, sleep where it's warm. I'll watch over thee while I study thy mother's quilt. I want to make sure we didn't stray too far from course today."

He half expected her to argue, especially since he'd laid out his own pallet for her, but she limped over in silence. Once she was settled, he laid the quilt over her. She yawned again, snuggling inside the thick pallet.

"Why couldn't thee have been this kind when we were children?" Her sleepy voice floated between them.

It was a simple question and direct. How could mere words lance him with renewed guilt? What could he say that would erase all the pain he'd caused her? He cleared his throat. "I was just a silly boy, Flora. I hope thee can forgive me."

"I've already forgiven the boy in thee." She smiled and rolled over onto her side, closing her eyes. "It's the man in thee that I'm trying to figure out if I can trust or not."

"Flora, it's time to go." Irene's gentle voice broke through Flora's groggy state. "Bruce says we must go."

She forced her eyes open to see Irene's dark form towering over her. The fire had fizzled to tiny embers. Beyond the tree branches above, white stars twinkled against the black sky. With a tired sigh, Flora rubbed her eyes and raised up on an elbow. Her body screamed in protest, still aching all over. She brushed strands of hair from her face, annoyed they had fallen from her braided coil.

Bruce poured water on the remaining embers. They sizzled until the drenched pile swam in a puddle. The smell of lingering smoke drifted in the air.

"How is thee feeling?" Irene asked.

"Sore, but I'll manage." Flora's voice cracked with recent sleep. She shivered as she threw the quilt aside and tried to rise without wounding her knee further.

"Here, let me help thee." Irene took her elbow and tried to help lift her up but staggered under the extra weight.

"I've got her." Bruce appeared beside them, taking a steady hold on Flora. "Will thee see to dusting off the quilts and folding them?" He looked down at Irene.

Irene nodded.

"Easy." Bruce placed a strong arm around Flora's waist and hoisted her against his side, using his body as an anchor. The scent of burning smoke from the campfire had settled in his clothes, mingling with a mixture of fresh cedar from their cedar chests. She found the unexpected aroma endearing.

"Thanks," she murmured, trying to steady herself. "I can walk."

"Indeed." He didn't let go of her. "But can thee climb upon the wagon by thyself?"

She hadn't thought that far ahead. As Flora took a step, the stitches in her knee were tight, pulling against her skin. What a horrible place to need binding.

Flora tried to keep her leg straight, bending it as little as possible when walking. Pain pierced her bruised bones as her muscles contracted and expanded in spite of her efforts to still them. She gritted her teeth to keep Bruce from noticing her discomfort. The pressure of her weight upon her leg caused her to limp—that she couldn't hide.

"I need to check on Marta." They reached the back of the wagon, where she paused.

"I already did, right before Irene woke thee," Bruce said. "Jim assured me that she's sleeping soundly, which is more than I can say for thee. Thy snoring was quite profound."

Embarrassment heated her neck and face to the roots of her hair. The sensation tingled all over her head. "Is this another cruel attempt to tease me?"

Even if she had snored, a gentleman would have kept the matter to himself out of respect for her feelings. Flora eyed him with disdain. One thing was certain: Bruce Millikan may be dependable in a crisis, and a tender charmer when he chose, but he still delighted in vexing her. "I suppose thee hasn't changed as much as thee would like me to believe."

Flora tried to jerk free of his hold, but he kept a firm grip on her and chuckled. "Wait a minute! If thee were to fall, I suppose I would be blamed for that as well."

She hobbled toward the front of the wagon, eager to be free of his assistance. If he had been anyone else to witness her humiliation, the sting to her pride might not have been so fierce. Her snoring was inappropriate and not ladylike. What must he think of her now? She knew she needed to cast down her pride, since it was a sin, but she needed more time to deal with her wayward emotions.

"I don't snore," she said through clenched teeth.

"I beg to differ." He chuckled again. "Ask Irene." Bruce tilted his head and gestured at her sister following close behind with a folded quilt in her arms. Flora met her sister's gaze, but Irene dropped her eyes to stare at the ground, unable to hold Flora's gaze. The simple action confirmed the truth. Another wave of humiliation spread throughout Flora, overheating her limbs in spite of the cool temperature.

She said nothing as Bruce helped her climb into the wagon. His hands were a steady comfort around her slender waist. To her mortification, she had come to depend on him more than she should. As Flora leaned forward, she wondered if he was disgusted that her behind was in such close proximity to his face. She closed her eyes, feeling for the seat, and managed to twist around and settle on the bench without bending or hurting her knee.

Irene climbed up from the other side to sit in the middle so Flora could stretch out her leg over the edge of the wagon. This arrangement suited her just fine. At least it would give her a reprieve from being so close to Bruce. If only she could make herself not care one bit what he thought of her.

They rode for the next couple of hours in silence. Flora longed for something to lean her back against. Soon her bottom felt like someone had paddled her with a two-inch thick board.

"My back hurts." Irene reached behind herself and rubbed her lower back. "I sure wish we had taken the train. I'd be feeling much better right about now."

Biting her tongue, Flora kept quiet. They were all tired and uncomfortable, but no one had voiced their complaints except Irene.

"Perhaps thee would feel better about thy circumstances if thee would concentrate harder on what thee has to be thankful for." Irritation laced Bruce's voice. "For instance, thy sister returning to us safely."

"Of course I'm grateful that Flora is safe with us." Irene looped her arm through Flora's. "I was quite distraught when I thought she might drown."

"I know thee was." Flora patted her sister's hand as an owl hooted in the distance. "Friend Bruce, she's a bit young and everything on this trip is so new to her. At least allow her the liberty to share her discomforts and concerns."

"Only if it's something of substance," Bruce said. "A train is something I can't do anything about."

"No one expects thee to do anything." Flora leaned around her sister, trying to see his expression. It was no use. A cloud had covered the moon and left them in utter darkness. "I don't know why thee would think any different."

"I'm a man of solutions. If thee brings me a problem, it's my desire to fix it. I've little tolerance for whining. Time is better spent on solving problems, not basking in them. And that's what I like about thee, Flora. I've yet to hear thee whine about anything, in spite of thy wounds and obvious discomfort."

Did Bruce Millikan just pay her a compliment?

"Huh!" Irene's sharp intake of breath regained Flora's attention. "I was hardly whining."

"Indeed," Flora said. "Irene was merely stating a thought aloud. Think of it this way. Women often voice their thoughts in their journals. It helps us get our feelings and emotions out so we won't be as tempted to complain—or whine, as thee calls it."

"Well, why didn't thee say so sooner?" Bruce's tone lightened. "A journal *is* something I can do. When we arrive near Lynchburg, I'll ride into town and get thee both a journal and some ink."

"That won't be necessary," Flora said. "I don't need a journal."

"I'm definitely getting thee one," Bruce said. "I want thee to put all thy feelings down on paper, every bad deed I've ever committed against thee. That way, thee won't be tempted to keep reminding me about them."

Flora's mouth dropped open, but this time she didn't have a ready reply.

Bruce cut through the underbrush, clearing a path for Irene to follow close behind. He carried a small empty barrel in one hand and his fishing net in the other. The morning sun had already risen, and fresh dew was still on the leaves and foliage around them.

"Help!" Irene called from behind. "I'm stuck."

With a frustrated sigh, Bruce turned and made his way back to her. He leaned to the left and then to the right. "I don't see anyone or anything holding thee."

"Something has my skirt." She tugged at the material, but it didn't move. "See?"

Bruce walked behind her and burst into laughter. "I see, all right. Thee is caught in a briar, naught more." The wiry plant scaled the back of her gray skirt, digging its claws into the garment.

"It may seem funny to thee, but I'll be heading into Lynchburg for more clothing if my skirt is ripped. Since thee insisted that we leave other clothes behind, we don't have much to spare."

"I saw Flora with a sewing kit the other day. I'm sure your skirt could be mended." Bruce gave her a pointed glare. It wasn't that he minded helping Irene out of her predicament, but the underhanded way she tried to dramatize the situation grated on his nerves.

"Oh, I'm sure Flora will be able to patch it up just fine, but the skirt itself will be quite ruined for anything beyond this trip." Irene glanced over her shoulder and down at the offending briar.

"I meant thee, Irene. Not Flora. Thee can borrow her sewing kit and patch up thy own clothing." He bent and set the items he carried to the side. "But I'll do my best."

"Flora's the one with all the sewing talent. I'm only decent with seams, hemming, and replacing buttons. She can sew an entire outfit from scratch."

Afraid of causing Flora additional work, Bruce plucked out the briars with care. He wished Flora's knee had been well enough for her to make the trip to the river with him. She wouldn't have dallied about or whined over a simple briar.

"I believe that should do it." He rubbed his chilled hands together and blew warmth on them before picking his items back up.

"Thank thee." Irene whirled with a bright smile, staring down at him. The innocence in her wide eyes shifted his irritation to discomfort. Flora was right. She was young and innocent of so many things. It wasn't fair to compare the two sisters—even if only in his mind. Besides, any woman he'd ever mentally compared to Flora came up quite lacking in his estimation.

Irene crossed her arms and stared down at him at an angle, tilting her head as if studying him in close scrutiny. Bruce tried to ignore her as he gathered his things and stood to his full height. She lifted her finger to her chin in thoughtful silence as she continued to stare at him. Bruce shifted his weight to his other foot.

"What?" The single word came out more harshly than he'd intended.

"Nothing." She turned on her heel and started walking. "It's just that I was thinking that perhaps Flora is wrong about thee."

Stunned, Bruce lurched into motion and caught up with her. "What did Flora say about me?"

"Lots of things." She shrugged, adjusting her purple cloak. "Most of which thee would probably rather not know."

Disappointment sagged in his chest. "I'm quite aware of how much Flora loathes me, but I had hoped we'd made some headway over the last few weeks, or at least come to an understanding." He concentrated on the woods ahead, where the sun brightened in an opening. "What was she wrong about?"

"That perhaps there is a gentle heart somewhere inside thee in spite of all the mean things thee has done, especially if thee truly has a calling to serve the abolitionist movement."

"I was a boy back then." Frustration edged his tone. "When will she realize that we've all grown up? Some childhood memories are meant to be forgotten—forever." Bruce walked along the bank looking for the best place to cast his net. He needed a good current to catch the most fish.

"Scars are constant reminders. Perhaps if thee hadn't scarred her with so many unpleasant memories, Flora would find it easier to forget them." Irene dropped to her knees. "This looks like a good place to fill the barrel."

"I realize my mistakes, but I refuse to live in the past. I won't tolerate being reminded of it constantly." Bruce bent to hand her the barrel. A hawk squawked overhead. The wind blew and yellow leaves flew into the river and floated down the stream.

"Friend Bruce, if thee would really like to erase all the bad memories Flora has of thee, then I would suggest thee create new memories, filled with happiness."

Bruce paused, staring at her in surprise. "That's a very wise suggestion for someone at thy age."

Irene smiled, her blue eyes shining bright. Her blond hair framed her face beneath a white bonnet. Her smooth skin and heart-shaped face made her delicate and pretty in her own way, but it was blue-gray eyes and a square face framed with coffee-colored hair that consumed his mind.

"Well, I must confess that I borrowed it from Mother. She has the best advice of anyone I know. I distinctly remember her saying something of the sort to Flora when she discovered thee would be escorting us on this mission."

"I see," Bruce said. "And what was Flora's response?"

"That isn't important." Irene waved her hand. "She came, didn't she?"

"Indeed." He nodded. "I think I'll take thee up on the advice and start with catching us all some good-tasting fish for breakfast." It was time Flora knew how well he could catch fish now that he was a man.

9

While Bruce went fishing and Irene went with him to retrieve more water, Jim paced as Flora examined Marta in the privacy of the covered wagon.

"Don't know why I couldn't go with Bruce. We'd catch a lot more fish and do it faster with the two of us." Jim's irritated voice drifted inside.

"That's my Jim." Marta grinned between spasms of pain. "Always wanting to be useful and important."

"Just be on the lookout for any strangers," Flora called, loudly enough for him to hear. "That's what I need thee to do right now."

"Listen, Miz Flora, I don't want Jim to be fretting over me." Marta held her stomach in a protective manner as she leaned against a trunk. "But I hurt for a while last night."

"Was the pain constant without ceasing, or did it come in spurts?"

"Mostly in spurts." Marta shook her head. "But my back ached something awful, it sure enough did."

"Did thee manage to get any sleep?" Flora felt her forehead with the back of her fingers, but it was cool to the touch.

"A little. I feel better on my side. He's got good legs. Jim could feel him kick." Marta rubbed her belly, a fond expression on her smiling face. "But those other pains . . . they's bad."

"Show me where." Flora adjusted the lantern light. Marta moved her hand below the round part of her swollen stomach. Low . . . too low for Flora's comfort.

By the time she finished Marta's examination, Flora was convinced Marta had started the early stages of labor. Hoping she was wrong, Flora gave Marta her own pallet in the comfort of the covered wagon, rather than the hard, dark compartment she'd been staying in with Jim.

"How's she?" Jim stopped short as she emerged.

"She's resting. I gave her my pallet so she'll be more comfortable." Flora held out her hand, struggling with her sore knee. "Help me, please?"

"Yes'm." Jim sprang into action, stretching out his long arm and offering his support.

Flora swung her leg over the back of the wagon in awkward discomfort. Her skirt slipped up to her knee. She shoved it down with her other hand, grunting with the effort.

"I'm gotcha."

Strong hands reached around her waist and swung her down. Flora yelped in surprise, but didn't have time to argue as her feet landed on solid ground. She brushed her hair from her face—it was unkempt because she hadn't had time to redo it.

"Tell me the truth. Is the baby coming early?" He lowered his worried voice. "Will Marta be okay?"

"I'm going to do my best, Jim. That's all I can offer thee."

"Come here," he whispered, pulling on her elbow to lead her away from the wagon. "This may sound bad, but if it comes down to it, Marta has to live. She can have other babies when we're safe and free."

Rebecca had warned Flora that a situation such as this might occur. Men often saw things differently than women. The thought of losing a child they'd never seen or gotten to know didn't put as much fear in them as losing a wife they'd come to love and know. Still, the outcome wasn't in her hands, but God's.

"Jim, it's too soon to be thinking like that. Both Marta and the baby may be just fine when the time comes. The best thing thee can do right now is pray and make sure that she eats and gets plenty of rest."

"I can do that." He pumped his dark head up and down and backed away. "Mr. Bruce done give me a Bible and started learning me how to read. I'll practice while Marta sleeps."

"That's a splendid idea." Flora smiled, wondering when Bruce had done that. The gesture not only pleased her, but once again improved her opinion of the man himself. "If thee should need any help with the words, just let me know. I'll be right over there building a small fire and making some coffee." She pointed to a flat spot Bruce had cleared before he left.

"Yes'm." He went over and sat on a log. With his elbows propped on his knees, he opened the small Bible and began sounding out the words in a whisper.

Once the fire was built and the coffee made, Flora paced in a semicircle around the fire. Shouldn't Bruce and Irene be back by now? The morning sun now shone bright through the trees surrounding them. Colorful leaves fell in a graceful rhythm with the slight breeze. Those that fell in the fire were consumed with a quick sizzle.

Mumbled voices pricked her ears. She rushed over, following the sound. Movement caught her attention, and she recognized the outline of Bruce's black hat and jacket. In one hand he carried a small barrel that she assumed was full of water. He walked at an angle, his other hand hauling something else.

Flora gathered her shawl close around her neck. A moment later, she saw her sister's purple cloak maneuvering around something behind Bruce. A sigh of relief escaped Flora. "Thank you, God," she whispered.

As they drew closer, she realized Bruce and Irene were each carrying one end of a stick with a full net of fish hanging from it. Flora pinched her nose as the stench reached her nostrils, realizing why her sister wore a frown of disgust.

"I wondered how thee planned to fish without a pole." Flora followed them as Bruce gave her a proud grin, his green eyes shining with triumph.

"I gave up useless poles a long time ago." Bruce and Irene hung the net on some hooks on the back of the wagon.

"That's so disgusting!" Irene wiped her hand on her skirt as if she'd been carrying the fish right in her hand.

"One evening when I was reading how the disciples cast their nets into the sea," Bruce turned to Flora with a shrug, "I realized I'd been going about fishing the wrong way. That's when I got the idea to build my own net and cast it in a good, flowing stream."

"Bruce Millikan, thee definitely has thy own way of doing things." Flora laughed, then wrinkled her nose. "Now thee must invent a way to get rid of the smell."

Bruce's broad smile faltered. He looked down at himself and sniffed. "Indeed, what would thee suggest?" He raised a red-gold eyebrow, watching her reaction.

Gold whiskers had started filling out over his jaw and his upper lip. It made him look older, more distinguished. Warmth pooled in the pit of her stomach, and a light-headed sensation washed over her. She let her lips curl into a playful smile. "Perhaps a long bath in a cold river?"

He leaned forward, his warm breath caressing her ear. "This time I caught more than enough for thee . . . and everyone else."

⸺⸺

Bruce woke with a start. Movement caught his attention a short distance away, in the nearby woods. He blinked and rubbed his face, rising with caution where he'd been dozing against the trunk of a tree.

He glanced to the right. Jim still snored, leaning back against another tree. Irene and Marta had retired inside the wagon. Rather than climbing back in and out with her wounded knee, Flora had elected to sleep on a pallet near where they had cooked their breakfast earlier. He peered over at the empty spot and rolled his eyes. Where had she gone?

A quick scan under the wagon told him she wasn't anywhere near where she should be. Inching toward the direction of the noise he'd heard a moment ago, Bruce took quiet steps on the fallen leaves to keep from announcing his presence.

He paused to listen. A feminine gasp bounced in the forest, followed by a sharp intake of breath. Had she hurt herself? He rushed toward the noise. A moment later a stick came hurling at his head. He ducked.

"Bruce!" Flora slammed her hand to her chest, her eyes wide and her mouth gaping in shock. "Thee scared me. Why is thee prowling around in the woods?"

"I could ask thee the same question, Flora." He swallowed, shoving a hand through his hair. He'd been so worried, he'd forgotten his hat—again.

"I could have hit thee in the head." Her hand trembled as she gathered her cloak tightly around her neck.

"Whatever happened to the fact that thee doesn't believe in violence?" Bruce quirked his lips into a twisted grin, taunting her.

"Thee frightened me." Her gaze faltered from his. "I had no idea I would react like that."

"Which is why thee shouldn't be here in the woods all alone. I thought we agreed on that the last time thee and Marta were nearly discovered?" He stepped closer. She backed away, but the acute pain in her eyes wasn't something she could hide. He could also tell she was in pain by the way she braced her whole body when she stepped on her injured leg and by her wrinkled forehead.

"What's wrong?" He stepped closer.

"Nothing." She half-turned from him, her shoulders stiffening. "I needed some privacy and didn't see any reason to wake Marta or Irene. That's all."

"Look at me." He meant to speak the words in a softer manner, but they came out sounding like an order. Her lips thinned in defiance. "Flora, I need thee to trust me."

"Never." She shook her head. "I realize thee helped me the other day, and for that I'm grateful, but I don't want to be dependent on thee." Flora shivered and rubbed her upper arms as if to ward off the chill. "That would be a very bad habit and quite unwise on my part." Her voice lowered at the end, almost to a mumble.

Bruce scratched the side of his head. "I'm sorry that my assistance seems so abhorrent to thee." He took a deep breath and straightened his spine. "Nevertheless, I'm all thee has at the moment. Come, let's go back where it's safe."

She stared at his outstretched hand but didn't take it.

"After what almost happened the other day, I refuse to leave thee here alone." He stepped forward. This time she stood her ground and lifted her gaze to his, her chin set at an angry angle. "Flora . . . please." He rubbed his eyebrows and pinched the bridge of his nose.

"No, I have a personal matter that needs tending to. Please go away."

Bruce hesitated. Was he being insensitive? With an elder sister, he was quite aware of a woman's personal needs, especially during their monthly courses. Could he be intruding in that regard? Heat flooded his face. He stepped back, uncertain.

"I'll wait over here, within shouting distance." He pointed his thumb over his shoulder. His throat constricted, almost choking him. "Or perhaps I could go back and get Irene?"

"No! She'll just faint at the sight of blood."

"How is that?" Bruce raised an eyebrow. "Doesn't she have the same . . . condition?" He said the last word so low it sounded like a whisper. Discomfort shifted through him in a wave of mixed emotions as Flora's skin turned a crimson shade, and he realized he'd been mistaken.

His gut instinct made him walk toward her. She backed away and tripped over something. He reached out to steady her, his hand gripping her elbow as he pulled her toward him. She landed against his chest with her hands pressed over his heart. They both paused, gazing at each other in awkward silence.

As before, a fresh scent of cedar drifted to his nose from her clothes having been folded away in her chest. Blue-gray eyes gazed up at him in a sea of confusion. Lost from the impact of his own frayed nerves, Bruce held her rather than releasing her as he should have done. It was just like the other day. He enjoyed the feel of her in his arms. How could he help it? Flora challenged and disturbed him in ways no other woman ever had.

She blinked. Her eyes shifted to blue ice and her mouth twisted into disgust. He held his breath, waiting for the blow, but instead she shoved away from him.

"Don't hold me like that." She hugged herself as she trembled. "Bruce Millikan, thee should know better. I'm ashamed of you." She looked away, avoiding his gaze. "I always thought thee would be revolted at being anywhere near me."

He closed his eyes and swallowed the cotton that had suddenly swelled up in the back of his throat. He missed the warmth of her body next to his, the scent of her being so close. It was as if that one brief moment had given him a taste of what he craved, and he wanted more. "Things change."

"Not for me . . . please leave."

A deep ache pierced his chest at the rejection. Is this how he'd made her feel so long ago? If so, he deserved it. But he wouldn't leave.

"No."

"I hate thee." She whirled from him, but not before he saw the sheen of tears in her eyes. Flora limped away from him. The movement revealed a small brown box that her skirt had been covering.

"What's this?" He stooped to retrieve it.

"That's mine!" She gasped, hurrying back toward him. "I'd forgotten about it. Thanks to thy interruption."

"It's what thee tripped over, wasn't it?" He twisted to the side, holding the box high over her head. Now he would discover why she was so eager to be rid of him.

"Bruce Millikan, I'm warning thee . . ." Her hands clenched at her sides as she tightened her jaw. "Give it back."

"What have I got to lose? Thee already hates me." He winked at her before popping the lock and lifting the lid. Needles, thread, small scissors, laudanum, and other medical supplies were tucked inside. His heart beat with trepidation. "Flora, what has thee done?"

"I busted my stitches and it hurts like the blazes, but I'm having to stand here and argue with thee rather than take care of it like I should." She blinked back tears and swallowed. Then he realized her red nose might not be from the cold.

"Why hide it? I could have taken care of it for thee. I'm not so much of a brute as all that." He pointed to the ground. "Sit down."

"No." She shook her head. "I'll take care of it myself. Thee shouldn't have sewn me up the other day. It's inappropriate." She lifted her chin. "I'm in better condition today, and I'll take care of it myself."

"Is it infected?" He raised an eyebrow as he waited for a response.

She looked away, and that was answer enough.

"Flora, out here we can't afford to take chances on propriety. Thee can think of me as a brute or hate me all thee wants, but I'm tending to thy leg." He pointed again. "Now sit down."

"Humph!" She sat with a puckering frown.

Bruce blinked to clear his mind as she slid her brown skirt up over her creamy calf. Red blood trickled from the gash on the side of her knee. Indeed, the first four stitches were ripped open, and pink swelling surrounded the wound, the first indication of an infection trying to set in.

"Propriety is not worth losing a leg over—or worse, dying." He spat the words out before he could stop himself. Pulling out the flask of water she'd brought, he cleansed the wound.

"Clint Roberts showed me how to sew stitches. I could have handled it." She bit her bottom lip, wincing in pain. "He's an excellent doctor. I've always admired doctors for the work they do."

Her voice took on a dreamy tone, causing Bruce to glance at her. Flora's lips curled into a smile as she concentrated on an object in the distance. Was it doctors whom she admired or this Clint fellow?

"Who's Clint?" Bruce asked in a casual voice as he threaded the needle. He assumed he was the doctor she had mentioned once before.

"We'll probably meet him in Charlottesville when we arrive at my aunt and uncle's."

"He's a cousin, then?"

"Oh, no." She laughed. "He's my aunt's nephew on her side of the family. He's no blood relation to us."

"How does thee know we'll see him since we're only passing through?" Bruce risked a quick glance in her direction. He disliked the glow now on her face.

"Because I wrote him and told him. We've been writing for two years since my last visit."

"I see." He took a deep breath, trying to concentrate. "Hold still. This might sting." Just like his heart, now that he knew what he knew.

***

Flora leaned on Bruce as they arrived back at camp. Irene rushed over from where she'd been pacing. "Where has thee been?" Irene's blue gaze shifted up to Bruce, standing behind her. "Marta woke up in a fitful state a while ago. It seems she had a bad dream about the baby." Irene sighed. "No one has been able to console her. Not even Jim. She's been asking for thee."

"I'll see what I can do." Flora stepped around her sister and headed toward the wagon. She grabbed her skirt, preparing to lift herself into the back of the wagon.

"Flora, thee should be careful. If thy stitches break again, I don't know if we'll be able to hold off that infection any longer." Bruce had been quite somber since he'd stitched her up and they had walked back to camp. She wondered what had really been bothering him. Had she angered him with her defiant behavior?

"I'll try, but I must climb into the back of the wagon to assist Marta. It's nearly impossible to move about without bending my knee."

"Then allow me to at least help thee." He settled his fists on each side. "Or does thee intend to keep being stubborn?"

She couldn't mistake the irritation in his voice, and she wasn't sure if she blamed him. Out here in the middle of nowhere, it was hard to figure out where the boundaries between propriety were drawn and where they should be ignored for necessity's sake.

"Fine." She gestured to the wagon. "Thee may lift me up. I'll do my best to cooperate with thee until my wound heals and the stitches can be removed."

Without another word, Bruce strode over, swept her up into his arms, and deposited her inside the wagon. He left her staring after him.

"Flora, yous back!" Marta sat up and reached out for her. Tears stained her cheeks. "It was awful." A flood of new tears poured from her eyes.

"She won't tell me the whole thing," Jim said. "Just keeps crying, and I don't know what to do." Jim sat beside her, lifting his large shoulders and shaking his head.

"Jim, would thee mind giving us some privacy?" She looked around their cramped quarters between all the trunks. "I need to stretch out my hurt leg and there isn't much room. I'll do my best to calm her."

"Yes'm." He nodded, moving up onto his knees. He took Marta's face between his two hands and looked into her eyes. "It's going to be all right. No matter what happens. I loves you. Don't forget that." He gave Marta such a gentle kiss that Flora's heart melted in longing. Would she ever have someone look at her with that much love?

Lord, please let it be so.

"I love you, too." Marta clung to him as tears squeezed past her lids. "More than you know."

Jim crawled out, leaving them alone.

"What are these tears for?" Flora straightened her knee and slid closer to Marta. "Tell me."

"I had a bad dream—a nightmare." Marta's voice was strained. "I can't tell Jim 'cause I don't want him to think it'll happen, but I'm scared jus' the same."

"Has thee ever had a dream that came true before?"

"Naw." Marta shook her head.

"Then what makes thee think it'll happen now?"

"I don't know. It just scared me is all." Marta placed protective hands over her swollen stomach. "I've been having so many pains today."

"What about when thee is lying down and resting?" Flora asked, wiping away the tears on Marta's cheeks with her shawl.

"I feel better." Marta sniffled. "Thanks, Miz Flora. I dreamed my baby was stillborn and all stiff-like." Her voice broke again.

"No, Friend Marta." Flora shook Marta's shoulder with a gentle hand. "Let's have none of that. Thy baby will be fine. He's in God's hands just as he ought to be." Flora looked around and thought of something that would cheer her friend. "I was going to save this for his birth, but I might as well give it to thee now. It might cheer and inspire thee with some hope."

"Oh, no, yous don't have to do nothing for me." Marta straightened and wiped her eyes with the back of her hands. "I be all right."

Flora leaned on her good knee and opened one of the trunks. The hinges groaned. The smell of cedar drifted through the air. She reached inside and pulled out a cream-colored baby gown.

"I made it for thy newborn. Whenever thee is tempted to think about that dream or to worry, hold onto this and know that thy baby will soon be wearing it."

"Oh, it's beautiful!" Marta's fingers covered her mouth as more tears filled her eyes—this time happy tears.

"I made it just for him or her, whichever the good Lord plans for thee to have." Flora held the gown up with a smile of pride. "Here, take it." She handed it to Marta.

"Thanks." She accepted the tiny outfit and hugged Flora. "I'll always be grateful to yous Quakers. There ain't anyone on earth as kind, and I mean dat."

"We are plain and simple people merely trying to live as we believe." Flora fluffed up a pillow and set it under Marta's head. "Now I want thee to get some rest. Thee will need thy strength when it comes time to have this baby."

"Yes'm." Marta hugged her baby's garment to her chest and laid back, settling in comfort. "I thank the Lord my child a-be born in freedom." She sighed with contentment and closed her eyes.

They rested that afternoon until evening. Irene and Bruce prepared a simple supper of bread cakes and beef jerky. Flora took out the Midnight Star quilt and studied it by the firelight. It smelled of home. Longing embraced her as she unfolded half of it and spread it out over her legs. As she traced her mother's labored stitching, she realized they would soon reach Lynchburg if her calculations were correct.

Irene sat between Flora and Bruce, allowing Flora to stretch out her knee as they traveled through the night. By dawn, they had rolled into their next station right outside of Lynchburg. An older Quaker couple greeted them with two lanterns and a warm breakfast. More than anything, Flora longed for a warm bath.

Once they were inside the couple's house, Flora tugged on Bruce's coat sleeve. She leaned up on her tiptoes to whisper in his ear, "Would it be possible for a short trip into town to mail a letter to my parents? I'm sure they're wondering how we're all doing." Bruce didn't answer right away as he looked at her and scratched his beard. "There would be nothing suspicious if Irene and I were to go to town with thee—not if Marta and Jim stay here."

"Would thee happen to be mailing a letter to Clint Roberts as well?" Bruce's voice was thick with unusual sarcasm. "Perhaps that is why thee is so eager to go into town after all this time, especially now that we're drawing close to Charlottesville."

10

As soon as Bruce strode away from Flora, he slammed his fist into his other hand, mentally chastising himself for his petty jealousy. What had gotten into him? Allowing such a dangerous emotion to take root in his heart could wreak havoc with his judgment and his ability to carry this mission through.

Besides, he'd jumped to conclusions. Just because Flora had been writing the fellow for two years didn't mean they were romantically involved. Perhaps they only had the medical field as a common interest. He massaged his aching temples. The one thing that wouldn't ease his concern was the fact that he'd heard rare admiration in Flora's tone. She'd never spoken of *him* that way.

As he walked down the hall, following the Browns to the kitchen, his anger dissipated with the smell of bacon, sausage, biscuits, and eggs. He rubbed his hands together in anticipation of a warm meal.

"I made milk gravy as well," Ida Brown said, carrying a bowl to the table. "Please, have a seat and enjoy thyselves."

Throughout breakfast, Flora kept her attention tuned to Marta as she answered Ida Brown's questions about their journey. Their hostess was a plump, elderly lady with gray curls beneath her bonnet. She wore a pair of spectacles on the bridge of her nose, and she missed few details. In spite of her advanced years, she lacked no energy as she bounced around the kitchen, refilling plates and cups as soon as they were half empty.

Harvey Brown was a round fellow with a short white beard and a mustache. He also wore a pair of spectacles and often tilted his head to peer through them at Bruce.

"So . . . which map is thee using for this mission?" Harvey asked.

"It's the Midnight Star quilt that Flora's mother made. I've studied it a few times, especially after being chased by a suspicious man and his dog. It helps that the map includes landmarks and rivers. We were able to find our way back to the main road and keep to our route."

"We received word that thee was on the way a few days ago, along with the bad news that Jim and Marta's master hired a bounty hunter to track them," Friend Brown said. "I wouldn't worry too much about it. I've been told it's common practice. I just wanted thee to be aware."

"I appreciate it." Bruce gave him a nod of appreciation. His chest tightened with unwanted tension. While it wasn't uncommon for a slave owner to hire a bounty hunter, it was less so once escaped slaves had likely traveled beyond state borders.

"I knew he wouldn't let us alone." Jim's voice rattled with fear. "What's we gonna do?"

"Nothing," Bruce said, keeping a calm tone and his gaze steady for Marta and Jim's benefit. "We've taken every necessary precaution. That's why thee has managed to elude him through the Carolinas and into Virginia. We don't have much farther to go."

"Bruce is right." Flora covered Marta's trembling hand with her own. "Try not to worry. Let's eat the nice meal Friend Brown went to the trouble of cooking for us."

"We're quite thankful," Irene said, grabbing another biscuit. "I was nearly famished!"

"Thee may eat as much as thee wants." Ida Brown set another plate of bacon before them. "In the meantime, we'll prepare thy baths. Who would like to go first?" Her gaze traveled to all of them.

Irene's mouth was full or Bruce was certain she would have been the first to speak up. Instead, Flora cleared her throat. "I'd like Marta to go first. She's been experiencing lots of worrisome pains of late, and I'd like her to have a chance to relax and rest as much as possible."

"Of course." Ida Brown rose to her feet. "Thy water is already warming, and I'll have it ready in a moment."

"We have two tubs." Harvey Brown smiled with pride and slid his thumbs beneath his black suspenders. "While the women bathe upstairs, the men may bathe downstairs in our basement by the large hearth."

"We're much obliged," Bruce said. Using Flora's admirable example, he turned to Jim. "Thee should go first."

"I couldn't." Jim shook his head, dropping his gaze.

"Yes, thee can. I insist. That way thee will be ready to retire when Marta is ready."

"Come on." Harvey Brown stood from the table. "I'll show thee where to go."

Flora rose with Marta, helping her lift her bulky form from her chair. Marta held her belly with one hand and clung to Flora with the other. Now only Bruce and Irene were left at the kitchen table.

She was in the process of finishing her biscuit when he glanced over at her. Perhaps she would be able to tell him a little more about Clint Roberts.

"When I was stitching up Flora yesterday, she mentioned a man by the name of Clint Roberts had taught her how to stitch up a wound." Bruce pulled another biscuit apart and kept busy spreading strawberry jam on one half. He hoped she would volunteer a little information without him having to be too obvious.

She finished drinking her water and set her cup down. "Yes, he received his doctorate this year, but was still in school when Flora met him two years ago. He was out on holiday while we were visiting our aunt and uncle." She giggled. "He wrote and asked if he could court her once he finished school and set up his practice."

Bruce choked and reached for his water. Flora had mentioned that a doctor in Virginia wanted her assistance with his medical practice, but she hadn't said anything about a courtship. And why would she? Until this mission, the two of them hadn't been on very friendly terms, in spite of how close their families were in their Quaker community.

"Is thee all right?" Irene frowned at him in concern.

"Yes," he managed to squeeze out as he coughed again. He hit his chest, more irritated with himself than anything else. "I'm sorry, please continue."

"Well, I think it's strange that he would want to carry on a long-distance courtship." She shrugged. "Unless he plans for one of them to move."

"Interesting." Bruce didn't know what to think.

"His last letter said he would like to visit us, but we had already planned a trip to Virginia. Flora wrote him back and told him of our plans."

"He knows about the mission?" Bruce leaned forward. "What sort of man is he? Can he be trusted? Is he Quaker?"

"Oh, yes." She waved a hand to dismiss his concern. "He's practically family . . . by marriage, that is—our aunt's nephew on her side of the family."

"What does Flora think about all this? I mean, she hasn't seen him in almost two years. People can change in that amount of time."

"That's what I said." Irene propped her chin on her hand. "Besides, I don't want him taking my sister away to live way up here. I'd hardly ever get to see her."

That made two of them. The thought turned his stomach. His hands felt cold all of a sudden. He dropped them into his lap and gave Irene a direct look. "Does that mean she's considering it?"

"Flora says a match with a doctor might suit her, since she is destined to be a midwife." Irene rolled her eyes heavenward. "Something about how he understands her and they have mutual respect for each other. It's so unromantic. I hope to marry for love."

"Flora has always been the practical sort." He tried to ignore the ache in the back of his throat and the gaping hole that had been drilled through his chest. "Still, I'd hate to see her settle for less than she deserves. I wouldn't want her to be unhappy."

Something struck his heart like a lit match, and he realized how true those words were. He couldn't stand the thought of her being unhappy.

"She says everyone in Greensboro will always think of her as Beaver Face." Irene pointed at him. "Thee contributed to that image she has of herself. To her way of thinking, Virginia would give her a fresh start where no one knows of her past."

"I don't know how many times I can apologize for the same thing. If I could, I'd go back and erase every bit of it, but I can't.

What's done is done." And now he could lose Flora Saferight due to his own folly. He rubbed his eyes, fatigue claiming the remainder of his strength. "If thee really believes this man isn't right for her, thee could try to persuade her otherwise," Bruce said. "Flora will listen to thee."

"I love my sister and wouldn't dream of standing in the way of her happiness." Irene dropped her hand and straightened in her seat. "I want to meet him again and see what I think of him now."

"I see." Bruce stood, feeling more defeated than ever. "I'm going downstairs to await my bath."

Flora smiled, thinking how refreshing some rest in a decent bed had been for all of them. Even Bruce seemed to be in better spirits as he conversed with Friend Harvey by the wagon.

Now that dusk claimed the sky, they prepared to leave. The only consolation Flora had about being back on the road and camping out in the wooded countryside was the knowledge that they would soon arrive at her aunt and uncle's home.

"I keep telling myself that getting back in that dark box is our way to freedom." Marta patted her round belly and took a deep breath.

"Here, take this quilt with thee. The weather is colder tonight, and I don't want thee to be freezing," Flora said.

"Thank you, Miz Flora." Marta accepted the thick quilt, hugging it to her chest. "Truth be told, I'm a little cold just now."

"My mother made this quilt. She included an extra layer of padding that will keep thee and Jim warm."

Flora ran her hand over the quilt, remembering how her mother had packed their trunks full of her handmade quilts.

It was the one thing she wouldn't let Flora and Irene compromise on when Bruce had insisted they lighten their load. Flora appreciated her mother's foresight and wisdom. A sudden longing for home filled her soul, and a deep ache throbbed inside her.

Their good-byes to the Browns were brief but heartfelt. Soon they were back on the road traveling into the increasing dark. Now, as she glanced up, she couldn't find any stars twinkling in the dark sky.

"Where are all the stars tonight?" Flora asked. "It's rare we don't see any—not even the moon is showing."

"That's what Harvey and I were discussing earlier," Bruce said. "Thick clouds have rolled in. He gave us some extra oil lanterns in case we need them."

"It's cold, too." Irene shivered, leaning close to Flora. The two of them huddled under a quilt. "I hope it doesn't snow on us."

Bruce chuckled. "I don't think we have any worry of that. A storm might be in store for us, though. The winds have picked up."

It was true. The tree branches swayed and brushed against each other as the wind pressed against Flora's face. Perhaps they should have stayed another night on the Brown farm. She glanced over at Bruce, but all she could see was the outline of his form and the hat upon his head. Thunder growled in the distance. They had traveled in rain before, and it had been miserable, but never in a bad storm. Flora swallowed her rising fear.

"Did thee hear that?" Irene sat up. "A storm's coming."

"Indeed. We'd better brace ourselves," Bruce said. "Flora and Irene, go ahead and get inside the covered wagon. It's liable to begin raining any minute. And mind those stitches."

"Go on, Irene. I'll be a moment longer," Flora said.

Irene didn't argue as she crawled over the back of the bench and fell inside the wagon with a thud. A double flash of lightning lit the sky. She scooted closer to the middle of the bench, near Bruce.

"I can pull over if thee needs me to so thy stitches won't bust." Bruce turned toward her. She swayed as they rode over a bump. He reached out a steady hand and pulled her against him. "The last thing we need is for thee to fall out and get hurt again."

"Bruce Millikan, thee cannot ride through this storm. Pull over and wait it out. Once the rain starts, we'll be sloshing through mud and could get stuck."

Thunder rumbled closer as more wind gushed. Bruce almost lost his hat. He slammed his hand over the top, catching it in time. Pulling it off, he handed it to her. "Here, throw this inside."

"What about pulling under the cover of a large tree?" Flora asked as she turned and tossed his hat inside.

"That's the worst thing I could do. I've seen too many storms bring down large limbs and whole trees." Bruce shook his head. "No, we'd be better trying to ride it out as far as we can and if we have to park, to do so on a hill so we don't get caught the bottom of a slope where rain would drain into a puddle and cause a mud hole around us."

"I trust thy judgment." What he said made sense.

"That's a first." Surprise carried in his tone and it made her smile.

"In this storm," she clarified. "See? I can be reasonable sometimes."

The wagon tilted to the right as torrents of rain slashed against them from the side wind. Flora reached for Bruce's arm, but feared jarring him and grabbed for the seat instead.

"Thee can hold onto me. I prefer it so I'll know where thee is." He said something else, but booming thunder drowned out his voice.

The horse struggled to pull them as they climbed a hill. Rain beat upon her bonnet and face until she ducked behind Bruce's shoulder. Cold wetness soaked her bonnet and matted her hair to her crown. The quilt provided little warmth as it grew saturated with rain.

They finally crested the hill, and Bruce steered them to a flat spot off the side of the road to a patch of grass. He set the brake. Flora gripped the bench on both sides of her lap to keep from losing her balance. More lightning and thunder exploded above them.

"Flora!" Irene poked out her head. "I can hear Marta screaming something fierce. I think she's gone into labor. Jim's banging on the wagon floor begging for us to let them out."

Ice settled in the pit of Flora's stomach. This was exactly what she had been dreading. If they hadn't already been traveling for several hours, she would demand that Bruce take them back to the Browns' house. Now she would have to make do with the resources she had available.

"Dear Lord." Flora touched her forehead. "I can't even build a fire to boil water in this mess. Please help me. Show me what to do to keep Marta from infection."

"What?" Irene yelled over the pouring rain.

"Get my medical supplies ready from my trunk!" Flora scooted to the edge of the wagon and prepared to jump, but strong arms lifted her. She gasped in surprise as she realized Bruce held her. She clung to his arms as he swung her down to her feet.

"Flora, thee can do this. If thee needs me, I'll be right here keeping Jim calm as best as I can." Bruce gave her arm a gentle squeeze of encouragement.

She could hardly see as she hurried to the back of the wagon, reached under, and unlatched the hidden lock. The door opened, and Jim slid out as Marta screamed in pain.

"Put her inside the covered wagon!" Another clap of thunder bit off her words.

Jim must have understood her. He bent, reached inside, and pulled Marta's writhing body out and into his arms. She buried her face in Jim's chest, muffling her cries. Jim crawled into the wagon and laid her on the pallet Irene had prepared.

"Takes good care o' her, Miz Flora." He backed out into the rain and left them.

"God, please help me," Flora whispered.

⸺⸺

Marta cried out in agony, her voice lingering in a wail. Jim cringed. The poor man leaned his forehead against the trunk of a tree, his face contorted in the pouring rain as if someone had him against a whipping post. Bruce shuddered and prayed. He didn't know all that was involved in bringing a new life into the world, but he'd known enough women through the years who didn't make it when things went wrong.

The agony went on for hours throughout the night. Coaxing voices drifted from the wagon when the cries quieted. Bruce assumed Marta had run out of energy to cry out. He exchanged worried glances with Jim as they passed each other in their pacing. The storm had raged on for a couple of hours. Bruce blew on his hands, unable to feel them now.

"Why ain't we hearing nothing?" Jim shoved his large hands through his thick hair and bent over, slamming his palms against his knees. Bruce placed a sturdy hand on his shoulder as his friend tried to catch his breath.

"I'm sure all is well or there would be weeping." Bruce gave the man's shoulder a reassuring squeeze.

Jim nodded, accepting his words as truth. Bruce swallowed, hoping he was right.

"I know it can take hours. On the plantation back home, other women could take all day and night." Jim stood and stretched his arms above his head. "I keep reminding myself o' that."

"My sister was in labor with her first one for over twenty-four hours. And they both did fine," Bruce said.

The thunder and lightning had waned, but a light drizzle still showered them. Bruce went over to the two buckets he'd set out to capture fresh rainwater. The buckets were now full. At least if they needed more water, he'd have it ready.

A piercing scream ripped the air, and Bruce's gut clenched in fear. He glanced at Jim, a similar expression of anguish creasing his young face as their gazes crossed.

"Irene, hold her tighter. I can't do this if she's wriggling away from me." Flora's strong voice rose.

"I can't. I'm going to be sick!" Irene said, as the sound of shuffling ensued. A moment later, Irene emerged. She leaped to the ground holding her mouth with one hand and gripping her skirt with the other. Running past Bruce and Jim to a line of bushes, she fell to her knees. Her shoulders heaved as the horrible sounds of retching broke through the soft pattering rain.

"Irene, come back here!" Flora's angry tone demanded. "Please."

Bruce was torn. Should he go comfort Irene or see if he could assist Flora?

"Marta? Oh, no." Jim ran to the wagon.

Bruce lunged after him, catching him before he could haul himself up into the covered wagon. He grabbed the man's shoulder, but he jerked free. Bruce gripped his arm. "Jim, wait. Marta may be fine."

"Bruce, I need thee!" Flora's frightened voice caused both of them to pause. He'd never heard fear in her tone before.

"Flora, I'm right here." He shoved past Jim, who now stood still, rooted to the earth like a one-hundred-year-old tree. He leaned inside to see Flora brushing Marta's hair back from her forehead in a comforting manner.

"I've got to turn the baby, and I've never done this before." She bit her bottom lip and blinked weary eyes where circles had formed in the last few hours. "I need thee to hold Marta as still as possible."

"Jim, Marta is fine, but I need thee to stay out here." He leaned back to see the man staring at him with wild eyes. "See if Irene is all right." Bruce climbed inside and took Flora's place in comforting Marta. "Thee can do this," he said to Flora. "The Lord is with thee."

Flora nodded and moved past him in an awkward manner, trying to keep her stitched knee from bending too much. She moved between Marta's legs and took a deep breath as she stretched out her leg to the side. "Marta, Bruce will hold thee while I turn thy baby. There will be lots of pain."

Bruce leaned over Marta, who stared up at him with glazed eyes. He wasn't sure how much she could hear or understand at this point. It looked like she'd already lost a good deal of blood. With a silent prayer, Bruce held her shoulders against the floor. "Go, Flora. I've got her."

She bent and worked hard, groaning and clenching her teeth as she struggled with her task. Tears streamed down her face as she set her expression like flint and wrinkled her forehead in determined fortitude.

Marta bit down on the cloth in her mouth, but it didn't stop the writhing cry that escaped from deep within her throat. Her body rose and twisted, contorting against Bruce's palms as he used the force of his weight to keep her down. Irene would have never had the strength to do this. Marta mustered some internal power and tried to lurch upward, but Bruce braced his knees and forced her back down, grunting with the effort it took.

"I've got it." Flora glanced up at him, their eyes meeting with mutual respect and gratefulness. "It's done. Let's give her a moment to recover, and she can push with the next series of contractions."

Marta calmed, breathing heavily and going as limp as a blade of grass. For a moment, she lay so still, Bruce worried. "Lord, give her more strength to push this baby out."

"Yes, Lord, please," Flora said, her voice joining his as she rose back up on her good knee and hunched over, prepared for the next phase. "Here it comes, Marta. Picture thy baby. Get a clear image of him in thy mind and push with all thy might. He needs thee, right now. Go, Marta. Push, now!"

Marta leaned up on her elbows, threw her head back, and closed her eyes as she scrunched up her face. "Argh!" She stopped to take another breath.

"Keep going, Marta. Don't give up now." Flora reached down with both hands and waited. "I can see his head."

Marta braced again. Bruce helped steady her back. She pushed, her voice straining under the pressure of what her body continued to endure.

"I've got him." Flora caught the stiff child in her arms. She grabbed a pair of scissors and snipped the umbilical cord. Blood spewed as Flora turned to work on the baby. "Well done, Marta."

No anticipated crying followed. Flora blew in the child's face, and when that didn't work she slapped his bottom.

"Why . . . ain't he crying?" Marta's tired voice rasped out after she took another deep breath.

"Bruce, let Marta rest and then press down on her stomach. The afterbirth still has to come out."

"What 'bout my baby?" Marta reached out her arms. "Let me have him."

Bruce repositioned himself beside Marta and set his hands on her stomach. "Marta, brace thyself for the pain." He did the best he could with no proper training, while Flora continued to work on the baby. Marta screamed, half-rising and curling up her body. He pulled out the messy afterbirth as he had done when he and his father had assisted with the birth of a new colt.

Still the baby didn't cry. Flora continued to work, and he maneuvered around to peer over her trembling shoulder. The stiff child lay in the crook of her arm, all ashen and gray. "Breathe!" she whispered. "Oh God, make him breathe."

Bruce's heart sank like a cannonball had hit him, knowing he would have to first convince Flora and then the child's labor-beaten mother of the truth. He swallowed the lump of cotton that drained the back of his throat dry. Laying a gentle hand on Flora's shoulder, he reached out with his other hand.

"Flora, give him to me."

"I can't . . ."

"Flora, he's gone."

"No." She shook her head. "I won't give up. He'll breathe. I know he will." She blew in the child's face and popped him on the bottom again as if to shock him into breathing.

"Give me my baby!" Marta cried, tears already lacing her voice.

"Marta . . . I'm . . . so sorry." Flora choked as a sob burst from deep in her chest. This time when Bruce reached for the child, she relinquished him without a fight and doubled over, silencing her grief as Bruce turned toward Marta.

11

With mind-numbing movements, Flora managed to clean Marta while Bruce broke the news to Jim. Marta curled into a ball and wept as she held the child to her chest.

"I should give him a name, don't yous think?" Her tear-strained voice pierced Flora's awareness. "He deserves that much."

"Yes," Flora nodded.

"Will yous put his outfit on him, the one yous made?" Marta wiped her red eyes. "I want him dressed like a proper baby boy when Jim sees him for the first time."

Flora swallowed and cleared her throat, but no sound came. She nodded a second time and reached for the outfit on top of a nearby trunk where Marta had laid it in the midst of her labor pains.

"Here's Jimmy," Marta held up the wrapped bundle. "I named him for his daddy."

"I think that's very wise. Jim will be proud." Flora accepted the silent baby and did her best not to feel as she tried to dress him. None of her previous training had prepared her for this. What had made her think she could do something so important as deliver new lives into the world?

"I kept my promise to him," Marta said. Flora paused to give her a puzzled look. "He was born . . . free." Marta's eyes swam in fresh tears, but she lifted her trembling chin, proud of her accomplishment.

Overcome with emotion, Flora kissed the top of Jimmy's tiny head. It took several moments before she could speak. "Indeed, thee did." Her bottom lip quivered as she offered Marta a comforting smile and handed back her son.

"If thee is ready, I'll go get Jim."

Marta wiped her swollen eyes and brushed her hair from her face. She straightened her shoulders and clenched her jaw. "I'm ready."

Flora scooted to the edge with her awkward knee and climbed down. She walked over to where Jim sat on a log with his head hanging in his hands. She touched his shoulder. "Jim, thee may go in now."

He bolted to his feet and rushed past her. Bruce and Irene approached from opposite directions. Bruce was quiet and resolute, while Irene wept, shaking her shoulders.

"Flora, I'm so sorry. Please . . . please forgive me," Irene said, choking out the words.

Shrinking back, Flora folded her arms over her middle. "It isn't thy fault, Irene. There's nothing to forgive. We both know thee has always had a weak stomach. Bruce was able to help me, so all is well."

Bruce took a step toward her and opened his mouth as if he wanted to say something, but hesitated when she held up a hand to stay him.

"I'm sorry, but I need a moment to myself. Please . . ." She turned on her heel, the tears in her eyes blinding her. Flora walked to the water barrel and cleaned herself as best as she could. The cold air made her fingers and limbs as numb as her heart. Without a word, Bruce draped her cloak over her shoulders. She clutched it over her chest and strode away.

"Don't go far," Bruce said. "It will soon be dawn and we must move on to a more hidden spot."

As she walked, the numbness gave way to an aching pain deep inside. Hot tears blazed a trail down her cheeks as the back of her throat throbbed. Her insides quaked with the sobs she finally released into the air. So many thoughts ran circles in her mind. Should she have demanded they stay at the Brown farm? Perhaps she should have tried to turn the baby sooner? What else could she have done to prevent little Jimmy's death? On she walked, mindlessly following the dirt road, not caring where it led.

Ignoring the pain in her bad knee, she lowered herself to sit and let guilt wash through her with each sob that shook her body. If she could feel like this, how much worse must it be for Marta and Jim? She sobbed even harder for the depth of grief her friends must be feeling.

"God . . . for—" The words lodged in her throat, but she had to force them out. He was the only one who could help her bear the guilt. "Please . . . f-forgive me."

"Flora!" Someone called her name, but the mire of confusion prevented her from caring. She dropped her chin to her chest, waiting in silence for God's comfort to ease her distress as He had in the past.

"Flora." Bruce touched her shoulder and bent beside her. "Dawn is here. We must go."

She shook her head. "Thee was right, Bruce Millikan. I was the wrong person for this mission. Their baby died because of me."

"No, Flora, listen to me." Bruce moved to his knees in front of her, lifting her chin. He looked into her eyes, his gaze deep and assessing. "I was wrong. God knew this would happen and thee would be the best one to handle it—to help console Marta. It would have happened no matter who tried to deliver him. And you likely saved Marta's life."

"I don't believe it. Someone with better skills could have saved him. I didn't have enough experience, and I'm not a doctor."

"That doesn't matter." Bruce leaned forward, touching his forehead to hers, his voice lowering, "Flora, after watching thee work so hard to save his and Marta's life, I've developed respect and admiration for thee. I promise, no one could have done better—not even a doctor."

"But I feel responsible."

"Don't do this to thyself." He cradled her face with both hands. "I was there. I saw what happened, and none of it was thy fault. Grieve if thee must, but no guilt or blame belongs to thee."

Having him near brought warmth to her shivering body, a strange comfort from a man who had spent so many years making her miserable. She wanted to believe him, but the idea of trusting Bruce Millikan wasn't easy. "Thee is only hoping to calm me, so we can get moving now that it's dawn." She tried to back away, but he held her face and lowered his head.

Bruce's cool lips touched hers, surprising her into silence, a rare submission. His tender touch gentled without him losing his firm hold on her. It was as if he willed Flora to believe in herself as he did. Caught in a whirlwind of unexpected passion mixed with a deep desire to be loved and valued, Flora allowed her emotions a moment of free rein. It felt so good to finally be cherished—to win the approval of Bruce Millikan.

This was Bruce!

Flora stiffened as familiar fear slithered up her spine, breaking the dangerous spell he'd cast over her. She jerked back.

How could she be so gullible? Would Bruce now taunt her with the liberties he'd taken and she'd given?

He stared at her in wild confusion, blinking as if clearing his thoughts. Flora laid a hand across her chest, bracing for some crazy accusation or angry retort. Instead, Bruce groaned and ran his fingers through his hair. Remorse etched his somber expression.

"Flora, please forgive me. I shouldn't have done that. I only wanted to console thee." He took a deep breath and looked away.

Of all the reactions she could have anticipated, his regret was something she hadn't considered. Fresh pain pierced her wounded heart. In a matter of seconds, Bruce had managed to resurrect her hopes, and then shatter them with one expression and an apology. What could the man be thinking?

Bruce mentally chastised himself over and over as he and Flora walked back to the wagon. He didn't touch her. Instead, he kept a respectable distance. He couldn't trust himself not to take her in his arms again. Nothing could change the fact that he had wanted to comfort her and take away her pain. His timing was wrong, and he shouldn't have taken advantage of her in such an emotional state.

Still, he couldn't bring himself to regret kissing her. His apology had been forced, but he knew when she pulled back that she was uncomfortable. He'd worked so hard to rebuild her trust. How would she feel about him after this?

For a moment, Flora had responded favorably. Their shared intimacy would always be a treasured memory. He prayed she would see past his desire and recognize the growing feelings he had for her. She wasn't some passing fancy that would disappear with the end of this trip. What he felt for her was lasting, and he suspected had started years ago, even if he hadn't been wise enough to realize it until now. He wondered if she could come to feel the same way about him.

Bruce cast a sideways glance at her. Flora kept her gaze on the dirt road before them. Daylight grew brighter by the minute, and they risked being seen if he didn't find a hiding place for them soon. He sighed from the heavy burden on his mind. Today they would have to bury Jim and Marta's little one. This was one part of the mission he'd hoped would never come.

They arrived back at the wagon before any riders or coaches met them on the road. Flora didn't want Marta to move, so she rode with her inside the covered wagon, while Irene accompanied Bruce up front. Jim agreed to ride inside the secret compartment as Bruce hunted for an appropriate spot to hide them.

He spied some bushes leading to a thick pine forest. Bruce swung wide and maneuvered them through, stopping long enough to cover their wheel tracks with some shrubbery and leaves. They rode deep into the woods. Once he had parked and set the brake, he turned to Irene. "I'm going to scout the area to make sure no one is within hearing distance. Don't build any cooking fires or unpack anything until I return. Thee can let Jim out, but keep him hidden inside the covered wagon."

It took him over an hour to walk a wide circle around the area as he climbed up and down steep hills, careful not to slide on the thick bed of pine needles and cones lying about. Bruce didn't see any houses or evidence that there were people living nearby. On the way back, he found the perfect spot to bury the baby. There was a wide pine tree with a deep crevice at the roots, resembling a cradle.

Once Marta saw it, she agreed. Bruce dug a hole as deep as he could with his knife and carved little Jimmy's name into the bark of the tree trunk. They found several rocks to cover the tiny grave. Bruce read a passage out of the Book of Psalms as they bowed their heads in prayer.

The rest of the afternoon passed in somber silence with the exception of Marta's muffled weeping and Jim's soothing voice attempting to console her. While Irene worked on knitting a pair of gloves and napped, Flora read from her Bible and studied the Midnight Star quilt. At one point, she bent over and cradled the quilt as if seeking solace from it.

Bruce lay on the front wagon bench and dozed after brushing down the horse and checking the animal's shoes. He watched Flora weep on her mother's quilt, using it to wipe her tears. His chest constricted. "Flora, please don't blame thyself. It wasn't thy fault."

She sniffled and glanced up at him. "I was thinking about the three babies my mother lost when I was a little girl. She grieved for months for each one. They were all two years apart." Her voice faltered. "That's when I decided I wanted to be a midwife—so I can save the lives of babies. This quilt is a reminder of Mother's faith in me. I'm afraid she'll feel that I let her down when I return and tell her I couldn't save Marta's baby."

"She'll feel proud that thee saved Marta's life, and that thee consoled her and was a true friend," Bruce said.

Two days later, they rode into Charlottesville. Until now they had ridden around towns to avoid people, but this time their station was inside the city. Mountaintops graced the skyline in the distance, showing a splash of yellow, orange, and dark red leaves mixed with the brown shades of empty tree limbs. He wondered if it was still the tenth month or if time had already passed into the eleventh.

Bruce kept a watchful eye on people as they nodded in passing. No one appeared too curious about the new strangers in town. Perhaps they were used to all kinds of people passing through. With a bounty hunter on their heels, the less they were noticed, the better.

Irene couldn't remember how to guide him through town to the Saferight farm, and the Midnight Star quilt didn't provide enough detail on individual streets.

"Flora, we need thy help," Irene called through the opening of the covered wagon.

"What's the matter?" Her head appeared a moment later.

"I can't tell what street we're on." Bruce pointed to the quilt spread out on his and Irene's lap, keeping them warm. He held the reins in his left hand, keeping an eye out for traffic in front of them.

Flora bit her lip as she assessed her surroundings. She squinted as the morning sun shone bright upon the melting frost still clinging to rooftops and the tops of trees. "I think it might be because this road didn't exist when Mother sewed the Midnight Star."

They came to a corner street with a wooden sign. Bruce turned right where more merchant shops lined the road. "Well, it looks like we found Main Street. Where is the Quaker church? Does thee remember?"

"There isn't one," Flora said. "Not many Quaker families live here, and the few here meet at my uncle's house. There's the courthouse up on the hill." Flora pointed straight ahead to a brick building with white columns. "I believe that steeple over the other buildings to the left belongs to the Presbyterian church. That means thee will need to turn left on the next street."

They passed a tavern, a tailor shop, a print shop, and a gunsmith, then made the turn. At the second block, a wooden sign indicated they were now on Church Street.

"Is this the right way?" Bruce raised an eyebrow at Flora and Irene. They looked at each other.

"I remember the church and the courthouse," Irene said, scooting to the edge of her seat. "At the end we'll take a right, and our aunt's house should be down that street."

"Yes." Flora lifted a hand over her eyes as she gazed down the street. "Although I don't remember some of these buildings. That must be a new tavern." She pointed to a brown building on the left where a woman swept the front steps. They rolled along, avoiding mud puddles in the street and dodging traffic.

They came to a gray house at a dead end. A red barn sat on a hill behind the house. As they drew closer, they could see a white cat with brown spots stretched on top of the porch, observing their arrival. A couple of round bushes were planted out front with a few flowers that had died with the frost.

"This is it." Excitement resonated in Flora's voice. "They live on a farm at the edge of town."

Bruce pulled around back so no one would see Marta and Jim. By the time they rolled to a stop near the back porch, Bruce realized the house was much larger than it looked from the front. Several rooms had been added to the original portion in back, lengthening the house into a *T* shape.

A blond-haired woman wearing a wide smile appeared on the porch. Bruce glanced from Irene to the older woman and recognized the resemblance.

"Aunt Abigail!" Irene bounced from the wagon, running with open arms to hug her.

A middle-aged man with gray hair approached from the barn. Two young men accompanied him; one looked to be near Bruce's age and the other a few years older. The brown-haired one whistled as he looked down at Irene and held out his arms. "Cousin, thee has grown up since I last saw thee."

"Of course I have. And Daniel, thee has grown taller." Irene walked into his embrace as he rubbed her head, knocking her bonnet slightly askew. She grimaced and gave him a playful pat on the arm.

Bruce leaped to the ground and walked to the back of the wagon to help Flora with Marta and Jim. As always, dependable Flora was the one who was taking care of others, while Irene pretended to be on a social visit.

"Flora, it's so good to see thee. I've been coming by every day hoping thee will arrive." Bruce turned toward the speaker, a young man with short black hair combed to the side. A few layers fell on his forehead from beneath his hat. The man had a square face and fashionable sideburns, but it was his gray eyes feeding on Flora that made Bruce tense.

"Clint, I'm so glad thee is here." Flora slipped an arm beneath Marta's shoulders, trying to help her sit up. Her strained features relaxed into a bright smile. "Marta had her baby a few days ago, but he didn't survive. She's weak, and I worry she may be hemorrhaging."

"I'll do what I can." Clint's gaze shifted to Marta, his expression turning serious. "First, let's get her into the house and in a comfortable position." He crawled inside.

Bruce stood outside, his hands empty and his heart full of worry. Flora and Clint worked together seamlessly as they shifted Marta into Clint's arms. He carried her out with Flora following, her attention fully focused on Marta.

Bruce stood still, his muscles taut like a pulley rope with a knot as he watched them disappear into the house. A knock from below the wagon bed jerked Bruce out of his stupor.

"Don't forget 'bout me!" Jim's muffled voice carried through the hidden compartment.

The house was quiet as Flora walked down Aunt Abigail's hallway. She stepped softly to keep her boots from waking the others. It was so good to see everyone again. While Bruce, Jim, and Marta had retired to catch up on some sleep, she and Irene spent an hour reconnecting with their cousins.

Exhaustion finally overcame them. With a yawn, Flora and her sister retired to their shared guest chamber. She slept for a few hours, then arose and left Irene slumbering.

Low voices carried from the back kitchen out onto the wrap-around porch. Flora followed the sounds to a plain white door. She turned the dark brass knob. It clicked and swung open with a slight creak.

"Flora, I'm surprised thee is awake," Aunt Abigail said as she rocked back and forth in her wooden rocker. "Thee could hardly keep thy eyes open early this morning."

"I know, but a few hours' rest did me a world of good." Flora stepped out onto the porch, closing the door behind her with a snap. She glanced from her aunt to her cousin, Belinda. Over the last two years, Belinda hadn't changed much. Her green eyes and blond locks beneath her white bonnet were still the same. The only difference was the fact that Belinda was plumper than she remembered.

Clint stood from where he had been sitting on the front step. He gestured to his spot and leaned against the white porch rail. Flora awarded him with a grateful smile and lowered herself onto the top step, fanning her gray skirt over her legs and feet. Only the toes of her worn black boots protruded.

"Thanks," Flora said, a warm blush heating her cheeks. Thoughts of the bold letters she'd shared with Doctor Clint flitted through her mind like a list of chastisements. At the time, her bold letters seemed appropriate, but now that she was once again in his presence, a strange awkwardness existed between them—a gulf she hadn't expected. To ease her discomfort, Flora turned to her aunt. "Where's Uncle Jeremiah and Daniel?"

"They're out in the fields back behind the barn. We harvested the corn a few weeks ago, but we still need to reap the carrots and cabbage now that we're at the end of the tenth month." Aunt Abigail pointed into the distance toward the red barn.

"Yes, I'll be helping with those crops when the time comes, aside from tending my patients," Clint said. "I haven't set up a practice around here, but as soon as the word got out that I got my doctorate, plenty of folks have been coming by with various illnesses and injuries."

"Why not go ahead and set up a practice?" Flora asked, glancing up at him, as the door opened and out stepped Bruce. He nodded in greeting to Clint and the others.

"I haven't decided if I want to settle down here. It all depends on . . . other factors." Clint gave Flora a direct stare, his eyes seizing hers. She gulped, wondering if he referred to the letter he'd sent her regarding a courtship between them. Surely he couldn't mean marriage—they hadn't even begun a courtship as yet.

Bruce cleared his throat as he walked to the other side of the steps, where Flora sat leaning against the opposite rail. He glanced down at her. She sensed him seeking her expression to gauge her reaction. Heat flamed her skin in a race to the top of her head. Dropping her gaze to her hands, which were folded in her lap, she said, "I'm certain thee will be an excellent doctor wherever thee goes."

"I was thinking about going south—to North Carolina."

Flora could hear the smile in Clint's voice. She didn't want to embarrass him in front of everyone, but she needed time to assess her feelings. Ever since she'd received his letter, she'd considered how beneficial a doctor husband would be for her desire to be a midwife. Their professions could complement each other. She wasn't a beauty and had no other outstanding qualities. Wouldn't she be wise to consider his offer of court-ship? How else would she know if they were suited? No one from back home had shown much interest. She wasn't getting any younger. Shouldn't she at least see where this opportunity would lead?

She forced a smile and looked up into Clint's hopeful gray eyes. "Then I'm sure that North Carolina would be pleased to welcome thee. There are many places that could use a new doctor such as thee." She chose words that didn't personally implicate her own feelings on the matter, but the sparkle in his eyes left her wondering if she had succeeded in being neutral.

"I realize thee will be leaving soon to finish thy mission, but I hope we'll be able to talk more about North Carolina when thee returns," Clint said.

"I'm not an expert on my home state, nor have I had the opportunity to visit far beyond Greensboro, but I'd be pleased to offer what knowledge I have."

Aunt Abigail stopped rocking and leaned forward with a satisfied grin. "I told Clint thee would be the best person to advise him." She clapped her hands together in a single slap. "I told him about New Garden Quaker school in Greensboro. For a steady income, he might want to teach while he builds his practice."

"What about the University of Virginia here in Charlottesville?" Flora asked. "It looks so impressive."

"It isn't Quaker," Aunt Abigail said, rocking again.

"I see." Flora scanned Clint's reaction, but he showed none. "I want to thank thee for examining Marta and trying to make me feel better about not saving her baby. The encouragement from a professional means a great deal to me."

"I told thee it wasn't thy fault. I've never seen anyone work harder than thee." Bruce's soft voice penetrated her soul like a healing balm. For so many years she had longed for his approval and now that he validated her efforts, she sought the approval of someone else. Confusion clouded her mind as his green gaze met hers. "It doesn't take a professional doctor to see the sincerity of someone's heart."

The slight chastisement stung, but rang true. Nor did she need the approval of any man. Why couldn't she be content with God's blessing? In the end, God would be the one she would have to stand before and give an account of all she'd done with her life, not either of these men.

Lord, forgive me, Flora whispered from her heart.

"Friends Bruce and Clint, I thank thee for thy words of wisdom," she said.

Hurt flickered in Bruce's eyes, and he looked toward the barn. She sensed it was because she'd referred to him in the same way as Clint, on a less intimate level. Her intention was to let Clint know that she hadn't yet decided upon a courtship. Perhaps she could later explain things to Bruce when they were alone.

"Did thee have Clint look at thy leg wound?" A hard edge had now entered Bruce's tone. "It might be best to have a professional take out the stitches in case I didn't do it justice." Bruce stepped from the rail where he'd been leaning and stood to his full height. He looked at Clint. "The wound is on the side of her right knee. She busted the stitches and tried to hide it. I caught her trying to restitch herself, so I really would like to know if there's any infection." His voice turned gruff as he cleared his throat. "I wouldn't want anything to happen to her. It's best if it's checked before we continue on our mission."

A mixture of anger and surprise swirled in Flora's chest as he stepped down, passing by her.

"Bruce." She grabbed at his arm, not caring what the others thought.

"I think I'll go for a walk and enjoy the beautiful day God has made." He pulled away from her and breathed in deeply, releasing a satisfied sigh.

She didn't want Clint examining her leg. In spite of what Bruce thought, she'd planned to ask him to remove her stitches. It wasn't that she distrusted Clint, but she felt more comfortable with Bruce—and he'd already seen her legs.

Flora wanted to run after him, but forced herself to remain seated for appearance's sake. She gulped and turned a half-hearted grin filled with guilt toward the others. How could she relieve their concern without giving in to Clint's doctoring her?

12

For the next two days, Bruce suffered through Clint Robert's attentions toward Flora. To his profound irritation, Flora didn't discourage the fellow. As he watched her smile up at him on their walks around the farm and observed their exchanged glances across the table during meal times, jealousy pinched his ego in a way he'd never experienced before.

Now as Bruce harnessed the horse and prepared to hitch the animal to the wagon, Flora stood alone with Clint. They talked under an oak tree, saying their good-byes. Fear spiraled through Bruce's stomach as worry pierced his soul.

"Lord, please don't let me lose her," he whispered as he bent, rubbing his faithful horse. "I know I don't deserve her. I was never good to her growing up. She made me nervous, and as a kid I didn't know how to react when she provoked me." He paused, adjusting his black hat on his head. "Things are different now. My feelings are so much deeper, to the point of feeling desperate. This jealousy isn't like me. Help me not to push her away."

He took a deep breath when Clint tilted his head toward Flora. Bruce's stomach clenched as nausea claimed him. The sick feeling rose up in his chest, closing off his air. He coughed.

The noise startled Flora. She turned and frowned with guilt, the same way she had once done when he'd caught her sneaking his grapes from his lunch at school. Clint's mouth twisted in frustration. Momentary satisfaction pooled in the pit of Bruce's gut. He didn't think he could have stomached seeing them kiss if that was about to happen.

He grinned and waved at them as he rubbed his throat, hoping Flora wouldn't be annoyed by the interruption. She gave him a half-hearted smile and bent her fingers, waving back.

They said their good-byes. This time Flora crawled up onto the wagon seat without the awkwardness she'd exhibited earlier. She settled between him and Irene.

"Did Clint remove thy stitches?" Bruce raised an eyebrow, watching her smooth her skirt and cloak over her lap.

"He did. I had hoped to ask thee to do it once we were on our way, since thee had already been exposed to my legs, but thee seemed eager to rid thyself of the unpleasant task." She sighed and looked away. "Sometimes I don't understand thee, Bruce."

He blinked, gripping the reins until his knuckles turned white. What had she expected? The wound needed to be checked for infection, and she had refused to cooperate with him after he'd restitched her. The last thing he'd wanted was Clint's hands upon her. If she had planned to ask him to remove her stitches, why not let him check her for infection? He snapped the reins in anger. "And sometimes I don't understand thee."

"Clint said that thee did an excellent job on my stitches. He assured me that he couldn't have done better. I'd have a lingering scar no matter who had stitched me."

"I'm sorry about the scar. Wish I could have prevented it," Bruce said, wondering if the scar had been the reason for her hesitation. He looked away, toward the lantern hanging on the side of their wagon. "Believe me, if I'd known that thee wanted me to remove thy stitches, I would have never said anything to Clint. I thought it was high time the wound was checked and feared thee wouldn't let me look at it since the good doctor was in town," he said, his voice lowered to a grumble.

"Bruce," Irene laughed, "thee almost sounds jealous. Doesn't he, Flora?" She elbowed her sister, nudging Flora into Bruce's side.

"Don't let him fool thee, Irene. Friend Bruce has never harbored anything for me but anger and frustration, although lately, I'm beginning to believe we've finally developed a real friendship." She laid a hand on his arm.

It felt like the air had been punched out of him as he covered hers. "Indeed we have. I care a great deal about thee, Flora. I always have, in spite of what thee believes."

"Which is why I told Clint that thee didn't interrupt us on purpose." She squeezed his arm with emphasis. "He believes thee is jealous, but I told him thee has known me thy whole life and is being overprotective, like a big brother."

"Thee does spend too much time alone with him," Bruce mumbled. He clenched his teeth, wishing he could say what he wanted to say without sounding jealous or making it seem as if he was being critical.

"We went nowhere that was improper." She removed her hand from his arm and folded them under her cloak. "We were always within view of someone, mostly thee." She emphasized the last word.

Not wishing to argue, Bruce dropped the subject, certain anything he said on the matter would serve only to infuriate her further. They traveled through the night; the horse's labored breathing grew heavier as they climbed into the hills toward the mountains.

Irene fell asleep on Flora, and eventually Flora's head fell against Bruce's shoulder. He reached his arm around her, holding her close against his side. His throat ached. This was where she belonged. A chill slid up his spine. How could he make her see reason? Whatever he did, he had only a few weeks to convince her to change her mind about Clint Roberts.

⋙

Flora placed an arm around Irene's shaking shoulders and tried to comfort her as the bobcat continued screaming in the distance. The fire put out a bit of heat, but the higher elevation meant colder weather. Across from them, Jim comforted Marta as they waited for Bruce to return.

Cold fear clutched Flora's heart as she worried for his safety. He had gone hunting, claiming that it was high time they had some meat and that Marta needed the nourishment as she continued to recover. It had been three days since they'd left her aunt's house. Their water was frozen each morning and they had to melt it by the fire before they could boil water and make coffee.

The sound of gunfire caused her to jerk. Irene whimpered. "What if he misses the cat? Couldn't it kill Bruce?"

"Don't think like that." Flora rubbed her sister's arm. It was bad enough that a similar thought had struck her.

"I'm could go after him," Jim offered. "I fought a black bear once."

"No, Jim." Flora shook her head. If Bruce was all right, he would yell at her for putting Jim in danger. She swallowed, listening for more noise. Several minutes passed before they heard another gunshot. It echoed through the forest, plowing at her already taut nerves.

"We should pray," Marta whispered. "Lord, please protect Mister Bruce. Keep him safe. Bring him back unharmed. We know you have all the power, in Jesus' name, amen."

Flora gazed at Marta, the fire casting a brilliant glow on her dark skin and hazel eyes. There were times when she seemed well beyond her years. The way she had grieved for her son and turned to the Lord for comfort had earned Flora's respect. This girl was only fifteen, and yet she had proven to be so full of wisdom—and strength. Flora marveled at her ability to overcome such heartache without letting bitterness take root or giving in to the temptation to blame God.

"I should have suggested praying," Flora said, looking into the dancing flames.

"Yous can't think of everything," Marta said.

The bobcat squealed again. Flora closed her eyes. Bruce hadn't killed the animal. They waited, but no further gunshots sounded. What if there were more than one bobcat? Why hadn't she thought of that before? Bruce was all alone. How could he manage more than one?

She shivered.

"What's wrong?" Irene glanced sideways.

"How much time has passed since the last gunshot?" Flora asked.

"I don't know. Maybe fifteen, twenty minutes." Irene sat back. "What is thee thinking?"

Bruce's voice came to mind when she'd first discovered his trunk of weapons. "I wouldn't fight for myself, but to protect thee, I would." How could she be willing to do anything less for him? An instinctive resolve swelled in her chest as she lifted her chin in determination.

"Bruce is alone. If he's injured, someone must help him." Flora stood up from the log and went to the wagon. She searched for Bruce's trunk with the weapons.

"Flora, no. Thee can't do this. He'll come back. Wait and see." Irene followed her. "It's too dangerous."

"She's right. I'm going," Jim said at the door flap.

"No. Jim, thee must stay here and protect Marta and Irene." She turned and threw a rifle into his hands. "Does thee know how to use this?"

"Naw." He shook his head. "My master never allowed us around guns afore." He turned it over, examining it closely, wrinkling his eyebrows.

"I'll show thee." Flora grabbed a small handgun. She pulled back the chamber and loaded it, then set the safety lock. Grabbing another oil lamp, she pulled her arm free from Irene. "My dad showed me this for protection against wild animals such as this bobcat. We have lots of them at home."

"Thee can't do this!" Irene said.

"I have to. I won't leave Bruce out there alone. I could never forgive myself if anything were to happen to him while we sit around this camp fire waiting." Flora grabbed Irene's shoulder. "I realize this is hard for thee, but I need thee to be strong. Dry thy tears and stay here with Marta and Jim."

"I'm sorry." Irene sniffed and wiped her cheeks. "I'm not as brave as thee. I love thee." Irene hugged her. Flora swallowed hard and embraced her sister.

Outside the wagon, Flora showed Jim how to load the rifle, the safety lock, and how to hold the gun, aim, and pull the trigger. "Jim, don't be afraid. Use this to save thyselves. There may be a family of bobcats out there nearby." Flora touched his arm. "Remember, when thee shoots, the rifle will kick back into thy shoulder. Just make sure thee sees thy target so thee won't mistake the cat for Bruce and I."

"I'll do my best, Miz Flora." He nodded. "Yous be safe." He patted her shoulder.

"I will." Flora lit her lamp, took her gun in hand, and set out in the direction of Bruce's last gunshot.

"I'll pray for yous, Miz Flora," Marta called after her.

Flora didn't respond as she stepped into the black night. The gun in her hand was cold. Fear coiled in her stomach, reaching up and clutching the back of her throat.

"Lord, please protect us, and lead me to Bruce. If he's hurt, show me what to do." The whispered prayer blew smoke in the lantern light. She trembled from a combination of cold and consuming fear as she crept forward into the unknown.

A howling wind swept the tree branches, swaying them around her. She listened, hoping for some sign that Bruce was alive and fine. The lamp only gave enough light for a few feet ahead of her. She had to watch her footing as she came to a fallen branch and stepped over it with care. Her skirt caught on something. Holding the gun away from her body, she reached down with the same hand and tugged her skirt loose.

Just as it gave way, a nearby sound caught her attention. Flora's heart hammered against her ribs as her breath left her in icy fear, freezing her voice to silence. She lifted the lantern, peering through the night.

"Flora! Woman, what is thee doing out here?" Bruce demanded a short distance away.

"I . . . I was worried for thee." Relief filled her, and she nearly collapsed in a puddle.

More grumbling followed that she couldn't decipher until he had reached her side. "Worried for me?" He rubbed his face as he looked down. "Thee will be the death of me before it's over."

"Don't say that." Anguish released in her voice. "I couldn't stand the thought of thee being out here all alone and wounded, if that bobcat got to thee."

"Shush." He placed a cold finger her over mouth. "Let's not draw attention to the cat. I left her a prize back there so she'll leave us in peace." His knuckles brushed her chin. "Did thee really worry for me?"

"Yes, but now I'm wondering if I should have bothered." No point in hiding her exasperation. Bruce vexed her when he wasn't busy confusing her.

"I'm thankful for thy concern, but extremely angered that thee would put thyself at risk." He leaned toward her ear, his warm breath fanning her neck. It was enough to make her shiver as a strange warmth pooled in the pit of her stomach. "How would thee have helped me?"

"I brought this for protection." She held up the gun. "I would have figured out something."

"Thee brought a gun?" Alarmed surprise changed his tone. He leaned his forehead against hers. "Flora, thy courage and instinct never cease to amaze me. Thy future husband will have his hands quite full. I've no doubt of that." He held out his hand. "Give me the gun."

Trying to interpret his words, she hesitated. "Thee sounds as if thee feels sorry for my intended."

"Hand it over . . . now, Flora."

With a sigh, she plopped it into his hand. "Judge me if thee will, but I had good intentions—even if they were for thee."

"Intended? Is thee engaged to that man?" He raised his voice, his tone harsher than she expected. Whatever happened to not attracting the bobcat's attention?

Bruce ushered Flora back to their campsite. Irene burst into tears of gratitude and hugged her sister. Jim and Marta both stood with relieved smiles.

"We're so glad you okay, Mister Bruce." Marta wrung her hands as Jim nodded beside her.

"Thanks, I appreciate it." He motioned for Jim to join him on the other side of the wagon. He glanced over to make sure Flora was occupied with Irene and Marta. "Could thee have not stopped Flora from making such a fool mistake as going out there in the dark woods with a bobcat prowling on the loose?"

"We tried to convince her not to go, but she's mighty stubborn." Jim scratched his neck. "I'm not used to arguing with a white lady. Where I come from, I could be hanged."

"True." Bruce rubbed his eyebrows, still in distress. "She can be the most stubborn woman I've ever known. I guess I've got to have a talk with her—and risk her wrath."

"Maybe it could wait when yous both calm down?" Jim scratched the back of his neck again and shifted from foot to foot.

"Jim, I'm not upset or disappointed with thee. I can't expect thee to control Flora if I've never been able to manage her."

"Uh, sir?" Jim's gaze slid over Bruce's shoulder.

"What does thee mean, can't control Flora?" a female voice demanded.

Bruce tensed. His skin crawled with tiny needles pricking him, traveling down his neck and shoulders. He pivoted on his heel, knowing he couldn't avoid her anger now. She stood with her hands on her hips, her hair cascading around her shoulders without a bonnet. Where was her bonnet? Didn't she know that all that hair distracted a man? His gaze followed the length of her long tresses.

"Explain thyself." She folded her arms across her chest and tapped her toes. Her lips protruded in a less-than-flattering frown.

"Flora, we both know that thee should have never come after me in those woods, especially knowing there's a wild bobcat on the loose nearby." He clenched his hands at his sides and met her gaze, unwilling to back down this time. When he thought about what could have happened to her, his chest spasmed.

"And if the bobcat had gotten thee, how would we have known?" She took a step closer, her eyes narrowing. "It was a risk I was willing to take." She pronounced each syllable with clarity and determination.

"It was unnecessary and foolhardy." His fast-beating heart pulsed with even greater intensity as his anger heightened. He wanted to grab her shoulders and shake good reason into her, but he refrained. Flora wasn't the sort of woman he could intimidate with threats or force. Such action would only fuel her fury. The only thing he knew to do was be forthright.

"How dare thee!" Flora leaned forward and poked him in the chest. His black coat took the brunt of her pointed finger. "I was worried sick for thee, but now I'm sorry I even gave thee a single thought."

The sizzling anger in him eased as her words penetrated his mind. A flutter of hope took root, causing his heart to beat faster. The situation struck him as ironic. Here they were angry at each other and arguing because each was worried about the other. He hid a grin as he rubbed his jaw. "I think I'm beginning to understand."

"Bruce, I'm not some animal thee can tame into submission," she blurted as if she hadn't heard him. Her nostrils flared as she took another deep breath to continue her tirade. "God gave me a mind of my own and the same free will as thee, and I intend to use it." She tilted her face toward him, now only a few inches away. "I will never be controlled by another."

"I, of all people, know that very well." He kept his voice low as he rejoiced in Flora's passionate spirit. It was one of the very things he loved about her. She ignited his senses, heightening a desire for her he'd been trying to fight for the last couple of years. Flora was everything he wanted in the woman who would stand through life by his side.

"Then why provoke me?" She tilted her head to the side and blinked up at him.

"It isn't my desire to provoke thee, and I'm sorry. All I want is to protect thee. I can't do my job in leading this mission if I've got to stop and worry about what danger thee might be putting thyself into. I need to know I can trust thy judgment."

"Thee really believes I'm foolish." She blinked as unshed tears floated in her wide eyes. "Thee called me foolhardy at the general store back in Greensboro and again just a few minutes ago." The tone of her voice lost its edge.

"That's not true." Remorse shot through his veins, pumping his blood even harder. He rubbed his eyebrows and glanced down at his feet before looking back up. "Why does thee always twist my words? That isn't what I meant. I don't believe thee is foolish, only what thee did."

She opened her mouth to say something, but her lower lip trembled and her words stalled. He waited, but she shook her head and stepped back. A sick feeling burrowed in his gut. He reached for her arm, but she jerked away.

"Don't touch me!"

"Flora, don't turn this into something it isn't. I've never thought as much of a woman as I do thee."

She shrank back and twisted her mouth in disgust. "Then thee must not think very highly of any woman. I truly feel sorry for the woman who will one day become thy wife. She will need a heart of steel and the confidence of a saint. As for me, I thank God he brought Clint Roberts into my life. Not once has he made me feel two inches tall, as thee has."

"He's not perfect either. I'm sure he'll say something to upset thee once he's spent enough time in thy company." He stepped forward and lowered his voice so the others wouldn't hear. "And don't ever compare me to him."

He leaned forward, his lips inches from hers. The scent of cedar drifted to him, and the warmth of her body being so near filled his senses with longing. If she intended to compare him with some other man, he would give her something she wouldn't soon forget.

Bruce closed the distance between them and pressed his lips against hers. Flora's resistance crumbled in surprise as a small gasp rose in her throat. Rather than backing away or slapping him, she kissed him back with the same fervor. He had intended to leave Flora with a lasting impression, but the woman had managed to turn his own lesson against him.

Breaking away to clear his dazed mind, Bruce breathed in cold air, allowing it to slice into his lungs like ice. It gave him the awakening jolt he needed. For once, he wanted to have the last word as he glanced at Flora with her similar dazed expression. She touched a pale hand to her chest.

"I want thee to remember *that* the next time thee is tempted to compare me with the likes of Clint Roberts." Bruce turned on his heel and strode away.

13

Flora stormed away from Bruce, her heart pounding so hard it echoed in her ears. She bumped into Jim as she rounded the corner of the wagon.

"I'm sorry." She stepped back, dazed and disoriented.

"It's okay, Miz Flora." He looked down at his feet, unable to meet her gaze after overhearing her argument with Bruce.

"Flora, what was all that about?" Irene whispered, pulling her cloak tight as she left the warmth of the fire. "I haven't heard thee and Bruce argue like that in a while."

"Well, some things never change." Flora wiped her eyes, angry that Bruce still had the power to drive her to tears after all this time. She touched her lips, still tingling from his kiss. The man baffled her. If he disliked her so much, why kiss her—twice?

"Miz Flora, may I say something?" Marta approached her.

Pausing, Flora turned to her friend with a nod. As much as Marta had endured on this trip, the least Flora could do was listen.

"I know it ain't none o' my business, but you have a long-time relationship with Mister Bruce, and a friendship like that is worth keeping." Marta twisted her hands in front of her and tears filled her eyes. "Yous folks have so many chances to love and spend time with each other. We risking our lives to have what yous got. Don't take it for granted. People can be 'ere one moment and gone the next, like my little Jimmy."

Marta's voice broke on her son's name. Her breath caught in her throat as she tried to swallow. Compassion swelled in Flora, convicting her of pride and some of the things she'd said to Bruce. How did he always manage to make her behave at her worst?

"Marta, don't worry. Bruce and I will be fine. This is the only kind of friendship we've ever had." She touched Marta's arm and offered a wry smile. "Just because we've known each other all these years doesn't mean we're true friends. It isn't the same as thee and Jim."

"Naw." Marta shook her head and glanced over at Jim with so much love in her tender expression that envy spiked inside Flora. "But I'm praying yous will. There's nothing like it in all the world."

"Maybe one day . . ." Flora couldn't keep her heavy thoughts from her voice. She doubted Bruce Millikan would ever find her suitable enough for what Marta alluded to, but perhaps Clint Roberts would. He didn't think her so lacking.

"Indeed, a love like thee and Jim have would be divine." Irene sighed as she gazed up at the tree branches and placed her hand over her heart. Her dreamy expression brought a reluctant smile to Flora.

"I accept thy advice and thank thee for caring." She laid a hand on Marta's shoulder. "Don't worry. I'll be fine, and so will Bruce."

Marta grabbed her hand and tightened her grip on Flora. "Don't miss what the good Lord brought. Both o' yous risked your lives fearing for the other. In spite of what you think of him, he means well."

Flora swallowed with difficulty. A fifteen-year-old girl had just chastised her. Marta was right, but why did Bruce have to be so arrogant? She closed her eyes and took a deep breath, feeling the full extent of her humiliation. "Please excuse me. I need a moment alone." Flora climbed into the covered wagon, where she brushed and braided her hair with trembling fingers. Weariness claimed her as low conversations were carried on outside.

Irene poked her head through the canvas door. "Flora, Bruce said we'll eat the rabbit meat he brought back. Jim is cooking it over the fire."

"I'm not hungry." Flora spread out a quilt and lay down. Her stomach rebelled at the thought of eating. How could she fill her belly when her nerves were tied up in knots? Confusing memories of Bruce's kisses danced through her mind while his words calling her foolhardy echoed in her ears. She dimmed the lantern on a trunk beside her pallet.

Flora longed to pour out her jumbled feelings in her journal, but dared not in case Bruce discovered it. He had bought a journal for both her and Irene while they were in Charlottesville. Even that action had proven how thoughtful he could be. She sighed and bowed her head in prayer, lifting her frustrating situation with Bruce to the Lord. Focusing on her thoughts, she asked for God's wisdom to help her make it through the rest of this mission.

As they traveled north, Flora stayed inside the covered wagon, claiming she had a headache. It was true. Pressure in her head pounded with each wayward jolt of the wagon. As hard as she tried, Flora couldn't rest. Her ears felt like someone had plugged them. Eventually they popped, opening up enough to clear her hearing and giving her relief.

"At the top of the hill, we'll stop and give the horse a break. He needs water," Bruce said. "Now that we're in the mountains, we'll have to give him rest more often to keep from wearing him out."

"Maybe we should have brought two horses," Irene said.

"He's strong enough to carry the load we have, we'll just have to be mindful of the steep hills." Bruce cleared his throat. "He's a good workhorse. He'll make it, but it might take longer than we'd like."

Flora pulled her mother's quilt over her head and tried to make Bruce's voice fade. She didn't want to hear about his compassion for a horse or admit that he might have been truly concerned for her. If she relaxed her guard, Bruce would choose that moment to strike again. His words could be deadly, criticizing and wounding her spirit beyond endurance.

Right now she would rest so she could be fresh and ready for whatever battles he would bring her way. She rolled onto her side, trying to find a more comfortable spot on the hard wagon bed.

"Lord, help me not to care about Bruce's opinion of me," she whispered. "Don't let anything he says hurt so much."

The peaceful rest she sought never came. Flora dozed into a fitful sleep.

Bruce set the brake and propped his foot on the side of the wagon and stared at the glory of the Shenandoah Valley. Mountain ridges spread out against the blue sky in shades of light and shadows. The brilliant colors they had witnessed in the past few weeks now faded to shades of brown and gray, marking the transition of autumn into winter.

"There's Harrisonburg." He pointed to a cluster of rooftops nestled in the valley below. "It's just past dawn, so we'll camp out up here, get some rest, and bypass the town tonight."

"It's beautiful!" Irene scooted to the edge of her seat and scanned the horizon. "Isn't it, Flora?"

Flora nodded, keeping her gaze on the scene below. It had been several days since her argument with Bruce, but she still went to great lengths to avoid him. The knowledge stung his pride, but not nearly as much as knowing he could soon lose her to that doctor when they returned.

He had hoped to spend the rest of the trip changing her mind, but none of his plans had worked out. She wanted nothing to do with him. If he asked her to help him with a task, she delegated it to Irene or Marta. She responded to his questions with one-word answers or claimed she needed to be alone for a while and would disappear into the covered wagon. He wondered what she would do if he crawled inside after her. Sooner or later, she would have to face him.

"Flora, would thee make some pancakes for breakfast?" Bruce held his breath, waiting for a snide response. When none came, he stole a glance in her direction. She turned to stare at him. Her blue-gray eyes assessed him with an expression he couldn't fathom. He decided to compliment her into action. "Thee knows how to make them nice and fluffy—just the way I like them."

"On one condition." Her lips curled into a smile that sent a ripple of interest through him.

"State thy condition." She wanted to bargain? What game was she playing? He kept a firm countenance, unwilling to agree to something before he knew the details.

"After breakfast, thee will take me into town to mail a letter."

"Who's the letter to?" Bruce raised an eyebrow.

"That's personal." Her smile faded along with her good humor. "Is it a deal or not?"

He knew she had written a couple of letters to her mother, since he had peeked at the pages while she wrote them by the fire. His other concern was that she would also post a letter to Clint Roberts. What would it take to get that man out of her mind?

Rubbing his chin, Bruce considered the matter and realized there was nothing he could do. Flora was a grown woman with an independent mind. He would have to place her in God's hands, and if she chose the doctor over himself, he would just have to accept it.

An hour later, he and Flora took off on horseback. The cedar scent of her clothes teased him. Having her warm body next to his made him yearn for a deeper relationship with her to ease the loneliness he felt when she wasn't around. He could get used to this. Wrapping both arms around her to hold the reins, Bruce leaned over her right shoulder.

"Is thee still mad at me?" he asked. Bruce hoped to wear down Flora's defenses now that they had some time alone. A lengthy silence followed, disappointing him.

"I suppose not, since God's word does command us to forgive." She glanced over her shoulder, but her bonnet kept him from seeing her expression, only her profile. "But that doesn't mean I trust thee. I promised Marta we would mend our feeble friendship, and so the first step I'm making is to accept the fact that thee believes I'm foolish."

Bruce clenched his teeth and swallowed as he considered his next words. "I don't consider our friendship feeble. And I didn't say thee was foolish. I said what thee did was foolhardy." He laid a hand on her shoulder. "Flora, if I hurt thee, I'm sorry. Will thee forgive me?"

"Of course, but thee will say something similar at some point. The only way I can keep forgiving thee for doing the same thing over and over is to accept that it's how thee sees me."

"That's not how I see thee." Frustration sliced through him, threatening the gentle patience he wanted to show her. He took a deep breath as their horse descended a steep hill and they both leaned back for balance. The change in momentum jostled them more than usual. He longed to wrap her in his arms and hold her tight against him. An overwhelming feeling of love burst inside his chest, and he could do nothing about it.

"Flora, I admire thy independent spirit, the way thee cares for others, and thy conviction for freeing those in bondage to slavery. The way thee fought for little Jimmy took courage. While thy sister is busy getting sick at the sight of blood, thee rose up to the challenge under stress and did all humanly possible. No foolish woman could have done that. I only said what I did because I was angry and worried about thee."

"I'll never understand thee, Bruce." She shook her head in disbelief. "Thee is the most contradictory man I've ever known."

He would have to surrender his pride if he hoped to convince her of his sincerity. Maybe sharing his heart would win her over. His heart thumped heavy, like a burden weighing him down.

"Fine. If thee would really like to know why I've annoyed thee all these years, it was because I always liked thee. I loved getting a reaction out of thee when I said something to shock or frighten thee. Now I realize how cruel I was, but I never meant to hurt thee. But Flora, at some point thee must let the past go. We have to move on and create new memories that we can cherish. I kissed thee because I can no longer hide how I feel about thee."

Bruce closed his eyes, fear seizing him as the words floated in the air and penetrated her mind. He waited. No sound. He must have shocked her . . . again.

"Flora?"

She stiffened and leaned forward. He opened his eyes, not sure what to make of her lack of reaction. She lifted a hand to her face and sniffled.

"Flora, say something."

"Bruce Millikan, thee is impossible! One minute thee is criticizing me and in the next praising me." Anger laced her voice as she crossed her arms. "I don't know what to think. Is thee teasing me?"

"No, Flora. I've never been more serious." Alarm pierced his chest as he tried to make sense of her reaction. Was his behavior as contradictory as she made him sound?

"I'm not sure I believe thee." She gave a sarcastic laugh. "Listen to thyself, Bruce. Thee annoyed me because thee liked me? What kind of nonsense is that? Let's not ruin the fragile friendship we've developed on this trip. Once we deliver Jim and Marta to Pennsylvania, our mission will be complete. We'll go home on better terms than we were before we left, and in many ways that's more than I'd hoped for."

It wasn't enough. Bitter disappointment rooted in his gut. He closed his eyes and tightened his arms around her. *Lord, help me, I don't want to lose her.*

Flora gritted her teeth and blinked back moisture as they rode into Harrisonburg. While waiting for some logical explanation with his confession, hope died within her. What had she expected? It was obvious he didn't know why he'd been so cruel, but his regret seemed sincere, and since she forgave him, that should be enough.

From this moment, she would let the past go, embrace the friendship Bruce offered, and forge a path into her future that would be better than a dream. It would be realistic, something obtainable.

Unlike in Charlottesville, their presence didn't go unnoticed in the small town. People stared at them as they rode down what looked like the main street. They passed by a general store, church, and tavern before they came to a small building with a Post Office sign on the door.

Bruce tightened his arms around Flora as a man rode past, his gaze concentrating on her. He tipped his hat with a crooked grin that made Flora shiver.

"It's all right," Bruce assured her, his voice near her ear. "I won't let anything happen to thee."

"I'm sorry, but you look familiar." The man had turned his horse around and now rode beside them. He leaned one hand on his pommel and tipped his brown hat with a brief nod. His blue eyes peered at Flora until she wanted to demand he look away.

"How can we help you?" Bruce asked, discarding the Quaker speech. His arms felt like a protective shield around her, and for that she was grateful.

"You don't sound Quaker. I thought you might be. You both have that look about you."

"Before I answer personal questions, I like to know who I'm talking to," Bruce said in a firm tone. Flora had never heard him speak to anyone like that. She kept her gaze averted lest the man suspect anything.

"Sorry. Let me properly introduce myself." The man chuckled. "My name's Carson Steele. I'm a bounty hunter, and right now I'm tracking a pregnant slave couple. A farmer south of here spotted a pregnant Negro with a Quaker woman, who fits this little lady's description . . . right down to the clothes." His penetrating gaze slid over Flora. Goose pimples rose upon her skin.

"Did he get a close view of this woman?" Bruce asked. "Lots of women have brown hair and wear practical clothing, unless they belong to the wealthy. I'm sorry to disappoint you, Mr. Steele, but we have things to do. And as you can see, no Negro couple is traveling with us."

"Which reminds me," Mr. Steele's grin faded into a sober expression, as he leaned toward them in a manner intended to intimidate them. "Do you both live around here? And if not, where's your camping gear? How do I know you didn't leave the Negroes behind?"

Flora trembled as Bruce tensed behind her. He chuckled, keeping up a pretense of innocence. "Mr. Steele, we have nothing to hide. If you intend to bring us in for questioning, by all means, do so. Right now all you've managed is to state suspicious claims with no valuable evidence."

"You didn't answer my question." Mr. Steele clenched his jaw, his tone displaying frustration.

"You're not wearing a law badge, or at least you didn't show it," Bruce said. "Therefore, you're a private bounty hunter hired by a private citizen. And even if you had been hired by the law, you would be out of jurisdiction up here. We're under no obligation to you."

"Don't forget you're still in the South. Even if I don't have jurisdiction here, no lawman would defend the Negro slaves. They're runaways, and if caught would be handed over to their rightful owners." Mr. Steele turned and spat in the dirt, his anger burning with intensity in his dark eyes.

"Again, you lack evidence." Bruce gestured around him. "I don't see any slaves."

"I'll be watching you." He pointed a crooked finger at Bruce and Flora, before flicking his horse's reins and moving on.

"Go ahead." Bruce laughed. "And while you're wasting time with us, they could be getting away," Bruce called after him.

He leaned toward Flora's ear and whispered, "Maybe that will plant a seed of doubt in him so he'll watch others, and not just us."

"Thee handled that well. I wish I had hidden my Quaker speech back at the river the way thee just did. Then that farmer wouldn't have been so suspicious or have a reason to give a description of me."

"Don't worry about it, Flora. It was merely a test. He's not sure it was you or he would have been more forceful in bringing us to the sheriff for questioning." Bruce patted her shoulder. "He only wanted to gauge our reaction and see if he could intimidate us into revealing something. We'll go on to the post office as planned. No need to raise further suspicion."

As they continued, Flora pondered Bruce's valiant behavior under the stress of almost being discovered. Images of him swimming with her on his back, carrying her, and sewing her knee played across her mind like a vision. She couldn't have felt more safe than if her own father were here with her. She trusted Bruce with her life. Dare she try to trust him with her heart?

He brought the horse to a stop in front of the post office, dismounted, and reached up for her. Without a word, Flora leaned toward him, treasuring his grip around her waist. She gazed up at him with a new perspective, wondering how much she'd misjudged him. He stared into her eyes with his hands still on her sides. Was he going to kiss her again?

"I suspect thee is going in to mail a letter to both thy parents and Clint Roberts. Don't send him anything. Please . . ." His green eyes searched her face, but she couldn't discern his thoughts, only his serious mood. "I wasn't teasing thee earlier before Mr. Steele interrupted us. I meant every word. If thee can somehow just forget the past and forgive me, I'd like to start a new future with thee. Allow me a chance to prove that thee can trust me."

"Bruce Millikan, I trust thee with my life, of that I can assure thee. And I have forgiven thee. As for the rest, thee has given me much to think about." She pulled two sealed letters from her skirt pockets, beneath her gray cloak. Flora kept the letter she'd written to her friend, Rebecca, beneath the one to her parents. Until she could figure out this change in Bruce, she would let him think what he wanted. "In the meantime, I intend to mail these."

With a fluttering heart, Flora stepped around Bruce and strode toward the small brick building. Behind her, Bruce released a heavy sigh, but his booted feet followed. She climbed the steps and opened the wooden door. A bell dangling on a thin rope rang, announcing their arrival.

"Mr. Steele might try to question the postman, so don't sound like a Quaker," Bruce whispered in her ear. She nodded.

Rows of box shelves hung on the right wall with stacks of letters in each, a number written above each slot. On the left wall were notices of land sales, event announcements, and hand-drawn pictures of the faces of two wanted men. Below them was an image of what looked like Marta and Jim. She gasped. Now that they had a description of her, would her image be next? Bruce draped a comforting arm about her shoulders. Flora took a deep breath, lifted her chin, and squared her shoulders, determined to recover.

A woman stood at the counter paying for her postage. Flora stepped in line behind her as Bruce left her side to pick up the town paper lying on the counter. He read the headlines and scanned the articles as he turned the pages. How could he concentrate on reading at a time like this?

She studied his profile. Bruce Millikan had always been handsome, even as an awkward boy. Now, as a man, he appealed to her even more. In spite of being a loner, he had the innate ability to lead people, and at times it made him seem like a bully. As a wiser adult, she'd come to realize that he wasn't really a bully, but one who took his responsibility to heart—even to the point of taking on responsibilities that weren't his to bear—like her.

His mouth twisted as he read something that didn't suit him. She liked him better without a beard and appreciated him shaving it off while at her aunt's house.

While Bruce wasn't an overly large man, his chest and arms were solidly muscled from long hours of farming out in the fields. His tan was a testament to his time spent in the sun. She'd always thought Bruce was too smart to waste his talents on farming. He should have been in a lab somewhere, inventing farm equipment rather than small machines in his father's barn. How could she not respect a man like him?

"Miss? May I help you?" a middle-aged clerk asked. His gray hair was combed to the side, and he stared at her through silver-rimmed spectacles.

"I'm sorry." Flora stepped forward, realizing the woman ahead of her had finished with her business and was now walking away from the counter. Heat climbed her neck. She cleared her throat and stepped forward, handing him her letters. "I'd like to mail these, please."

"That will be two pennies." The clerk accepted her letters and tossed them into a box behind him.

"Thank you." Flora reached into her skirt pocket, produced the correct change, and dropped the coins in his outstretched palm. One clinked against the other. She strolled over to Bruce. "That newspaper must be full of news. Your expressions have mirrored everything from perplexity to disgust."

"Indeed." He sighed, folding the paper and setting it back on the counter. "It seems the debate over slavery is growing intense. Some Southern states are threatening to secede from the Union."

"And that worries you?"

"It does for many reasons." He offered his arm, and she took it, proud to be by his side. If only things between them could be as real as appearances might seem to others who passed them. "I wasn't so engrossed in my reading that I missed you mailing both those letters. I had hoped you would consider my words and not write Clint."

"Did I promise not to mail them?" She waited as he opened the door and held it wide enough for her to cross the threshold.

"No, I've never known you to lie." Bruce closed the door, and it clicked in place. "I despise liars, and your honesty is another one of the virtues I love about you."

"Bruce, who says the other letter was to Clint?" She grabbed his arm. "You made an assuption."

"Then who was it to?" He paused on the step to give her his full attention. His green eyes widened in curiosity.

Flora didn't answer as she gave him a mysterious smile and descended the steps. It felt good to be the one teasing him rather than the other way around.

14

Bruce took a detour on the way back to camp until he was certain they weren't being followed. That night they waited past midnight to pack and continue their journey. They didn't light the lanterns, but relied instead on the moonlight. For days, they traveled over the mountain terrain through gusts of wind, cold rain, and moments of sunshine. Bruce grew anxious. He worried Mr. Steele would be more determined as they drew closer to the Pennsylvania border.

As the gray dawn turned bright with daylight, Bruce glanced down at Flora's sleeping profile where she lay in the crook of his shoulder and chest. Pieces of her dark hair had fallen past her white bonnet now askew on her head. He pulled her close, worried this might be the last time he could hold her like this.

Flora never told him who the second letter was addressed to, leaving him to wonder and speculate. He didn't know what to do other than pray, and he spent many hours sitting next to her praying God would show her the truth in his heart.

The wagon rattled and rolled up a hill toward a painted sign nailed to an oak tree. It said "Welcome to Pennsylvania" in red paint on a white background. A rustling noise scared the horse. Bruce pulled the reins to calm the animal, as a man on horseback rode out from the cover of nearby bushes. He aimed a rifle at Bruce. Mr. Steele joined him, an arrogant grin broadening his face.

"Good morning." Mr. Steele touched the brim of his black hat and inclined his head. "Remember me?"

The sudden jolt of the wagon stirred Flora, and she groaned. Bruce kept her steady, hoping neither she nor Irene would give them away due to a startled slumbering state. At least Irene was still inside the covered wagon.

"What do you want?" Bruce asked.

"I'm Sheriff Brady Jackson," said the man with the rifle. "We figured you might be heading this way, so we thought we'd wait for you."

"Have I broken the law, Sheriff?" Bruce kept his gaze steady but humble as he stared into the man's piercing blue eyes. The sheriff wore a brown hat over his gray head.

"Well, that remains to be seen." He glanced at Mr. Steele. "Carson, here, believes you're Quakers harboring runaway slaves." He flashed his bronze badge, clipped to his black jacket. "And that, my friends, is a crime."

"Bruce?" Flora raised her head, her bonnet askew, and her eyes widening. "What's going on?"

"Mr. Steele is back, this time with the sheriff." Bruce slid his hand up and down her arm to comfort her. "Don't worry, *you* will be just fine." He emphasized his speech, hoping she would catch on to not sounding Quaker.

"Oh!" Flora bolted upright and tried to straighten her bonnet.

"I'm sorry for disturbing you, ma'am, but we have a few questions, and we need to take a look inside the wagon." The sheriff's gaze drifted down to her hands. "I noticed you're not wearing a wedding band. It's my duty to make sure you haven't been taken against your will." His gaze slithered over to Bruce in an accusing manner.

"He's my brother," she croaked, still waking up.

The sheriff threw his head back and laughed in a deep rumble. Mr. Steele joined him. When he had calmed and his shoulders had stopped shaking with mirth, he fixed his liquid blue eyes upon her. "Forgive me, ma'am, but I've seen the way this man stares at you, and I'd bet my whole ranch that he ain't your brother. Now tell me your names, both of you."

"Flora Saferight."

"Bruce Millikan."

Both answered in unison, resulting in more laughter from both men.

"Brother and sister with different surnames?" The sheriff raised an eyebrow in disbelief. "An unlikely story. What am I to think of that?" He leaned on the saddle pommel with one hand holding the reins and motioned to Flora with the other. "Your name was verified with the postman on your letter. I checked before we left. As for you," he motioned to Bruce, "I'll need to do a little more investigation."

Bruce sighed, set the brake, and gave him a level stare. "All right, I'm escorting Flora and her sister up north to a friend's house. When we first set out, I told her we would travel as brother and sister, as we did when we came to town to post her letter. It would be safer and better for her reputation, especially since her sister stayed behind with the wagon." Bruce shrugged. "If you believe she's here against her will, question her privately if you must."

"No!" Flora grabbed his arm, holding tight enough to cut off his circulation. Bruce glanced down at her pale face, her blue-gray eyes wide with fright. Did the woman honestly believe he would put her in harm's way?

The men chuckled again.

"Well, Sheriff, I don't reckon she likes that idea too much," Mr. Steele said. "Looks like she trusts him too much to be taken by force."

"Sure does." The sheriff nodded. "Let's get a look inside. Shall we?" He dismounted and Mr. Steele followed.

"Wait!" Flora called as she scrambled down behind Bruce. He turned to grab her arm in time to keep her from losing her balance. "My sister is sleeping in there. Please, let me make sure she's at least decent."

The sheriff hesitated, unexpected surprise lighting his face. He glanced at Mr. Steele, who shrugged. "I don't see the harm in it. Unless she's a magician, she can't make any Negroes disappear," Mr. Steele said.

"No, but the two of them can load a gun," Sheriff Jackson said. He stroked his chin in thought. "Tell you what, I'll give you a few seconds to warn her to cover herself with a blanket, but not enough time to dress or load a gun. And," he pointed at Flora, "you stay out here. Just poke your head inside. No climbing in, or someone will get hurt. Don't force me to assume the worst."

"Thank you." Flora nodded. She hurried to the back of the wagon. The rest of them followed, but Mr. Steele motioned for Bruce to stay back. He pulled out a handgun, cocked it, and aimed it at Bruce. Flora leaned through the canvas doorway. To Bruce's relief, whispering and movement could be heard, but no actual words. He hoped Flora had been able to warn Irene to lose the Quaker speech.

Irene's head appeared, her blond waves a mass of tangles and her groggy eyes swollen with sleep. "I'm coming," her voice shook with fear, but only Bruce and Flora knew her well enough to notice it.

"Show your hands and climb out slowly," Sheriff Jackson said. When she held up her palms, he steadied his elbow, helping her climb out. Irene had wrapped the Midnight Star quilt around her, inside out so as not to give away the map on the other side. This way they wouldn't find the quilt map in the trunks. Bruce's heart pounded. If anyone gave them away, it would be Irene or that quilt.

Once Irene was out, Sheriff Jackson climbed inside. Irene ran to her sister, and Flora draped a comforting arm around her shoulders. The sheriff rummaged through their things. A lock clicked on one of the trunks, and Bruce gritted his teeth, assuming the man was now rifling through their personal trunks.

A few moments later, he reappeared and climbed out. He rubbed his hands together as if dusting his palms. Pulling out a pair of gloves from his coat pockets, he said, "Folks, I'm sorry for the inconvenience." He glanced over at Mr. Steele. "Carson, it looks like your instincts were off this time. We've found nothing, and I don't have any reason to detain them further."

"But things don't always add up." Mr. Steele followed the sheriff to the spot where their horses were tethered. "They're hiding something."

"Whatever it is, it doesn't concern us. Now mount up." Sheriff Jackson touched the brim of his hat in a brief nod. "We won't be bothering you folks again. Please accept my apologies." He guided his horse around. "Come on, Carson!"

With an angry glare at Bruce and a sigh of disgust, Mr. Steele did as the sheriff ordered.

Irene burst into tears, clinging to Flora, who met Bruce's gaze with a hint of a smile and something else he couldn't quite decipher.

He laid a hand on both women's shoulders. "Well done. Now let's get out of here. I don't trust that Mr. Steele. They were hoping to stop us right here at the border. I'll feel much better once we're on the other side."

They climbed back into the wagon and passed the Pennsylvania sign. Bruce scanned the landscape, looking for an indication they were nearing Charlestown. While the leaves had fallen from all the trees, the valley still displayed brilliant shades of color. Scattered farmhouses surrounded a tiny village nestled in the valley below. From their vantage point on the hill, he could see a couple of churches, a few stores, and a building with a long red roof that resembled a factory or mill. This had to be it. A mixture of excitement and relief seeped into his weary soul.

"Flora, look. We made it." Bruce pointed to the valley below.

"I see it." She leaned forward. "It's beautiful."

Sharing this moment with her blessed him. He reached for her hand, and to his surprise she didn't pull away. Instead, she linked her fingers through his.

"Now that we're over the border, I thought it would be appropriate to let Marta and Jim out. They deserve this moment—to ride into town with dignity," Bruce said.

"That's so thoughtful." A smile brightened her face as she gave his hand a squeeze before releasing him. "I'm glad I got a chance to see this side of thee."

With his heart pounding, Bruce pulled the reins, slowing the wagon to a stop. Had Flora seen the change in him? Dare he hope it wasn't too late?

Flora turned and leaned inside the covered wagon. "Irene, we're here!"

As he set the brake, Bruce grinned at the excitement in Flora's animated tone.

By the time he had jumped down and walked to the back, Flora was there, waiting for him. She folded her hands in front of her as she swayed from foot to foot. Bruce reached under and pulled the switch. The hidden door creaked open. The sound of shuffling movement could be heard, and then Jim's booted feet appeared. Jim slid out and then bent to help Marta crawl out of the cramped quarters.

The two of them stretched and blinked, squinting to adjust their eyes to the light. Bruce waited a few minutes, then said, "I want to show thee something." He held out his hand to lead them around the wagon.

"Oh, it's something!" Marta's jaw dropped open. "I ain't never seen nothing like it."

"Welcome to thy new home," Bruce said. "Down there in that valley is Charlestown, Pennsylvania. Thee are standing on free soil as a free man and woman."

Marta put her hands over her mouth as silent tears streamed down her face. Jim stood behind her and planted his large hands on her shoulders. Similar tears swam in his red eyes. He sniffed and gulped, overcome by emotion.

"We free, Marta. We did it!" He wrapped his arms around Marta's thin frame and squeezed her. She laughed and wiped at her face, but more happy tears kept flowing.

Bruce closed his eyes on the moisture blinding him. "I thank thee, Lord." He bowed his head.

Marta turned and took Jim's hands between her own. "Bruce is right. The Lord did it. He made it all happen."

Jim lowered his head, and they shared a tender kiss that touched Bruce's heart. The two of them had borne much in their short lives, but it seemed to have drawn them closer. He didn't envy them as much as he wanted to remember them as an example for his own future marriage. As soon as the thought slammed his mind, his gaze traveled to Flora standing beside her sister.

Flora laughed with tears in her eyes as Jim swept Marta up into his arms and twirled her in circles. The two of them laughed more than they had probably ever been allowed, more than they thought they would ever do again after little Jimmy's death.

When Jim set Marta down, she rushed toward Flora with outstretched arms. Jim strolled over to Bruce and stuck out his hand. Bruce shook it. "I don't know how I'll ever be able to thank yous."

"No thanks necessary. God intended life to be a free gift for every man and woman. I pray that will soon be the case for everyone, and as long as I draw breath, I'll do what I can." Bruce leaned forward and drew his friend into an embrace. "Remember, thee is my brother in Christ. There is no color in God's kingdom."

Jim's shoulders trembled against him, and Bruce knew Jim wept with the overwhelming power of God's love. Bruce held him tight for a moment. Jim wiped his eyes as he looked down at the fading white frost on the grass.

"I'm sorry. Don't know what's come ova me," Jim said.

"I do." Bruce smiled through his own tears. "Thee has just witnessed the power of God's love, and sometimes it can bring a grown man to his knees at the most unexpected moments, but I wouldn't trade it for anything else."

"Marta and Jim, both of thee will sit in front with Bruce when we enter Charlestown. Thee will not arrive hidden like fugitive slaves. Irene and I will sit in the back," Flora said.

"We couldn't." Marta shook her head, her red eyes growing wide with disbelief.

"We insist." Flora nodded. "Go on." She motioned her fingers to direct them away. They walked around the wagon, glancing back with obvious reluctance.

Irene remained, looking from Flora to Bruce.

"Could I have a moment alone with Bruce?" Flora asked.

"Sure." Irene nodded, eyeing them with suspicion before turning to climb into the back of the wagon.

Flora walked toward Bruce. He waited, unsure of her intentions.

"I just wanted to let thee know that witnessing thee with Jim a few moments ago gave me more respect for thee than I ever thought possible. Now I understand thy passion for these missions."

"I was wrong, and Pastor John was right. Thee is perfect for this mission, and I'm glad thee came along." His stomach tightened, realizing how true his words were and all the other things he wanted to say but couldn't.

—◦◦◦—

Flora wrapped her shawl tight around her shoulders as she stepped outside Red River Meeting, the local Quaker church in Charlestown. She walked toward the large fire pit where a pig turned on a spit. People had arrived on wagons and by horseback from all around. It looked like this would be a well-attended feast in honor of Marta and Jim. The church had welcomed the young couple with open arms and was helping them get settled in the community.

Marta and Jim had stayed the night with the pastor, Isaiah Davidson, and his wife, Maryanne, while Flora and Irene were taken in by another couple, Herbert and Lesley Taylor. Bruce had stayed at a local boardinghouse run by Mrs. Murray, an elderly widow.

"Flora!" Marta hurried toward her, wearing a clean, new gown that someone had given her. "I've never known such kindness in all my life."

"This is the way it should be, Marta." Flora sighed, breathing in the crisp, cold air and allowing it to fill her lungs with freshness. "At home, even Quakers have to be careful. If we don't support our abolitionist beliefs in secret, we could be fined or imprisoned."

"Do yous fear prison?"

"No," Flora shook her head. "Probably not as much as I should. I agree with Bruce, there's little good we can do for God in prison. With freedom we can do so much more. I don't want this to be my last mission. It's changed me. I can't explain it."

Little Isaiah Davidson ran toward them and wrapped his tiny arms around Marta's legs. The force of his momentum knocked her off balance enough to step back. She laughed.

"I'm sorry," his mother said, out of breath as she hurried toward them. "He may be three, but I can hardly keep up with him." She touched her swollen belly with her other hand. Flora guessed she'd be expecting another little one in about three months.

"Oh, it's all right." Marta rubbed the boy's blond hair. "He just reminds me o' my little Jimmy and what he would have been like at this age." Tears swam in her dark eyes when she looked back up at them.

"Come with me." Maryanne said. She turned and walked to the other side of the church. As Maryanne lead them up a hill, Flora realized they were heading toward a cemetery. They passed the first two rows, where Maryanne stopped in front of a small gray stone. The inscription read, "Our little angel is home with the Lord."

No one spoke as Maryanne dropped to her knees on the faded grass. "She was our first child. I only had her for three days before she died. The doctor said her heart was too weak. I never even got around to naming her." She touched the headstone, running her fingers over the engraved words. "Marta, I share thy grief. While thee will go on to have other children, none of them will take the place of the one that is buried in thy heart. The Lord will give thee enough strength to heal with each passing day. The healing is gradual and slow, but one day thee will wake up and it will be more bearable than right now."

"I . . . didn't realize . . ." Marta's voice faded into sobs as her shoulders shook. "I'm sorry." She inched closer to Maryanne, who reached for her hand. They stayed like that for a while. Flora lingered behind them, not wanting to intrude on their moment of shared grief. God had brought her and Jim to the right family, people who would understand. Her heart swelled with relief, knowing it would now be easier to leave them here. God's plan had begun to take shape and make sense.

"My sister." Isaiah went to the stone and hugged it.

Flora swallowed with difficulty, realizing that there could still be peace and beauty even in the midst of such grief and pain. The scripture "with God all things are possible" came to mind, and for the first time it was real to her, more real than mere words. She could see it right in front of her.

Leaving them alone, Flora turned and started back down the hill. Bruce stood talking to Pastor Isaac Davidson, little Isaac's namesake. Both of them wore the typical black Quaker hat, but Isaac's tall, slender frame in no way mirrored Bruce's medium height and muscular form. Isaac also wore a brown beard with sideburns. To Flora's relief, Bruce sported a fresh shave and shorter sideburns.

He looked up, smiled, and gave her a brief nod. Flora angled around them, unwilling to interrupt their conversation. She would go see if she could be of some use to the women organizing all the food that each family had brought. The roasting pork smelled enticing. Her stomach grumbled.

"Flora!" Bruce took his leave of Pastor Isaac and hurried toward her. "What does thee think about everything?" He fell into step beside her.

"I had no idea how welcoming to Marta and Jim the community here would be. I wish things were more like this back home." She stared ahead as she considered her next words. "I envy thy ability to go on more mission trips."

"Then come with me." Bruce grabbed her arm and stepped in front of her. She paused and stared up at him in confusion. "We could be a team leading more slaves from the South to freedom."

"I . . . can't. Irene says she won't go on another trip like this, and we can't travel alone. It wouldn't be right." She shook her head and crossed her arms.

"Then marry me. Be my partner in life. We could do this together." He lowered himself to one knee. "I'll do it proper."

"Get up!" She hissed through her teeth, as sudden warmth flooded her with embarrassment. Flora pulled at his arm. "A partnership in freeing slaves is no reason to wed."

Bruce rose to his feet and smiled down at her. "Flora, I don't know how to be the romantic sort. All I know is not once has any other woman come to mind when I think of my future wife. It's always thee."

Shock vibrated through her system, robbing her of speech. She touched her neck and slid her cold hand to her chest. Was he serious? He couldn't be. Was this a dream?

With God, all things are possible.

"But," she said, shaking her head, "I'm going to be a midwife and I'd planned . . ."

"To marry a doctor, yes, I know." Bruce's lips thinned. "But thee doesn't love him. The idea of marrying because a midwife complements the career of a doctor is even more absurd."

"It didn't seem so absurd when no one else wanted me." Flora lifted her chin, angry at the confusion blurring her judgment. "I don't understand. I finally forgave thee, let the past go, and resigned myself to accept thy new friendship. My future is supposed to be in Charlottesville, with a fresh start and where no one knows me as Beaver Face."

"I'm sorry, Flora. We'll both put the past behind us and create a new future." He gripped her shoulders. "Please, Flora, give me a chance. Thee must admit that this trip has been different. It's changed things between us."

"It has." She nodded. "But it's also changed *me*, in unexpected ways. What will it be like when we return home and things go back to normal? Will thee think of me as the old Flora? Out here in the wilderness we were forced to depend on each other for survival. I do forgive thee, Bruce, but that doesn't mean I should marry thee."

"My feelings for thee won't change when we go back home. I've been in love with thee for a long time." He squeezed her shoulders in emphasis and searched her face.

"And that's what scares me, if that is true. I never felt loved by thee before." She forced the hoarse whisper as she groped for a steady voice. "Right now I don't know how I feel about thee. I can't agree to marry thee when I feel this uncertain. I'm sorry. This time thee will have to forgive *me*." She pulled away and rushed toward the church, seeking a private place to cry.

The next day their good-byes to Jim and Marta were bittersweet. The trip back was somber, with furtive glances between Bruce and Flora. If Irene hadn't been with them, Bruce might have lost his resolve and stolen more kisses from Flora.

Now, back at the Saferight farm in Charlottesville, Bruce poked at the wood in the fireplace, wishing he and Flora were anywhere but here. He hovered over the heat as Flora's family concocted ways for her and Clint to spend more time together. He knew by their conversations that Flora had not told them about his proposal.

While he was disappointed that she had not yet answered him, she hadn't given him false hope and promises. Flora was too honorable a woman. Bruce rubbed his eyebrows as he laid the poker back in the corner. While he had been forgiven of his childhood sins against her, forgiveness didn't necessarily erase all the consequences. He feared he might spend the rest of his life regretting them.

The others left the dining room and joined him in the living room. Flora's Aunt Abigail and Uncle Jeremiah settled on the dark blue couch. Flora and Irene sat in identical wingback chairs on the opposite wall facing them. A long, narrow cherrywood table separated them. Belinda plopped down in the wooden rocker, while Daniel took the wooden chair in the corner near the hall.

Clint stood in the wide doorway and surveyed the room. His eyes rested on Flora. He disappeared, and returned a moment later, dragging a wooden chair next to Flora, where he deposited himself.

Bruce leaned against the mantel and stared into the fire, pretending he hadn't noticed. He crossed one booted foot over the other, forcing himself to release his breath in a slow, quiet manner that wouldn't gain anyone's notice. Inside, his gut twisted like a taut rope.

"Bruce, thank thee for stoking the fire so we'd be warm when we retired in here for the evening." Abigail leaned forward, offering him a warm smile.

"Thee is welcome." He gave her a nod and sat down on a cushioned chair in the corner by the fireplace. Forcing his gaze to the floor, Bruce was determined not to stare at Flora and Clint.

"Bruce is always thoughtful like that," Flora said. "The whole time we were traveling, he thought of things the rest of us would have never considered." He could feel her blue-gray eyes upon him so he looked up. A pensive expression crossed her face as her forehead lifted in a questioning line.

"That reminds me," Irene interrupted. "Now that the mission is over, I'd like to stay here a fortnight. If we had come by train, we would have visited a whole month. It doesn't seem fair that we should have to leave so soon."

"We'd love to have all of thee stay longer." Abigail clapped her hands, grinning at both Flora and Irene. "Thy visits are far too few for my liking. Friend Bruce, please say thee will consider it."

"Why not return by train?" Clint asked. "Flora and Irene need not be camping out in the woods if it isn't necessary." Clint nodded toward Bruce. "I'm certain Bruce would agree, wouldn't thee?" Clint lifted an eyebrow, no doubt hoping to corner Bruce into agreeing with his plan.

"I do, except for the fact that I promised their parents I would take care of them and see them home safely." Bruce shrugged. "I can't leave the special wagon here and also escort them on the train."

"We wouldn't need to be escorted. Flora and I are together." Irene wrung her hands in her lap. "Right, Flora?"

"I understand the need to keep thy word, Bruce." Jeremiah nodded at him, giving his approval. "It's an honorable thing."

"But Aunt Abigail could write Mother and Father with the change in plans. It isn't as if we'd be deceiving them." Irene scooted to the edge of her seat, unwilling to let the matter drop.

"What is thy opinion, Flora? We've not heard what thee thinks." Belinda tilted her blond head and pinned her cousin with a green-eyed stare. She was only a couple of years older than Flora. In his short time with the family, Bruce had noticed that Belinda was often overlooked, while her brother's animated personality charmed everyone. Belinda had time to study everyone and spoke when she had something significant to say.

Flora's gaze traveled around the room to all the expectant faces watching her. When her eyes strayed to Bruce, he leaned forward, planting his elbows on his knees and linking his hands in the middle. To keep his expression from showing his distress, he concentrated on clenching his hands tight. Regardless of what she decided, he didn't want to leave without her. A sinking feeling filled his gut. He couldn't afford to wait long. The winter weather could turn nasty without notice. Indecision battled in his heart and mind.

"Irene, thee is only trying to figure out a way to travel by train. I realize that traveling by wagon and camping out has been an inconvenience, but it wasn't that bad. Besides, it could take a fortnight for Mother and Father to receive our letter and by then we'd already be on our way home." She shook her head. "I really believe we should stick with our plans, but I don't see why we couldn't stay a few extra days."

In truth, he wanted to be gone as soon as possible. The fire crackled. Any further delay would risk their lives out in the elements. As much as he hated to admit it, the train would provide them more warmth and comfort. Bruce cleared his throat, unwilling to take a chance with Flora's and Irene's health. He would have to place his and Flora's fate in God's hands.

"I'm afraid delaying could jeopardize the women's health. The weather is unpredictable this time of year."

"True." Jeremiah nodded. "Does thee recommend the train?"

"I do." Bruce struggled to breathe as his chest tightened. It reminded him of the time he'd had pneumonia as a child. This decision took more faith than he'd anticipated. If leaving Flora here with Clint caused her to choose Clint, then he and Flora were never meant to be. Still, the realization didn't ease the emotional pain torturing his heart.

"Why don't they all stay? Through the whole winter." Daniel waved a hand in the air, a broad grin on his face. "Then I'd have three chums to pal around with."

Belinda rolled her eyes at her brother and gave a dramatic sigh.

"Daniel, this is serious." Jeremiah's firm tone sliced through the room.

"Of course it is, Father." Daniel blinked brown eyes in feigned innocence. "It will solve all the problems and make things more lively and interesting around here."

"I'll go with what Bruce has suggested," Flora said. "I trust his judgment."

"Really?" Irene slid to the edge of her seat in her excitement. "I can't believe it. We'll finally get a chance to travel by train!"

Flora turned her gaze to Bruce. "I must admit traveling home in the comfort and warmth of the train is inviting, but I worry about thee being out there all alone. Why not leave thy wagon here? Thee will not be making more trips through the winter and thee could return for it in the spring."

"Flora, if it was my wagon, I wouldn't hesitate, but I feel obligated to return it to Pastor John. I don't want to betray his trust in me."

"I don't like it, but I understand." A wistful smile crossed her face. "In fact, I'm almost sorry the mission is over. I believe I'd like to go on more." Her gaze met his with intense purpose. Bruce held his breath, hoping she meant with him. Did this mean she was still considering his proposal?

15

Excitement bubbled inside Flora as she placed her hand in Clint's outstretched palm and descended the small steps of his black carriage. He had invited her to accompany him on a house call to a family in the neighborhood. The honor thrilled her. While women were still confined to nursing and midwifery, she dreamed of a day when they could be doctors.

Together they climbed the steps to the white two-story home. Clint lifted the brass knocker and rapped it against the door. A few moments later, footsteps sounded on the other side. The heavy door opened to reveal a stern-faced man with a dark brown mustache. His black formal attire made Flora assume he was the household butler.

"May I help you?" he asked.

"I'm Dr. Clint Roberts, and this is my assistant, Miss Flora Saferight." Clint gestured to Flora standing beside him. She offered a friendly smile.

"Yes, we've been expecting you." The butler stepped back and opened the door wider. "Please, come in."

Flora followed Clint into the foyer. The wood floor sparkled under the lit crystal chandelier above them. A mirror with a gilded frame hung on the wall to the left. Flora imagined it was used by the ladies of the house to make last-minute adjustments to their hats and bonnets before they left the house.

"You may leave your coat and hat there. I'll announce your arrival to Mrs. Crouch." The butler pointed to a cherrywood hat-and-coat rack in the corner behind them.

Clint shrugged out of his black overcoat and set it on one of the arms of the rack, while Flora unfastened her gray cloak and did the same. Next he pulled his hat off his head and placed it over his coat. He stood holding the double handles of his black doctor bag in front of him and looked over at Flora with a curious glint in his gray eyes.

"Is thee uncomfortable? Thee didn't take off thy bonnet."

Flora touched her head, feeling for her white bonnet. "Oh, I forgot." She untied the strings and set the bonnet on her cloak. "Their house seems so fancy," she whispered. "I was just noticing the pretty colors." She pointed at the wallpaper decorated with strange designs of blue and gold. Quakers rarely used colorful wallpaper.

A woman appeared wearing a gorgeous wine-colored gown with a net of lace lining the neckline. The sleeves extended an inch beyond the wrists, coming to a peak over the hand. Muslin and petticoats swished as she walked toward them, an expression of concern filling her swollen eyes.

"Thank you for coming." Her tense shoulders relaxed in relief, and her lips trembled into a forced smile. "My boy got a simple cold about a week ago, but then he started running a fever two days past. His breathing is labored, and he's hardly spoken a coherent word since."

"How old is the lad?" Clint asked.

"Five." A pool of liquid filled her dark eyes. "He's so small and frail."

"May we see him?" Clint tilted his head and raised an eyebrow.

"Of course." The woman turned and led them to the staircase in the hallway. She held onto the rail as if she needed the support, while using her free hand to lift her gown to climb the stairs. Her weary shoulders bent forward in obvious exhaustion. Compassion filled Flora as she followed.

"I stayed with him through the night, but his nurse is now with him so I could oversee tonight's dinner preparations." She reached the landing and paused. "I feared leaving him even for that short period of time."

"I understand," Clint said. "But one of the things I caution parents about is getting enough rest themselves so they have strength for their child. Thee won't be much help or be able to make clear decisions if thee collapses. It's good thee has his nurse to help."

Rather than joining the conversation, Flora listened and observed. She wanted to comfort Mrs. Crouch, but she had no idea what to say. They stopped at the first door on the right. The hinges groaned as Mrs. Crouch opened the door.

With only a lit lantern burning on a bedside table, the rest of the chamber was shrouded in darkness. A plump woman sat in a wooden rocker by the bed, where she read aloud from a small Bible. She looked up as they entered the room.

"There's been no change." She spoke in a low voice as she closed the book and set it aside. Pushing to her feet, she stepped to the foot of the bed and folded her hands in front of her.

Mrs. Crouch went to stand next to the nurse. Flora noticed a small rocking horse over in the corner, as well as a ball on the floor. Heavy breathing came from the tiny figure in the bed. Her heart ached for this child she didn't even know.

Clint touched the lad's forehead. "Still feverish. Has he had any hallucinations or visions?"

"No, but he does call for me from time to time." Mrs. Crouch bit her lip in worry.

"Good. I want thee to keep talking to him when he calls for thee. If he has a nightmare, thy voice will soothe him. I was once very ill as a child, and I can assure thee that I could hear my mother even though I didn't have the energy to open my eyes."

Clint pulled a stethoscope from his bag. He inserted the two ends into his ears, then listened to the child's chest. After a moment he moved the contraption over his heart.

"Flora, I want thee to come hear this. First, listen to his lungs here and then his heart, here." She noted where he pointed and nodded as he removed the stethoscope and handed it to her.

Using the device she could hear a slight rattle with each breath. His heart beat in a steady rhythm. Once she had listened, she tried to commit the experience to memory in case she ever needed this knowledge when a doctor wasn't around.

Flora offered the stethoscope back to Clint, but he shook his head and pointed to his bag. She dropped it inside and waited for the verdict.

"He has pneumonia, but the good news is that his heart is beating strong and steady. I wish there was some medicine I could give him, but right now the best thing we can do for him is to make sure he gets plenty of rest and keep giving him water and broth. He must eat to keep up his strength, and to keep his heart strong."

"Will you bleed him?" Mrs. Crouch tensed, her forehead wrinkling.

"No." Clint shook his head. "I concur with Dr. Pierre Alexandre Louis, whose studies a few decades ago proved that bloodletting only weakens patients and makes them die faster."

She relaxed with a nod. "My own mother died years ago after they bled her. As you said, it made her worse."

She paid Clint for his services, and they took their leave. As they walked back toward the carriage, Flora gave him a sideways glance. "What would thee have done if she had demanded a bloodletting?"

"I would have refused and suggested she call another doctor." He shook his head. "I can't in good conscience do something I feel would risk a patient's life."

Flora smiled, pleased with his answer. Today had been a good experience for her, and now she would include the family in her prayers.

Bruce strolled out to the backyard, where Irene was scattering feed for the chickens. They were penned inside a wire fence about three feet tall that surrounded the chicken coop. The construction didn't appear sturdy enough to keep out a sly fox.

"I was hoping to get a moment alone to speak with thee." Bruce shoved his hands in his coat pockets, waiting for a reaction from Irene. To his disappointment, she spared him no glance as she continued to toss more feed while chickens hustled to gobble up the seeds she sprinkled upon the cold ground.

"And why is that, when we've been traveling for months and thee has had ample opportunity to speak a private word with me?" Irene cut her blue eyes in his direction without giving him a direct stare.

"True enough," Bruce conceded, not wanting to waste any time while Flora was away with Clint and one of the others could appear at any given moment. "Let me be frank with my question. Does thee think Clint Roberts is the right man for Flora as everyone else seems to believe?"

"We've talked about this before. To be honest, I don't know." Irene shrugged.

"Does thee want her to move away?" Bruce forced a neutral voice. "Thee would hardly get to see her."

"What would thee have me do?" Irene threw a hand on her hip, turning to gaze up at him. "Besides, Clint talks as if he might be willing to move to North Carolina."

"What if he changes his mind?" He rubbed his chin, wondering how much he could trust her. He couldn't be sure that Irene would be an ally, yet there was no doubt that she held some sway over her sister. "First, let me ask thee this, does thee truly want thy sister to be happy?"

"Of course." A look of irritation crossed her face. Then a glint of suspicion narrowed her eyes. "What is this about? Is thee jealous?"

Several chickens bucked and flapped their wings. A slight breeze stirred the empty tree branches around them. Up the hill sheep bleated and grazed.

"Flora believes wedding a doctor would suit her because she has an interest in the medical field and wants to be a midwife." He paused, unsure how to continue without sounding selfish. He closed his eyes and rubbed both hands over his face. "Let's just say that I believe a profession isn't a reason to choose a spouse. I've not heard either of them declare a love for one another."

"That doesn't mean they haven't declared their love to each other in private." Irene tossed the rest of the feed and dusted her hands with a sigh. "If thee wants to know if she's confessed anything to me, I can tell thee that she has not."

They walked toward the hill where the sheep roamed. The mid-morning sun cast angled light across the faded winter grass, melting the white frost except in areas hidden by the shade.

"Bruce, thee forgets that I've known thee almost as long as Flora has." She squeezed his arm and blinked with an innocent smile. "I'm not blind or stupid."

"What?"

"I know thee kissed her the night of thy argument." Irene lifted an eyebrow. "And my sister hasn't been quite the same since."

"Different? How?" Bruce looked out over the fields, hating the tension rising inside him. He tried to relax as they walked. Irene could be toying with him. She was childish and enjoyed playing games.

"I don't know how to explain it. Don't worry." Irene patted the top of his hand with a reassuring smile. "Things will work out the way they're meant to. Look at me, for instance. I've been praying to travel by train, and in a fortnight, my prayers will finally be answered."

Bruce rubbed his eyebrows, trying to hide his frustration. How she could compare a train ride to his life with or without Flora? The silly girl gave him a headache. The only thing he'd managed to learn from this conversation was that Flora hadn't confided in her sister—and no wonder.

"Irene and Bruce!" Flora waved at them from the back porch. "We're back, and I have so much to tell thee!"

The bright excitement on her face filled Bruce with trepidation. Clint stepped out behind her, and she turned to give him a look of admiration. Bruce froze. His feet stalled. If she was about to announce their engagement, he couldn't hear it. His heart dropped to his gut.

Flora held out her frozen fingers to the blazing fire in the living room. While out with Clint, she had forgotten to bring her mittens, and her poor hands had suffered for it.

Footsteps brought her head around. Both Irene and Bruce came in with rosy cheeks. Seeing them walking arm-in-arm had been a surprise. What were the two of them discussing?

Belinda sat in a chair already working on the day's sewing. Uncle Jeremiah had taken Aunt Abigail into town on some errands. Flora turned to warm her backside while she gave them a secretive smile and linked her hands in front of her.

Bruce glanced around the room. His gaze paused on Belinda and then turned back up at her. "Where's Clint?"

"He went off with Daniel to park the carriage in the barn. I think the two of them might go horseback riding." She paused and tilted her head, realizing he might have felt slighted being left there among the ladies. "Did thee wish to go with them?"

"No, of course not." He shook his head and took off his hat and then his coat before carrying them to the rack in the hall. A moment later, he returned and settled into a chair. "I'm ready."

Irene kept her coat on as she crept toward the fire. Flora moved to the side, allowing her sister to warm herself.

"The first patient call Clint and I went on was for a little boy who has pneumonia. We must pray for him. The second call was for a woman who had been in labor for about eight hours. It was her fourth child, and the baby came fast. Clint allowed me to deliver her. He introduced me as the midwife."

"And thee finds that exciting?" Belinda gave her a horrified stare. "I would be scared half out of my wits."

"There's something enthralling about bringing a precious new life into the world." Flora met her cousin's green eyes. Belinda's fingers kept moving without pause as if she could sew in her sleep. She looked down at her work, her blond hair pulled back into a tidy bun. "It reminds me of the miracle birth of Christ," Flora said.

"I've no doubt that God has given thee the grace for the midwife skills." Belinda shook her head. "I'm glad He didn't call me to it, for I fear I'd be a huge disappointment. Cousin, it goes to show how very special thee is."

"Indeed, I feel much the same way," Irene said. "I tried to help with Marta on our mission, and I failed miserably. I don't know what Flora would have done without Bruce's help."

"Well, if we were all as pretty as thee, Irene, the rest of us wouldn't need to work so hard on our talents." Flora went to her sister and laid an encouraging hand on her shoulder.

"Flora, beauty fades." Irene patted her sister's hand and gazed into the fire, a rare pensive expression crossing her face. "What man would want a woman without talent? One who is afraid of childbirth?" Her voice faded on the last word.

Flora's heart lurched as she sensed a deeper fear in her sister than she'd realized. "Since when has thee been frightened of childbirth?"

"When mother lost three babes after us, and when Marta went through all that pain only to lose the very reward she'd labored so hard for." Irene's liquid blue eyes searched her own. "Never mind me, I just need some time to get over it. Sounds like a new life was brought into the world today and both mother and child are healthy and fine. Perhaps hearing thy story will make me feel better."

"Indeed." Flora nodded, her excitement returning. "The baby was a precious little girl with a patch of brown fuzz upon her head. She cried loudly, demonstrating a sturdy set of lungs. The only complication was a breech. I turned her in the womb and a moment later she was born. This time I didn't lose the child."

"Flora, little Jimmy wasn't thy fault." Bruce's soothing voice floated across the room. "It happened. That's all."

"Deep down I know that." Flora moved to sit in the same chair where Bruce had sat yesterday. In spite of Clint being there to encourage her, it was Bruce's comforting voice she kept hearing throughout the morning. How could she express that without sounding so strange? "I wish thee could have been there."

Something flickered in his gaze, but she wasn't sure what. He looked around the room as if in sudden discomfort. Now that she thought about it, he'd seemed quite preoccupied at breakfast.

"Bruce, is something wrong? Thee hardly ate this morning." She leaned forward. "Perhaps thee is hungry now? I'd be happy to make some sausage gravy and biscuits."

"No, that's all right." He held up a hand. "I didn't think thee had noticed anyone else before taking off with Clint." His voice took on a hard edge. Feeling as if he was once again displeased with her, Flora bristled and sat back.

"Perhaps it was foolish, but I was concerned that thee had only taken two sips of thy coffee, a bite of sausage, ate only half thy eggs and none of thy biscuit." Flora crossed a leg over her knee and kicked her foot back and forth.

"Wow, that's detailed." Belinda stared at her. "I don't think I've ever paid that close attention to someone else's plate before."

"It's only insignificant details," Flora assured her cousin as she folded her arms. The last thing she needed was for them to mistake the attention she paid Bruce.

"Well, then, tell me what I had and how much I ate of it." Irene leaned her elbows on her lap and watched Flora with a knowing grin.

"Don't be absurd." Flora waved a hand in the air. "I happened to notice he didn't eat much. That's all."

"What did Clint have?" Irene asked.

Flora paused. Not only did she have no idea, but she couldn't even tell anyone what Clint liked to eat. She knew all about Bruce's eating habits. He preferred scrambled eggs over boiled or fried, and sausage over bacon, biscuits over toast, and grits over oatmeal.

All eyes stared at her, as if waiting for a response. The truth would be giving them what they wanted. She couldn't admit to not knowing Clint as well as Bruce. How would it sound if she accepted his courtship? Truth was, she hadn't considered Clint's offer of courtship today, only Bruce's proposal.

"Don't be embarrassed, Flora," Bruce said, once again coming to her rescue. "I happen to know that thee had only half thy cup of coffee and another glass of water. Thee ate a biscuit with grape jam, all of thy scrambled eggs, two slices of bacon, and no sausage."

Irene clapped her hands. "That's even better than Flora's memory. I think it's so romantic."

"But I thought thee liked Clint?" Belinda paused in her sewing to glance back and forth at Flora and Bruce. "Is thee in love with Bruce?"

"Just because one happens to know what another eats, doesn't mean one is in love with that person." Flora jumped up from her chair with the intention of escaping before Bruce made her regret her blunder.

16

The next morning, Flora rose with the dawn and asked Bruce if he would step outside with her. It was then that he knew her answer. He nodded and followed her to the porch swing. Disappointment riddled him with a mixture of anger and fear as he sat beside her.

"I wish thee would come back with us on the train. Winter is coming, and I can't help worrying about thee out there in the cold," she said.

He nodded, not trusting himself to speak. Adjusting the hat on his head, he looked out at the sun rising over the ridge of the trees. The rooster crowed, breaking the silence of dawn.

Cold fingers slid over his. It was like a dagger piercing his heart, but he didn't pull away.

"Bruce, please don't be angry with me, but I need more time to pray about our future and to see how things go when we return home."

He didn't answer. He was angry, and lying would do neither of them any good. She knew him almost as well as he knew her.

"Bruce . . . please . . . don't hate me."

He swallowed the anxiety clogging his throat. "I could never hate thee, Flora." His voice sounded flat. At least it didn't reflect the pain aching inside him.

She pressed a sealed letter into his hand. "I wrote this last night when I couldn't sleep. Don't read it until thee is close to home. Traveling by train, Irene and I may even beat thee home."

"Be careful, Flora. Stay in sight of each other at all times. And trust no one." He chuckled with sarcasm. "Here I am telling thee what to do again." He lifted his hands as if in surrender and dropped them back on his thighs. The swing rocked them with the sudden movement.

"It's fine. I now understand that it's only because thee cares," she said.

"A lot of good it did me. I'd better go get the horse and wagon ready." He started to rise, but Flora grabbed his arm, halting him.

"My decision to stay isn't what thee thinks." She touched his chin and turned his gaze down to her. He looked into her blue-gray eyes. Fresh pain sliced his gut. Moisture filled his eyes. She leaned forward as if she was about to kiss him, but he pulled away. He blinked and stood with abrupt force. He wouldn't allow her to tease and torment him like this. It was too cruel, even if she did think he deserved it after all his childhood taunts.

"Bruce?" Confusion clouded her expression. "Read my letter. It will explain everything."

He clutched the paper in his hand, tempted to rip it up and throw it away. Perhaps he would throw it in the campfire he'd make later that night. Instead, he dropped his hands to his sides.

"I hope thee is happy with Clint Roberts." He turned and bounced down the steps.

"It isn't like that. Thee is mistaken." Tears now filled her voice, but he refused to turn around. He wouldn't be strong to do what he had to do if he saw her weeping. Forcing his legs to stride faster, Bruce hurried to the stables. First, he would see to his horse.

While his horse ate oats and drank water, Bruce pulled the wagon out into the yard. He checked the brakes and the wheels. A purple-cloaked figure floated toward him.

"What happened?" Irene asked. "Flora's inside crying and won't come out of our chamber."

"I'm glad thee came out. Is there anything thee would like to take out of the wagon and keep here? If not, I'll deliver it home to thy parents."

"We already have our trunks. That should be enough to take with us on the train. We appreciate thee delivering the rest." Irene sighed.

"It's the least I can do." He nodded.

"Thee didn't answer my question."

"To be quite honest, I've no idea why she's weeping." He threw his hands in the air. "I don't know what she wants from me." He stomped toward the stables to get his horse. "I'm getting out of here before I lose my mind and she manages to destroy what little is left of it."

"I don't understand." Irene followed him.

"I always thought Flora was so level-headed and sensible compared to all the other girls. Maybe I was wrong."

"Thee of all people should know the truth about my sister."

"Give my thanks to thy aunt and uncle." He led his horse from the stall and backed him up toward the wagon.

"Thee should tell them thyself." Irene crossed her arms.

"I think it's better this way, Irene." Bruce pulled the harness over the horse and fastened the buckles to hitch him to the wagon. "They all know that I'm leaving today."

"But not like this!" Irene tugged on his arm. "Listen, Flora doesn't love Clint. I know it."

"So do I, but I can't convince her to change her mind if she believes she'll be happier with him." Bruce jerked away. "And I won't stand around and watch."

"I'm afraid both Flora and thee will regret this." Tears filled her eyes, causing him to pause and reflect on his previous opinion of her.

"Don't worry, Irene. Remember what thee told me? Things have a way of working out." He tried to lighten the atmosphere between them, not wanting to make things worse. "Flora will feel better in a few days."

"This is all wrong." She blinked back tears. "Flora doesn't get upset very often."

"I know," Bruce said. "But I can't fix this for her. She's the one with a decision to make."

Bruce flicked the reins, and the horse stepped into action. It felt awkward not having Flora and Irene sitting on the wagon seat next to him. He scooted to the middle and stretched out his legs, but the emptiness lingered.

Over the next week, he covered a good distance since he didn't have to stop as often as he had when the women were with him. His diet suffered. He missed Flora's pancakes and biscuits, as well as her coffee. He missed the Star quilt. It would have been a nice map on the way back home. Instead, he stayed on the main roads, asked about his location when he came to small towns, and tried to remember the image of the quilt map as he judged distances.

On several occasions he pulled out the letter Flora had given him, but couldn't bring himself to read it. He feared it contained an explanation of her final rejection. As long as he didn't open it, he could keep hoping.

He read the Bible and searched for comforting verses to build his faith and ease his aching soul. By the time he neared the North Carolina border, he was tired of his own coffee and looking forward to seeing his family again. As he drove the wagon up the dirt road between his father's tobacco fields, a sense of belonging and home overwhelmed him. Perhaps once he greeted his parents and brother, he would find some time alone in his chamber to finally read Flora's letter.

⚭

Excitement charged the air as people said good-bye to loved ones at the train depot. Others looked forward to where their journey would lead them. As for Flora, she could scarcely get Bruce and his cold departure out of her mind. She wondered if he'd read her letter by now. If she'd hurt him as she feared she had, would her letter make a difference?

The train whistle blew, startling her out of her reverie. Irene laid a hand on her shoulder. "Why is thee so tense? I declare, Flora, thee hasn't been thyself since Bruce left over a fortnight ago."

"All aboard!" called a man in a dark blue uniform. He wore a jacket with bright brass buttons and stood by a set of portable wooden steps that had been hauled to the entrance.

"Come!" Irene pulled her elbow. "I've got our tickets." A porter had already secured their trunks in another compartment. Without a word, Flora followed her sister. The massive black engine up front let off a cloud of gray smoke.

"Hurry, ladies!" The man took their tickets. "Soon, we'll be taking off."

They walked down the aisle, smiling at strange faces until they came to a row with two unoccupied seats. Irene took the one by the window, while Flora sat next to the aisle. She set

217

her bag down by her feet. It contained the Midnight Star quilt and some drawings Daniel had made of Charlottesville. Flora hoped to use them when she returned home to make a memory quilt of her own.

She pulled out the Midnight Star quilt and hugged it to her chest, remembering how Bruce had studied the quilt map as they made their way north. She could only imagine how much harder it would have been without her mother's quilt. Burrowing her nose in the soft material, she breathed in the aroma of cedar. After this mission, she would not only think of quilts as a simple means to stay warm, but as a hidden path of freedom. This mission had not only freed Marta and Jim, but it had released Flora from her past, allowing her to love Bruce Millikan.

"This is so exciting." Irene rubbed her gloved hands together. "I've wanted to travel by train ever since the first one came to Greensboro earlier this year."

"Indeed, and I hope this experience is all that thee had hoped it would be." Flora offered her sister a smile, not wanting to dampen her spirits with her own less-than-cheerful mood.

The whistle blew again and the train lurched forward, slow at first, as the wheels on the tracks gained momentum. They pulled out of the depot and waved at their aunt, uncle, and cousins. Soon, trees were the only sight through the window. The bare limbs passed by in a blur.

Flora laid her head back against the seat and closed her eyes. Perhaps she would get a lot of rest on the way home if nothing else. She'd tossed and turned during the nights at her aunt's house until dark circles formed under her eyes.

"What did thee tell Clint? Why didn't he come with the rest of the family to see us off?" Irene asked.

Flora opened her eyes. Her sister stared at her. Flora sighed, having known this conversation would come sooner or later.

"I told him the truth—that I respected his profession and him as a person, but I didn't feel that I could love him the way a wife should love her husband." She shrugged. "I told him that I thought he deserved better."

"Good."

"Irene!" Flora gave her sister a scolding look. "Never take advantage of a man's affections. Compassion should always be of utmost concern."

"What I meant is, I'm glad thee didn't entangle thyself with him. I never thought he suited thee." Irene cleared her throat and laid a hand on Flora's. "I know that his profession was of great interest to thee, but I feared it wasn't enough to bind yourself to him. How boring."

"I'm not as shallow as all that." Anger rose inside Flora as she jerked her hand away. Keeping her voice down, she leaned toward Irene. "I only spent time around him to see if anything would come of it. It seemed prudent to at least give the man a chance. Even though he isn't meant for me, he isn't as boring as thee seems to think."

"Fine." Irene gave her a slanted smile. "But I believe Bruce suits thee much better."

"Ah . . ." Flora twisted in her seat and lifted her pointer finger. "Bruce did say something to thee, didn't he?"

"He did." Irene nodded. "But for once I've resolved myself to not interfere."

"But what did he say?" Flora grabbed her sister's arm. "I need to know."

"Nothing more than he told thee," Irene said. "He believes thee has settled on Clint. Just think how relieved he'll be when thee arrives home with thy news." Irene picked up Flora's hand and gave it a reassuring squeeze.

"True. I gave him a letter explaining everything before he left." Flora nodded, regaining her hope.

"Now get some rest," Irene said. "So those circles will go away." She pointed to Flora's eyes.

The rumble of the traveling train became a familiar sound that helped them sleep throughout the night. They ate in the dining car when they grew hungry. The window afforded them a beautiful view of the mountains and the countryside.

When the conductor came through to inform them that they would soon be arriving in Greensboro, anxious anticipation seized Flora. Would Bruce be with her family members to welcome her home? She hoped her letter had explained things and eased his temper. When next she saw him, she would know by his behavior if he had forgiven her.

As the train slowed, pulling into the Greensboro depot, Flora leaned across her sister to look out the window. People waited patiently to greet their loved ones; others waited to board. Flora scanned the many faces.

"There they are." Irene pointed at an angle through the window.

"I can't see them." Flora squinted and leaned forward a little further.

"Ouch. Thee is squashing me." Irene wrinkled her eyebrows in discomfort and elbowed Flora.

"Sorry. Just tell me who is there." Flora tapped her chin, trying not to be impatient.

"Why, Mother and Father, of course, but I don't see Bruce."

"Is thee sure?" Flora asked.

"Perhaps he intends to give thee time with Mother and Father and to settle down at home before he comes to call on thee," Irene said.

Acute disappointment filled her with sudden melancholy. She swallowed and shook her head. "No, he hasn't forgiven me. Otherwise, he would be here."

—⊷∞⊶—

Bruce walked home from an afternoon of hunting, carrying a wild turkey by the feet. At least his parents would eat well tonight. A cloud drifted in front of the afternoon sun, casting the field into a shadow and leaving the air cooler than before.

His brother rode toward him on horseback. The fast and steady pace indicated he had good news.

"What is it?" Bruce called as Silas drew to a stop.

"I just left Greensboro. Guess who I ran into?" Silas leaned down with a grin meant to taunt him.

"Must thee leave me in suspense?" Bruce asked, determined to keep his annoyance at bay.

"I ran into the Saferight family. They were returning from the train station. Both Flora and Irene were with them." Silas raised a dark eyebrow. "Flora inquired about thee—specifically."

Bruce dropped his gaze to the ground lest his brother see his pain. "And what did she wish to know?"

"She asked if thee had read her letter. I told her that thee hadn't mentioned it." His horse pranced in impatience, and Silas pulled back on the reins to calm him. "Her parents seemed a bit curious about it."

Confusion raced through his mind, bidding his heart to hope for that which he had not permitted himself to hope since he'd arrived home. Had he made a mistake by not reading Flora's letter? Could it have been something different from what he'd assumed?

"Bruce?" Silas leaned down. "Thee is acting most peculiar. What of this letter? Does thee have it?"

"Indeed." Bruce held the turkey out to his brother. "Please . . . take this home to Mother since thee is on horseback." He pulled out a sealed letter from the inside of his jacket pocket. "It seems I have a letter to read."

"Goodness man, has thee been carrying around that letter unopened all this time?" Silas shook his head in disbelief. "Thee has much more discipline than I could ever possess. Curiosity would have already done me in."

"I've no doubt of it." Bruce grinned. "Now, if thee will excuse me, I've a letter to read." Bruce turned and hurried toward a nearby oak tree. He lowered himself against the sturdy trunk and broke the seal on Flora's letter.

Dear Bruce,

I want to thank thee for being so patient and understanding in giving me time to properly consider thy proposal. I've always admired thee and have spent most of my life trying to prove myself to thee. No matter how hard I tried, I thought thee disliked me. Because of this, when thee proposed, I feared my feelings were somehow misguided. I wanted time to seek God's will, but tonight I can't rest. I need thee to know how I feel so I'm writing thee this letter since thee will be leaving in the morning.

This mission has been such a blessing and so different than I expected. In many ways, it seems unreal. I wonder if our common goals in the abolitionist movement and our dependence on each other to survive masked our true feelings for each other. I pray the truth will be revealed in time, especially once we return home and things are back to normal. Part of me fears thee will go back to thy old habits.

In addition to seeking God's will and spending time with my cousins, I stayed behind to refuse Clint Robert's offer of courtship. He is a decent man, but he's not meant for me. I don't feel for him what I feel for thee. After much soul-searching and prayer tonight, I'm convinced that I love thee.

When we both return to Greensboro, and if we still feel as deeply for each other as we did on the mission, I would be honored to accept thy proposal. If thee returns home and thy feelings have changed, say nothing, and I will know. All will be forgotten and forgiven.

Sincerely,

Flora

Bruce reread the letter several times, making sure he wasn't mistaken in her meaning. Finally, he looked up into the heavens and said, "God, I thank thee for this. Please forgive me for my lack of faith. I should have opened this letter and read it much sooner."

He folded the letter, slid it back into his jacket pocket, and jumped to his feet. He ran home, wishing he'd persuaded Silas to leave his horse with him. Arriving at the stables out of breath, Bruce bent over with his hands on his knees. Once recovered, he saddled his horse and rode west toward the Saferight farm.

By the time he arrived, Will Saferight was unhitching the horse from the wagon. He paused upon noticing Bruce riding up at such a fast pace. With a pat to his horse's neck, he shook his head in disbelief and flashed a knowing grin. "I suppose thee has read the letter that Flora mentioned to thy brother?"

"Yes." Bruce dismounted and took his horse by the reins. The poor beast breathed heavily and needed some water.

"I cannot pretend to know what that independent girl of ours has done now, but I only hope all is well." He held out his hand. "I'll see to thy horse if thee would like to go on inside and speak to her."

"I thank thee, Friend Will." Bruce handed over his horse, relieved that he would be spared the time it would take to tend to the animal. Bruce hurried toward the house and bounded up the porch steps, taking them two at a time. He knocked on the door with more enthusiasm than was appropriate. Friend Sarah opened the door, her gray eyes wide with fright.

"Goodness, is something wrong?" She touched her hand to her chest. "It sounded like a bull had come charging through the door."

"I'm sorry. I didn't mean to scare thee. Friend Will said he would see to my horse so I could have a moment to talk to Flora. May I see her?" Bruce pulled off his hat, determined to be as humble as possible.

"If thee has already spoken to Will, then I suppose it's all right." She opened the door wider. "Would thee like to come in?"

"I'll just wait out here on the porch. I don't want to inconvenience thy family any further."

"It's never an inconvenience to welcome our friends into our home." Flora's mother gestured for him to enter, but he shook his head.

"I was hoping to speak to Flora in private."

"I see." She paused, gazing up at him in bewilderment. He could see the unspoken questions in her eyes, but was thankful that she refrained from voicing them. "I'll get her for thee."

A moment later, Flora stepped out onto the porch, looking as beautiful as ever in a navy shawl and matching bonnet.

The only difference was the faint circles beneath her eyes. He stopped pacing, trying to ease the nervous tension that had been building inside him ever since he'd read her letter. Perhaps it was best he hadn't read it before now, for he wasn't sure he could have endured the suspense.

"Shall we sit on the swing?" Flora held out her hand, but he didn't see a swing. No matter, he nodded his consent. She led him around the corner of the house, where a long bench swing hung from the ceiling. He'd never known of its existence.

Without a word, Flora sat and waited for him to do the same. He obliged, dropping his feet to the porch floor and pushing them backward. They swayed front to back.

"I read thy letter," Bruce said. "And my feelings have not changed."

She took a deep breath, but kept her gaze focused in front of her. "I'm relieved to hear it. I was hoping I would see thee at the train depot. When thee wasn't there, I wasn't certain what I should think."

"Only this," he took her hand in his and lifted it, pressing his warm lips to her knuckles. "I love thee, Flora Saferight. Please forgive me for all my childish transgressions and marry me."

"I love thee, too. I've prayed about this and nothing would satisfy my heart more than to be Mrs. Bruce Millikan for the rest of my life."

Bruce twisted sideways and gripped the back of the swing for support. With his other hand, he tilted her chin toward him and kissed her as they swayed back and forth. Flora's lips were warm as she returned his kiss with unexpected fervor. Her cool hand reached up, cupped his jaw, and caressed his sideburn. All too soon she pulled away, leaving him in a heady state.

"Bruce Millikan, I've waited my whole life for thee to come to thy senses."

"I'm only sorry it took me so long." He brushed his lips against hers, unable to deny himself. "May we have a short engagement? It isn't as if we need to get to know each other."

"We shall have a proper engagement." She poked him in the chest. "I need to make sure thee won't turn back into the old Bruce."

"That lad grew up and disappeared, I assure thee." Bruce leaned forward and kissed the tip of her nose.

"I intend to make sure that thee has." Flora kicked her feet against the porch floor and sent them both sailing high into the air. "I want to go on more mission trips with thee, and I want to carry on my mother's tradition. For every mission we go on, I plan to make a map quilt for others on their path of freedom."

Bruce laughed, knowing his life with Flora would not only be complete, but a free and satisfying adventure.

Discussion Questions

1. The Quakers in *Path of Freedom* believe in plain-ness. How does this affect their character? What are the advantages of living a plain life and what are the disadvantages?

2. While Quakers don't believe in violence, Bruce says he would protect Flora, even if it means shooting some-one to wound them enough to stop them, but not to kill them. Does this go against Bruce's faith? Is this a human flaw in his character?

3. How does the Midnight Star quilt affect the mission? Do you believe a quilt could be used in something so important? What other ways could quilts be used for important purposes, either in the past or in the present day?

4. Marta showed exceptional faith and moral character at such an early age. Why do you suppose this is?

5. The fact that Mrs. Saferight lost three children in infancy has scared Irene away from childbearing, but has caused Flora to want to be a midwife. How can two people from the same family react so differently to the same events?

6. How can Flora trust Bruce with her life but struggle to trust him in matters of the heart? How does her faith in God help her overcome this flaw?

7. When Marta's baby dies, Flora blames herself. How does this event affect her faith and confidence? What helps her keep going?

8. At what point does Flora begin to see God at work through this mission? When does she begin to rely on God more and on herself less?

9. Bruce has a lot of guilt to overcome. What would have been his best approach to convince Flora of his sincerity? How does his faith play a role?

10. What other scary or difficult circumstances would they have faced traveling by night?

11. What did you learn about Quakers that surprised you the most?

Want to learn more about author
Jennifer Hudson Taylor and check out other great
fiction from Abingdon Press?

Sign up for our fiction newsletter at
www.AbingdonPress.com
to read interviews with your favorite authors, find tips
for starting a reading group, and stay posted on what
new titles are on the horizon. It's a place to connect
with other fiction readers or post a
comment about this book.

Be sure to visit Jennifer online!

www.jenniferhudsontaylor.com
http://jenniferswriting.blogspot.com
http://carolinascots-irish.blogspot.com

We hope you enjoyed *Path of Freedom* and that you will continue to read the Quilts of Love series of books from Abingdon Press. Here's an excerpt from the next book in the series, Loree Lough's *For Love of Eli*.

⎯⎯⎯⎯

For Love of Eli

Loree Lough

Learn to do good. Seek justice:
help the oppressed; defend the orphan;
plead for the widow.
(Isaiah 1:17 CEB)

1

Mother's Day Weekend at the Misty Wolf Inn
Blacksburg, Virginia

Taylor stood at the bottom of the stairs and held her breath. It only *seems* like a hundred steps, she told herself.

As she planted her foot on the first step, Eli whispered "You really goin' up there this time?"

His hand, warm and small, fit perfectly into hers. "I'm seriously considering it," she said, nodding.

The echo of his gasp floated up and disappeared around the first bend of the long, spiral staircase. "Can I come with you?"

She followed the line of his gaze to the half-door leading into the turret. It had been a source of fascination for him from the moment he'd moved into The Misty Wolf Inn, nearly a year ago.

"Please, Taylor? *Please?*"

Oh, how she loved the boy who reminded her so much of her brother! Peering into his trusting green eyes, Taylor wondered which excuse would work this time: *It's dirty and dusty up there. There are about a hundred ways you could hurt yourself. That big, bare lightbulb has probably burned out by now.*

But Eli beat her to the punch.

"If you let me come with you," he said, sandwiching her hand between both of his, "I promise to be careful and not touch anything without asking first. *Promise.*"

He'd been with her slightly more than a year now, and she could probably count on one hand the times she'd told him no. "Well, OK," she said, pointing at his bare toes, "but only if you put on your sneakers."

He did a little jig, then fist-pumped the air. "You're the best, best, *best* aunt a boy ever had!" He ran toward his room, stopping at the halfway point. "You won't go up without me, right?"

"I'll wait right here. *Promise.*" If she didn't know better, Taylor would have said Eli's smile had inspired the "face lit up like a Christmas tree" adage. Grinning to herself, she sat on the bottom step and said a silent prayer. *Please don't let me blubber like a baby—not in front of sweet Eli.* He'd lost as many loved ones as she had, and certainly didn't need to see her fall apart. Besides, if she allowed self-pity to distract her, even for a second, he could pick up a splinter, or trip on a loose board, or topple a stack of boxes. How would she explain *that* to his grumpy uncle?

The familiar *sproing* of a doorstop broke into her thoughts, followed by thuds and thumps that inspired a grin. She could almost picture Eli tossing shoes and boots over his shoulders as he searched for his favorite tennies. But so what if he made a mess in his own room? The last guest had checked out yesterday evening, and she didn't expect the next until Monday. Helping him re-tidy his closet was as good an excuse as any to give him her full, undivided attention.

He ran toward her, the soles of his shoes squeaking on the hardwood as he came to a quick stop. "See?" he said, showing her one foot, then the other. "Shoes!"

"Yep," she said, laughing, "shoes." Not the bright red high-tops she'd bought as his reward for mastering the art of tying his own shoes, but his old Velcro-closure sneakers. That he'd chosen to save time by wearing them told Taylor just how excited he was about exploring the turret's attic space.

"Well," he said, snapping on the light switch, "are you ready?"

Ready as I'll ever be, she thought as he darted up the stairs. She'd been putting this off far too long. It was long past time to face her past—the good memories, and the sad ones, too.

When she caught up with Eli, she found him grunting and grimacing as he wrapped both hands around the cut-glass doorknob. "It's . . . it's stuck." And as he rubbed his palms together, both brows disappeared into his blond bangs. "Or maybe it's locked."

Taylor hadn't been much older than Eli when her grandfather helped her hang the old skeleton key from the hook he'd hidden along the door jamb. She reached for it, then scooped Eli up into her arms instead. "Quick, grab the key," she grunted. "You're heavier than you look!"

It took a second or two for him to wiggle the key free, and when he did, Eli shouted, "Got it!"

Taylor gave him a little squeeze before turning him loose.

Eli held it up to the light. "Never saw anything like *this* before." One eye narrowed suspiciously, he looked up at Taylor. "You sure it's a key?"

Down on one knee, she showed him how to insert it into the keyhole. "I'm sure."

After a moment of wiggling and jiggling, the lock went *clunk*, startling Eli. "Whoa!" he said, giggling as he handed Taylor the key. "Bet Tootie heard that all the way over at her place!"

He grabbed the doorknob again, but this time his hand jerked back so quickly that she couldn't help but wonder if a chip in the glass had scratched him. Taylor was about to inspect his fingers when Eli said, "Is it okay if I open it, or do you want to?"

So, he'd been sincere about his promise not to touch anything without permission. . . . Smiling, she said, "No, *you* do it."

The old brass hinges squealed as the door swung open into the hallway. "It's kinda like the door on the Keebler elves' hollow tree, isn't it?"

"You know, you're absolutely right!"

Hands on his knees and shaking his head, he stooped and peered into the darkness. "No way we'll both fit through at the same time."

Translation: *"I'm scared to go in first, but I want to be first to see what's on the other side of this strange little door."*

"I have an idea," she said, taking his hand. "I'll go in just far enough to turn on the light, and that way, we'll both see what's in there at the same time."

"Good idea!"

Side by side, they ducked through the opening. Their entry stirred a thousand dust motes that danced like microscopic ballerinas on the beam of sunlight that poured in through the front-facing window.

"Wow," Eli said, straightening. "*Wow.*"

She knew exactly how he felt. As a girl, she'd spent hundreds of hours here, spinning dreams when the sun was up, wishing on the stars when moonlight painted everything—

especially that gigantic old steamer trunk—a strange and eerie shade of silver.

He turned in a slow circle. "Just *look* at all this stuff!" Then he noticed the rugged wood steps that led higher still in the turret, and pointed. "What's up there?"

"Oh, just more stuff." Taylor smiled, remembering how after Nonna's stroke left her unable to sew, Grampa stacked boxes of material and spools of thread as high as his arms would allow. "*Lots* more stuff."

"Man-o-man-o-man. It'll take days to see it all!"

Yes, it probably would—if she had any desire to rouse gloomy memories. . . .

Eli flicked a wooden whirligig, and, while giggling at its comical dance, blew the dust from a red metal fire truck. "Whoa. Co-o-ol," he said, picking it up. "Whose was it?"

"Careful, now," she warned. "There are lots of sharp edges on toys that were manufactured way back when." She held out her hand so that he could see the bright white scar in the web between her thumb and forefinger. "I got this playing with an old toy car that belonged to Grampa Hank's dad."

Nodding, he said, "I'll be careful." He touched the tarnished key on the side of the fire truck. "What's this thing do?"

"It makes the siren work. At least, it used to. It's an antique, and nobody has played with it in years."

He gave the key two quick cranks and grinned when the toy emitted a tinny, high-pitched wail. Down on his hands and knees, he rolled the truck back and forth. "Vroom-vroom!" he said, oblivious to the tracks its tires left in the dust.

Taylor knelt, too—in front of the cedar hope chest that had lured her up here in the first place. A wedding gift from Taylor's maternal great-great-grandparents to their only daughter, it had been handed down through the generations until, on Taylor's sixteenth birthday, it became hers. For years, it had stood at the foot of her bed, pestering her to look inside. Two days after hiring Isaac, she silenced the nagging by asking him to carry it to the turret.

And it had been here ever since. Would she have the courage today?

Eli put the truck back where he'd found it and went to the window. "Gosh," he said, using the heel of his hand to rub dust from the bubbly glass, "you can see all the way to the creek from up here."

"On a clear day," she said, tracing a burl in the trunk's rounded lid, "you can see even farther than that."

"Bet Uncle Reece would love this place. Wonder what he'd say if he came up here and saw all this. . . ."

Taylor harrumphed. No doubt he'd say something like, *"The boy should be outside, playing in the fresh air, instead of inhaling all this grit and grime. There are probably millions of dust mites up here, along with a hundred ways he could hurt himself!"*

With most people, Taylor gave people the benefit of the doubt. Why not Reece?

Maybe, she thought, because he acts more like a grumpy old codger than the thirty-something man he is.

But that wasn't fair, and she knew it. Eli was *Reece's* only living relative, too; it couldn't have been easy, finding out the way he did, that his sister hadn't named him Eli's guardian.

She remembered that day in the lawyer's office, when Reece's expression went from stunned to angry to anguished as the attorney read the paragraph in Margo's will that gave Taylor total control of the boy. The news had shocked and puzzled her, too. For one thing, she'd only known Margo since shortly before her marriage to Eliot. For another, Reece had changed his entire life to help out after Eliot was killed in Afghanistan.

Eli's excited voice pulled Taylor's attention back to the here and now. "Oh, wow," he said from his perch on the window ledge, "I can see our horses! There's Millie. And Alvin and Bert. And Elsie, too!" With each one he pointed out, Eli left a tiny fingerprint on the dusty glass. "And a whole bunch of deer. Taylor! Come see! There must be fifty of 'em!"

She loved how he called everything at the Misty Wolf "ours," from the big house, itself, to the land surrounding it. Taylor went to him, and, hugging him from behind, said, "That *is* a big herd, isn't it! And you're right—we *can* see the horses from up here." It still amazed her that, almost from his first day here, he'd started referring to the Misty Wolf Inn as *home*. Even more astounding was how quickly he'd accepted the fact that his dad had been killed by a roadside bomb in Afghanistan, and a car crash had taken his mom. *Oh, to have the pure, unquestioning faith of a child,* she thought, thanking God for the green-eyed blessing who stood in the circle of her arms.

"Can we go riding later?"

"Maybe . . . if there's time. It's Friday, don't forget."

"Oh, yeah. I almost forgot. An 'uncle Reece' Friday."

"Mmm-hmm." Uncle Reece Fridays—her least favorite nights of the month.

"Can I call him, see if he can come get me a little early, and maybe go riding *with* us?"

"I don't see why not. As my grandpa used to say, 'It never hurts to ask.'"

One of two things would happen when they got downstairs: Eli would get busy doing little boy things and forget to make the call, or he'd get his uncle on the phone only to find out that Reece still had patients to see and wouldn't be able to leave the office early.

Turning to face her, Eli looked up into Taylor's face. "So what's in the ugly ol' trunk over there?" he asked, using his thumb as a pointer.

Taylor kissed the top of his head. "You know, I honestly have no idea."

"Whose is it?"

"Mine."

"Whoa. No way. It's yours, and you don't know what's in it?"

Smiling, Taylor shrugged. "'Fraid not."

"But . . ." His eyes widened as he looked at the trunk. "Why not? Did somebody say you weren't allowed to?"

"No. . . ."

"That you'd get in trouble for opening it?"

"No, nothing like that."

Frowning, he said, "Then . . . then why haven't you opened it?"

How could she explain to this big-hearted boy—who'd lost both parents in less than a year's time—that she didn't have the guts to look at reminders of the people *she'd* lost?

"I don't have a good reason." In truth, Taylor didn't have *any* reason.

"You know that's just *weird,* don't you?"

"Yes, yes, I suppose it is."

Eli crossed both arms over his chest. "So, what do you *think* is in there?"

"Oh," she said on a sigh, "probably just a bunch of old junk. A few things that belonged to my mom and dad, and to my grandparents, and maybe even to *your* dad."

Eyes narrowed slightly, Eli said, "Oh. I get it. You don't want to see all that stuff 'cause you're afraid it will make you sad . . ."

"Well, I-I—"

". . . and remind you how much you miss them, right?"

She pictured Eliot's gap-toothed grin, her dad's playful wink, her mom's loving smile. "Right."

He took her hand, gave it a little squeeze. "You know what I do when I miss my mom and dad?"

Taylor didn't know if she had the self-control to keep her tears at bay if he continued.

"I hug their pictures *re-e-eal* tight."

". . . because that's all I have left of them," Taylor finished. Stirrings of resentment swirled in her heart. She'd never forgive his mom for giving away everything, except photographs, that might have reminded Eli of her and his dad. *Makes it real hard to believe your death was an accident, Margo,* Taylor thought. But bitterness quickly gave way to a blush of shame as she realized what Eli was *really* telling her: *"You should be thanking God that you have these things to help you remember your loved ones. . . ."*

"It'll be okay," he said, patting her hand. "I'll be right here with you. Don't worry, if you get sad, I'll give you a hug."

With that, Eli led her over to the trunk. "There's nothing in there to be scared of," he said, getting down on one knee. "There's probably nothing in there but old lady underwear!"

He giggled at his little joke as Taylor marveled at the depth of his perceptiveness.

"Bummer!" he said, tugging at the big padlock. "Did your grampa lock *everything* up?"

"Pretty much," she admitted, picturing dead bolts on the tool shed and barn, the garage, and the slanting doors leading into the basement.

"Oh, cool!" Eli said, pointing at a tarnished skeleton key. It dangled from a yard-long strand of twine that had been tied around one of the trunk's leather handles. "Must be something pretty good in there," he sing-songed, inserting it into the keyhole.

Her heartbeat doubled when the latch went *click,* because now, she couldn't turn back. The sound bounced from sun-faded bureaus, threadbare chairs, framed photos, and fading portraits that stood like somber sentries against the turret's curved walls.

Eli sat back on his heels. "Well . . . ?"

Taylor might have said, *"Well, what?"*—if she could have found her voice.

"You want me to open it, or are you gonna do it?"

What I want, she thought, is to go downstairs, right now, and put Isaac to work installing a big lock on the door to the turret. After which she'd throw away the key.

Eli must have read her hesitation as permission to open the trunk, because that's exactly what he did. "What's that smell?" he wanted to know.

"It's cedar, a much less stinky way to protect clothes than moth balls." Her hands shook as she removed a layer of tissue paper.

"What's that?"

"A cigar box," she said, peeling away the bulky burlap wrapper. Hands trembling, she handed it to Eli, who flipped up the lid to expose a jumble of gold chains, once-silvery earrings, bangle bracelets, rings, and a cameo broach the size of an egg.

"Oh, yuck," Eli grumbled, frowning as he handed it back. "Nothin' but *girl* stuff." Then he pointed. "Wonder what's in *there*?"

Taylor set the cigar box aside to retrieve a small wooden cedar chest. Inside, wrapped in brown paper, were dozens of scallop-edged photos, some still wearing the corner tabs that had once fastened them to the pages of an old-fashioned picture album. But sensing Eli's impatience, Taylor put the box down. She'd have plenty of time to look through the photographs after Eli left for his weekend with Reece.

In the next layer of the trunk, three elegant hats: a simple veiled pillbox, one adorned with ostrich plumes, and a straw sunbonnet trimmed in velvet. Here, a lacy-edged scarf, there, a crocheted shawl, and a single elbow-length glove that was missing one of its iridescent pearl buttons. Then, a white box filled with embroidered handkerchiefs, a package of seamed silk stockings, and finally, a wedding gown, veil, and size-five white satin shoes—all preserved to perfection in their blankets of cotton-soft tissue.

Eli exhaled a heavy sigh. "Aw, bummer. Is it *all* girl stuff?"

"Sorry, kiddo," she said, mussing his bangs, "but it looks that way. But just as soon as we put everything back the way we found it, we'll open another box. And who knows," she added, tapping the tip of his upturned nose, "maybe that one will be filled with all sorts of cool *boy* stuff!"

"Want me to help?"

"No, you go ahead and play. Just be careful—some of that stuff is sharp, remember."

As he busied himself with the whirligig and the fire truck, Taylor noticed a brown cardboard box at the very bottom of the trunk; on its lid, her mother's beautifully feminine script spelled out, "To Taylor."

Was it coincidence that Taylor had found the box today—the Friday before Mothers' Day—her very first as a substitute mom? She didn't think so. Hands trembling and heart pounding, Taylor eased off the lid. And under a blanket of pale pink tissue paper, she saw an unfinished quilt, scraps of cloth, spools of thread, and a pencil sketch of what her mother had had in mind when the project began. "Oh, my," she whispered, hugging it to her chest, "isn't it just lovely?"

Eli knee-walked closer to get a better look, lips moving as he counted a dozen colorful squares cut from satin and silk, cotton and flannel. Then he picked up a small, square envelope and handed it to Taylor. "What's this?"

Taylor's fingers were shaking when she took it from him.

"Is it a note? From your *mom*?"

Nodding, she bit down hard on her lower lip. *"Oh, Lord,"* she prayed silently, *"please don't let me cry. . . ."*